A NEW ENDING

Alyssa Dean Copeland

alyssa Dean Copeland

Publisher's Note: This is a work of fiction. Names, characters, places, and incidents are a product of the author's imagination. Locales and public names are sometimes used for atmospheric purposes. Any resemblance to actual people, living or dead, or to businesses, companies, events, institutions, or locales is completely coincidental.

Cover Illustration Copyright © 2015
Cover design by SelfPubBookCovers.com/Shardel
Edited by John Klocek
Book Layout ©2013 BookDesignTemplates.com
Printed by CreateSpace

A New Ending / Alyssa Dean Copeland. – first edition.
ISBN-13: 978-1492127123
ISBN-10: 1492127124

To my Pothos, my Lancelot, my Romeo.

Love looks not with the eyes, but with the mind,
And therefore is winged Cupid painted blind.
— William Shakespeare

I've completely screwed up this time." Rachel Weber paced outside of the college in downtown Denver. "I *can not* believe I let myself fall for him."

"You just need to find something to do to take your mind off of him."

The voice on the other end was Rachel's oldest friend, Christian Donaldson, a starving actor, and former curator old enough to be her father. During his prime, Christian had partied with some of the most famous people in Hollywood. Recently, he chose to move behind the scenes and start an independent film company.

"You're kidding, right? There's nothing left to do. I've done everything. I have my degrees, my house, my new car. What else is there to do? I don't want to commit to another long term project."

"Well you knew better than to fall for a married man." Christian joked, "You get men married, not divorced."

"I know. You're right. Maybe I should start wearing a sign that says 'Date me and meet the woman of your dreams'." All the men she had previously dated cheated on her with the women they later married. "You remember William?"

"I remember. I set him up with the top acting agency in five states."

"And he ruined his chance because he rescheduled twice and missed both appointments; then he got the lead actress in a low budget film pregnant, ending both of their careers."

Christian paused. "You just need to find someone that wants to be with you. It can't be that hard for someone like you."

"You have no idea. It's not hard to meet a man; it's hard finding the right one." Rachel brushed away a lock of long, blonde hair the breeze lifted into her crystal blue eyes.

"At least you don't need to go out to get a man to hit on you. You're lucky; you have a natural beauty and look younger than thirty-three."

Rachel joked, "How many times do I have to tell you? I'm still twenty-six." She looked down at the little finger of her left hand. The sun reflected off a simple gold ring that had belonged to her grandmother.

"You will always be twenty-six in my eyes. The guys always stare at your photograph in my office."

"You swore you would keep it hidden. I told you not to let anyone see it!" When Rachel created her modeling portfolio almost thirteen years ago, Christian asked for a copy of a photograph of her wearing a bikini. Reluctantly, she gave in. She didn't pursue the dream; she wasn't pretty enough. Now it was signed and framed, hanging in his home office.

"Don't worry, I have it hidden. Maybe you should consider dating one of the guys who's been hitting on you. What about the guy who sold you your new car a few weeks ago. Hasn't he been asking you to meet him for happy hour?"

Rachel sighed and moved the ring around her finger. "He can't be older than twenty-six."

"What about your contractor? How old is he?"

"He's twenty-nine and wants to stay and drink every time he works on my house. Look, it's not just about the age. I want more than a friend with benefits." The contractor was hot, and it took everything she had to say no. "I know what these guys are looking for and I want no part of it – not without a real commitment."

"Men can be dogs." Christian laughed.

Rachel went on as if she hadn't heard the amusement in his voice. "I just realized that I've been looking for Mr. Right for fifteen years and I haven't found him yet. Why should I believe that I'll find him sometime in the future?"

"Not *all* men are like the ones you have dated, Rachel. There are some good ones out there."

"I need to get back to work." Rachel changed the subject, not wanting to continue the conversation that she knew was coming.

"I understand." Christian paused. "We need more research on the new project; maybe that will take your mind off of him. I'll e-mail you the details. Take care of yourself."

"I'll call you tonight." Rachel hung up the phone.

She sat down on a bench in the courtyard of the campus. Rachel worked for a small, elite art university. It was the only job she had applied for after she received her MBA. She had moved up the ladder quickly, two promotions in less than two years.

The wind picked up on that peculiarly cool August day. She thought about going back upstairs to find her sweater. Instead she watched the branches of the red maple tree sway in the wind and her thoughts drifted to the man who had interrupted her life four months earlier.

CHAPTER ONE

Rachel rushed through the framing aisle of the hardware store, her cellphone balanced on her shoulder, arms full of tape, glue, caulking and finishing nails.

"You're kidding right? I emailed you those documents yesterday – and the day before that!" Rachel rolled her eyes; how many times did she need to send him the same paperwork?

"Check your e-mail again!" Her phone fell from her shoulder, its battery and case sliding across the floor in different directions.

"Can't anyone do anything for themselves?" She stomped her foot. Tears built up in her eyes and blurred her vision. Rachel stumbled in a daze toward the pieces of the broken phone.

"What bad thing did I do for all of this to happen to me today?" she mumbled.

She turned to locate the last piece of her phone and slammed into another customer. Tape, nails, and glue flew out of her arms. Rachel stood still, fixated on the painters tape rolling down the aisle.

"I am so sorry. I didn't mean to bump into you." She knelt down to pick up the mess. "This wouldn't have happened if I had grabbed a basket. That's what I get when I'm in a hurry."

She kept her head down. Tears ran down her face.

"Hey. Are you okay?" The man bent down and handed her the box of finishing nails.

Rachel nodded. She didn't want to admit that her life felt like it was falling apart. She averted her eyes and wiped the tears from her face.

"I don't think you are." He placed the rest of her items into his basket and stood up. "Come on."

Her eyes still averted, she shook her head no and tried to rearrange the items she held in her arms.

"Come on Rachel; let's find a place for you to sit down for a while."

Rachel looked up and temporarily forgot her embarrassment when she saw a familiar face. She had seen him on campus and remembered his amber eyes, light brown mixed with golden honey, but at the moment she couldn't remember his name. He took a few steps forward, stopped and turned back. "This way."

In a haze, Rachel followed him into the garden section of the store. He motioned for her to sit down on a cedar chair in a patio display next to a huge selection of roses. Rachel breathed in the fragrance and closed her eyes. He pulled up a matching ottoman and settled in across from her.

She couldn't explain why she felt drawn to him. Maybe she just needed someone to talk to. Rachel took a deep breath and eased back into the chair. Once she calmed herself down, she recalled that his name was Allen . . . Allen Sinclair; a few weeks ago he had come into her office to ask her a question about his account and his name was embroidered on his work shirt.

"I'm sorry. This has been a crazy few days." Rachel fumbled with the pieces of her cell phone. "I just hung up on my boss. He's probably going to fire me."

"I doubt it. Every time I see you, you're working. The campus would fall apart without you."

Rachel laughed; there were a lot of students that told her the same thing. "I hope you're right. Lately it seems like everything I touch goes wrong. Yesterday the bottom of my soda cup fell out, spilling all over my papers. My computer blue-screened so I couldn't print and the IT guy told me it would take a week to fix. The report is due tomorrow and the laptop they gave me doesn't have the appropriate software loaded. I ran late this morning and the minute I got to work someone handed me a list of supplies one of the departments needed. And now I just blew up at my boss. I guess I'm pretty devastated." She couldn't believe she had just told him all this. Her face turned red.

"Sounds like you've had a rough time." Allen smiled. "Things will get better, they always do."

Rachel took another deep breath and sighed. "At least most of the time."

"I know what you mean." His forearms rested on his knees, he looked at the floor and rubbed the palms of his hands together.

Out of habit, Rachel glanced down and noticed he wore a wedding ring.

"I'm sorry, here I am talking up a storm and I feel guilty that you're taking care of me. But you don't seem too happy either."

"I'm fine. Things will work themselves out." He took the parts from her hands, quickly replaced the battery and snapped the phone case back together. He turned it on to see if it worked before he handed it back to her.

"Thank you." She leaned forward, crossed her arms and gave him a questioning look. "But what about you?"

After a moment Allen sighed.

"I just got a new job. It doesn't pay much, but the day I started, my wife went out and bought a new truck. The one she had before was repossessed a month ago because she didn't make the payments. I have no idea who would finance her."

"Oh, wow. My day doesn't seem so bad."

He shrugged. "I know, but that wasn't the worst of it. A few days later I found out we were three months behind on the mortgage."

"Don't you see the bills?" Rachel oversaw the financial literacy program the college offered; making sure people understood their own finances was her passion.

"No. My wife has always taken care of the bills. Every time I try to get involved, she pushes me away."

"I'm so sorry."

"It isn't so bad, except her older brother Jim lives with us. He's been unemployed for years and doesn't help around the house. I don't even trust him to take care of our son. When I bring it up, she makes excuses and tells me to mind my own business."

"That's not cool. What are you going to do?"

"I just want a quiet life where the bills are paid and there's no drama. I'm getting divorced when I graduate." He picked up his basket and separated the contents.

"Are you sure you're going to be okay?"

Allen nodded and ran his hand over his shaved head. When he stood, Rachel stopped to take a good look at him. He was tall, about six feet, with a lean build. His full lips were surrounded by course, light-brown hair with hints of red on his goatee. The tattoos covering his arms gave him a bad boy image, yet he showed unusual sensitivity for a bad boy. He made her feel like they were old friends meeting for the first time. She felt she could tell him anything. When he glanced back, he didn't look at her in the same way other men had. It was as if he could see into her mind, into her soul.

He would be a wonderful man to be with, she thought to herself; the only problem – he was married. A married man, no matter what the circumstances, was off limits. She gathered her things and followed him to the front of the store.

Rachel walked into her office on campus. She couldn't get the last thing he said out of her mind. Tying back her long, blonde hair, she entered her office.

The office that she shared with Aimee, her assistant, was larger than most on campus. At one time it was a small classroom that held thirty-two students; with a large white-board still hung on the wall. As the campus grew, she volunteered to take the larger space that now held two desks and five mismatched filing cabinets. They were all hand-me-downs because she couldn't get anything new approved.

Aimee looked up from her computer. "I'm almost done, but I have a question on this account." She held out a sheet of paper for Rachel to look at.

Rachel surveyed the paper for errors but couldn't seem to focus on the numbers. "Give me a minute." She pulled the tie back out of her hair and sat down in her worn computer chair.

"Something wrong?"

"No. It's nothing."

"Don't tell me nothing. If it was nothing you'd already be fixing that account."

With a sigh, Rachel looked up from the paper. "I just blew up at the boss and hung up on him when I dropped my phone in the hardware store." And I just had a conversation with an incredibly attractive man, she thought to herself.

"That's not good." Aimee's cell vibrated on the table.

"Is your husband calling *again?*"

"Yes," she snapped, hitting the "end" button on her phone.

"How many times has he called today?"

"I don't know." Aimee shifted in her chair. "He always wants to know what I'm doing and calls for the stupidest reasons. Earlier he asked which shoes he should put on our oldest."

"That is a stupid reason." Rachel wanted to laugh but the mental image of events at the hardware store took over.

Aimee interrupted Rachel's thoughts. "My husband just wants to make sure that I am at work and not messing around."

"One of these days he will figure it out." Rachel raised an eyebrow. "Have you talked to him about going back to college to finish your degree?"

"I tried. But I think he's afraid that I'll make more money than he does."

Rachel shook her head and focused on the sheet of paper. Aimee's cell phone vibrated again.

CHAPTER TWO

A re you ready for this?" Madison Nichols quickly removed her baseball cap and checked the time on her cell phone.

Maddi, as everyone called her, started class on the same day as Allen Sinclair. Since then, they had attended almost every class together. At times, Allen felt that she knew him better than his wife did.

Allen nodded, his mind racing again. "I hope so."

Months of preparation and planning came down to this single day. Once a year, the college held an elaborate art show for graduating students, giving the community an opportunity to experience all types of art by various up-and-coming artists. Over one-hundred students from schools state-wide submitted works to the year's event, making competition fierce. Scholarships would be awarded by prestigious organizations in different categories later in the day. Both Maddi and Allen had pieces that made the cut for the final judging: Maddi's black and white sketch of an old woman in front of an English cottage portrayed a mischievous intelligence, while Allen combined computer graphics with hand-drawn art to create a simple and romantic book cover.

Family, friends, and potential employers came to the convention center in downtown Denver for a full day of demonstrations, presentations, and a bit of competition. Some students had been able to find employment with major corporations all over the country. Others were picked up by small galleries in Denver, though freelance work was the most common. A few years ago there was a bidding war going for one oil painting. Everyone had heard the story: the student walked out with a couple of grand in his pocket and a major gallery in New York commissioned him for a week's exhibit. The newspapers wrote he would be the next Picasso.

Allen wasn't looking for fame and fortune; he just wanted steady work that he was proud of to pay the bills. Looking around the room at the other displays, he began to feel out of his league, as if his work wasn't good enough. He straightened the business cards he made, hoping that he could impress someone important enough to offer him a well-paying position. And his wife Veronica wasn't helping. Whereas the week before Veronica seemed fully supportive, even excited – she had helped pick out the pieces to display – now she seemed opposed to going at all.

Last night when he got home from work she decided that the living room was cluttered, and shoved everything in the back of the garage, tearing the canvas on two of his paintings and breaking the frame on the poster-size book cover that won an entry into the contest. Thankfully, the computer generated piece and the oils on the canvas board and Masonite weren't destroyed.

Carefully, he set everything in the back of his Jeep, hoping that somehow he could fix the frame. Allen had spent hours custom-making the frame using tools in his father's garage, but he didn't have the time to drive there right then; he was already running late.

At least one person in his life had his best interest at heart; Allen didn't know what he would do without Maddi. When he arrived the night before, she had just finished setting up her display. He found his space with easels put together, a tablecloth covering the table, and Maddi had brought an extra extension cord for his laptop. The only thing missing was his artwork.

She didn't say a word when he showed her the damage to his entry. Grabbing her cell phone, she called her father who showed up an hour later with a new frame; somehow the man reframed it right there in the room.

"How did you manage to save my life?" Allen inspected the frame her father had fixed.

"It helps when your father is a curator."

Allen turned toward Maddi and tilted his head.

She laughed. "There are a lot of things that you don't know about me. Besides, I had a feeling that Veronica would try something to sabotage the exhibit."

This morning Veronica got out of bed late before sitting at the kitchen table, holding her coffee for over an hour. She took longer than normal getting herself ready as Allen dressed their son. Finally she decided that she wanted him to start looking for a better paying job since he was done with school. He tried to explain, as he had many times before, that the exhibit would give him exposure and he had one or two more months left, but she didn't want to hear his "excuses".

They were an hour into the exhibit when he finally spotted Veronica and Lucas across the room. Lucas looked bored standing next to her while she was texting.

"I just hope that Veronica doesn't cause any problems today. She didn't want to drive down here by herself, so we only brought one vehicle."

Maddi looked over. "I'm sure everything will be okay."

A strange sensation went through his body; his eyes were drawn to the front of the room. He turned and saw Rachel at the entrance on the arm of an older, distinguished looking gentleman with a graying moustache and beard. They greeted the director and a few of the sponsors. Allen knew he was someone important by the way he carried himself and the way the men shook his hand; and, instead of wearing jeans and holding an I-pad, the older man sported a dark-gray three-piece suit and a highly polished, cherry wood cane.

Before he could process the information Veronica walked up to him and handed him his son. "I need the keys."

Reflexively he pulled Lucas into his arms and dug his keys out of his pocket, handing them to her. "You forget something?"

She took the keys from his hands. "I'm tired of this place. I'm leaving."

When Allen tried to hand his son back, she stopped him. "You wanted us here, you keep him. I'm leaving."

"I thought you would at least stay until the award ceremony is over." Allen didn't like the pleading sound in his voice. He had hoped that once she got here, she would see how hard he was trying.

"Call your mom to get him. I've got better things to do today than stand around here." Veronica turned and walked out of the room, bumping into Rachel at the doorway, almost knocking her down. The older man caught Rachel as the other men reflexively reached for her. His wife gave her a dirty look and walked out of the convention center, leaving Allen to care for his son during the exhibit.

Allen was embarrassed; not only had his wife aban-doned him, but she also nearly floored someone in the process without an apology. Except Rachel wasn't just someone, he thought, and began to feel guilty. If he wasn't married, she would be someone he could spend the rest of his life with. During the last couple of months he had gotten to know her and everything he learned made him even more attracted to her.

"What was that about?" Maddi leaned over, trying not to cause another scene.

"I have no idea." Allen watched the group disband. Rachel and her companion walked directly toward him.

"Hi guys." Rachel smiled. "I want you to meet a very dear friend of mine. This is Christian Donaldson." The older man put out his hand while Allen tried to control his son who was kicking to get down.

"How do you do?" Christian formally greeted them, with the hint of an English accent.

Just then Allen felt his arms relieved of forty pounds when Rachel pulled his son out of his arms and talked to Lucas with the ease of someone use to dealing with chil-dren.

Nervously he rubbed his free hand over his head as he shook Christian's hand with the other.

"Christian is an Executive Producer of an independ-ent film company and he used to be a curator years ago.

The man's got an eye for art," she said, and tickled his son, making him squeal in laughter.

Instead of looking at the pieces Allen had on display, Christian walked over and flipped through his portfolio. Allen didn't know how to present himself, comparing his work to those of the other students he had seen this morning. Between the stiff competition, Veronica leaving, being left with his son, and then Rachel coming to the rescue, confusion had set in. Instead of using the elevator speech he had prepared, Allen just stood there wondering about the last three minutes.

Christian turned to Allen. "I like a man that does not have to explain each piece, who lets the patron enjoy the work quietly."

Slightly embarrassed, Allen smiled. The man knew what he was looking at. Allen appreciated that he was overlooking the chaos.

Glancing over, he saw Maddi quietly talking to Rachel. With nothing to do, he felt awkward and out of place. Lucas was pulling on her hair, trying to put his finger in her mouth and she looked comfortable holding him. Gently, she would move his hand and whisper in his ear, making him giggle. For a moment he couldn't help but think what a good mother she would be. She looked perfectly natural holding his pride and joy. He wondered what Veronica would do in the moment.

Allen sighed and rubbed his hands together. He knew what his wife would do. Dump their son off on him while he tried to find a job. He thought back to when he married her; there was a connection when they first met – when she was happy and wanted to be with him.

Allen glanced back at Rachel. Were the feelings he had for Veronica as strong as what he had for her?

The older gentleman whispered in Rachel's ear before he shook Allen's hand again and walked away.

"Thank you." Allen held his arms out to Lucas.

"You're not planning to keep him here the entire day?"

"No, my mother will be here in about an hour or so."

"Well, I'm going to be here all day. Why don't I take him to the kid's area for a while? I'll keep him entertained until she gets here."

"We should be fine."

Laughing, Rachel gave him a funny look. "I'm sure Lucas would rather run around and paint than try to sit still with you."

He looked over at Maddi who nodded in encouragement.

"I guess it will be okay. Let me know if you need me. Here," he grabbed Lucas's survival bag from under the table. "It's got toys, a change of clothes and some snacks."

Taking the bag, Rachel walked Lucas to the other side of the room.

Maddi stepped up and lowered her voice. "So have you told her you like her yet?"

"No, not yet, and I'm not sure I should." He watched Rachel until she disappeared into the crowd.

"She's better than your wife. She wouldn't leave you like Veronica did."

Allen sighed. "Yeah. I know. Veronica likes to pick random fights. She'll apologize later." He walked over to the table and straightened his business cards again.

Maddi followed him. "You need to quit covering for her. She's like a kid, using negative behavior to get your attention."

"She's not that bad," he said, trying to convince himself.

Maddi placed her hand on top of the business cards. "You mean like last Christmas when she pretended to overdose on pain medications?"

Allen shrugged and pulled his hand back.

She crossed her arms. "Or did *you* exaggerate?"

"No, I didn't exaggerate. She really did lock herself in the bathroom for over two hours. I broke it open and found her passed out with an empty pill bottle in her hand. That's when I called 9-11."

"That's what I'm talking about. They didn't find a trace of the medication in her system, did they?"

Allen rubbed his palms together. "No. And her seventy-two hour suicide hold is costing us a fortune. She still blames me for calling the paramedics. When they got there, she woke up and told them she was fine. But they took her to the hospital anyway."

"And how many times did she go to counseling before she said she didn't need it?"

"A couple of times. I guess I should've divorced her like she told me to that night."

"Well, you're a better man than that. She has no idea what she's messing up." Maddi walked away.

Allen looked back at the direction Rachel had taken. Maddi was right. Veronica had no idea what she had. It didn't matter how much he wanted to leave his wife, he couldn't.

* * *

The children's section of the exhibit was a tiny makeshift kitchen, complete with a sink, microwave, and several large round tables covered with white table cloths and chairs. The room was vacant other than one of the younger students helping out. Seeing Rachel, she asked to take a bathroom break.

Rachel covered Lucas in an old, tattered men's dress shirt. Luckily, they were available to keep the children's clothes clean.

Alone, watching Lucas smear paint on cheap canvas boards, Rachel sat down and pondered. Allen's wife had rammed right into her at the entrance. If Christian hadn't been there to catch her, Rachel knew she would've fallen. Instead of apologizing, she just flipped her hair, as if Rachel had done something wrong.

Maddi had told her who ran into her while Christian and Allen were talking. Allen's wife was beautiful but strange. Veronica's facial features reminded Rachel of a model in a fashion magazine. Her high cheekbones, button nose, and full red lips with her creamy white skin contrasted perfectly with her long, dark brown hair and eyes.

But the woman had just left her husband alone with their son on one of the biggest school events of the year. The students looked forward to this day more than the commencement ceremony for the networking opportunities alone.

She sighed and picked up another blank mock-canvas for Lucas to smear paint on. The boy was giggling and had red and blue paint all over his hands and face.

"How's it going?" Maddi asked from behind.

Smiling, looking over at Lucas, Rachel replied, "We have a future artist on our hands. If we could only teach him how to use a brush instead of trying to eat it."

Maddi laughed, but then seemed to remember something and looked behind herself. "I need to talk to you about something."

"Okay." Rachel began to look around to see if anyone in the vicinity had made Maddi nervous.

Maddi leaned forward and whispered in her ear, "He has a crush on you," then jerked her head toward the exhibit.

"What? Who?" Rachel blushed when she realized Maddi meant Allen. "How did you find out?" That was the last thing she thought she would hear today.

"He told me. He's been attracted to you for a very long time."

"Wow." Rachel lifted her eyebrows. She wondered if it would it be safe to tell Maddi or if she should keep it to herself. "I um . . ." She stuttered and finally decided to say it before she lost her nerve. "I'm attracted to him too. But, we have a policy where . . ."

Maddi cut her off in mid-sentence. "I know. He told me he had already asked you out. What about when he graduates?"

"Well," Rachel thought out loud, "then he is not a student."

Maddi grinned. "I wish he would go through with the divorce. They're toxic together. He's been frustrated with the things she's been doing since we started college together."

"Like what?" Rachel wondered what more there was to this woman that Allen hadn't mentioned.

"For one, she always goes through his phone looking at who he called or texted. She was really upset when she found out that I was a girl. I don't know how many times he told me that he had deleted my number just to avoid a fight." Maddi looked around again and lowered her voice. "You're exactly what he needs. Maybe you can get him to leave his wife."

"I don't know." Rachel rolled her hands nervously in front of her. "He has told me more than once that he plans to divorce her when he graduates but hasn't followed up with anything."

"Don't tell him that I told you. He needs to tell you. I need to get back. I'm sure he's wondering where I am. They're going to announce the winners in a couple of minutes. I just thought you might want to know." With a wink, Maddi walked back into the exhibit.

Rachel couldn't describe the emotions she felt. Her palms started to sweat and she felt a funny sensation in the pit of her stomach. He's attracted to me, she thought to herself. Is it possible that he has the same feelings? Maybe there is hope; maybe I won't spend the rest of my life alone – if he gets divorced. Could he be the one?

She gathered Lucas in her arms and walked him over to the sink to wash his hands. "Let's go back to Papa and show him your paintings."

Lucas giggled and squirmed out of Rachel's arms when she started washing the paint off of his face. Instead of letting her finish, Lucas ran toward his father. Rachel picked up his bag and latest masterpieces and chased him across the floor with the wet towel in her hand.

When she reached his father, Rachel was out of breath and wondered if she really wanted to have kids. They were a lot quicker than she thought.

Rachel handed the pieces to his father, then knelt down to get the last bit of red paint off of his son's face. Lucas giggled when his father proudly set his artwork on the table for everyone to see.

"He's a handful." Allen took the wet towel from her hands.

"I'm sorry, I tried to clean him up but he ran over here before I could finish."

"Lucas isn't the only one needing cleaning."

Rachel jumped when the cold damp cloth touched her face. Tilting her chin, Allen gently wiped paint off of her face. She couldn't help but gaze into his beautiful amber eyes, knowing that he shared her feelings, her desires.

The intercom buzzed and they both jumped. "The winners will be announced in five minutes."

Everyone migrated toward the podium at the front of the room. An older woman approached them and Lucas screamed, "Na Na!"

Rachel watched Allen's mother pick the boy off the floor and give him a loving hug. She thanked the heavens Lucas didn't have to depend on her to keep him entertained for the day. I'm just going to have to figure out how to entertain a three year old, she thought to herself, before realizing what she was thinking. Allen was married and the last thing she wanted to do was be the "other woman". They would just have to wait until he got divorced.

Standing there alone, feeling out of place, Rachel didn't know what to do. She didn't want to leave, especially after what Maddi had said, yet she felt awkward waiting for him to finish talking to his mother. She stepped to the table and flipped through his portfolio.

Allen walked up beside her. "Have you seen the entries?"

"No. I've been a bit busy." Smiling, Rachel nodded to the newest masterpieces on the table.

"Come on." He took her by the hand. "There's something I want you to see."

The competition had dozens of pieces in several different categories. Everything from oils, sketches, and watercolors, to computer-generated designs. The talent in the room was overwhelming and the rivalry was in fun, for the most part, but now there was a more serious feeling in the air as everyone awaited the results with bated breath.

Allen walked her over to a poster-size print portraying a novel cover. The white-satin fabric looked real. Rachel wanted to reach out and touch the soft, delicate folds which appeared to shimmer in the light. An old painter's pallet splashed with various colors brightened the simple but romantic piece. An exquisite mother-of-pearl ring, framed with a silver antique finish, sat next to an old-fashioned paint brush. The title and the author's name were in a stunning silver. Had it been a real book, she would have picked it up and read the back.

"The milgrain details of the ring were hand drawn," Allen stated proudly as he pointed to the image. "It took me a while to draw the antique finish, but I finally got it right."

Rachel gently squeezed his forearm. "It's beautiful."

The Director of the campus stepped up to the microphone and thanked everyone for attending. He gave a small speech and introduced representatives from the companies and organizations who made the event possible. After several quick speeches, the winners of the competition were named. Maddi won first place for her pencil sketch and received two scholarships. Allen won second in the graphic design category.

With a few more hours of the exhibit, the students wandered back to their displays and the patrons approached the winning pieces to see what they might have missed.

When Rachel and Allen made it back to his display, Christian was waiting for them with a serious look on his face.

"I like an artist that can express all types of work." Allen gave him a questioning look when Christian laughed, pointing to the newest pieces with his cane.

"My son." A bit embarrassed, Allen lowered his head.

"I believe the small fingerprints gave it away." Christian shook Allen's hand and leaned over to kiss Rachel on the cheek. "It's time for this old man to leave. Have a good day, my dear."

Allen turned toward Rachel after Christian had left and whispered in her ear. "He's a character."

"Of course he is. He used to be an actor in Hollywood."

Before she could say another word about Christian, one of the instructors walked up and handed Allen an envelope. "Your piece had a lot of interest. A few people kept coming back to admire it. And one guy was interested in buying the rights. I told him I would introduce you but he said he had your card."

Rachel could not help but feel pride for Allen. He deserved to have a better life and maybe this exhibit would help him find it.

Watching him open the envelope, she saw surprise come over his face. She knew what was inside because she had ordered the checks and put the envelopes together. Inside was a scholarship for $1,000.00 that he could apply to his outstanding tuition charges.

Caught up in the moment of excitement, Allen put his arm around her. Reflexively, as if it was the most natural thing to do, she hugged back. When they touched, she felt something that she had never felt before. A spark of energy shot through her body giving her a pleasant tingling sensation. When she pulled away, he didn't let go of her. He looked into her eyes, and for a brief second there was only the two of them.

Suddenly, they heard a scream in the back of the room, and chaos broke out. Children wearing small cowboy hats, coveralls and boots dashed down the aisles chasing several sheep, one of which wore a little, blue bow and which ran straight into Maddi, almost knocking her down.

The students grabbed their works from the easels as the animals knocked other displays over.

A voice came over the intercom: "Please stay calm. The sheep are not a threat."

Eventually, they were caught as the kids put leashes around their necks, leading them outside to the appropriate building.

Word had got around that the backdoor was left open to ventilate the room, and a driver delivering the animals had pulled up behind the wrong building; one of the kids unlatched a trailer, and . . .

Laughing, Allen looked at Rachel. "Time for a beer?"

"Absolutely," she laughed, knowing they would have to wait a couple months, when he graduated.

CHAPTER THREE

Allen tried to control his anger once he was home. He hadn't exactly had the most wonderful day.

After work his Jeep ran out of gas in a busy intersection; with a little help from a pedestrian, he was able to push it into the gas station on the corner. It didn't help his mood when the traffic behind him continued honking, and one guy drove by yelling obscenities.

He knew he should've filled his tank this morning before work. If he had, he would've been late, again. Fine, he could take responsibility for the tank being empty. It was his fault for waking up late. But he was not the one who drained the bank account in less than twenty four hours.

When the debit card was declined at the pump he walked into the convenience store and handed it to the clerk. After three declines, the kid told him to call the bank. It was absolutely embarrassing to have a teenager with six piercings on his face and purple hair tell Allen that his card was declined. Luckily, his mother lived five minutes away and the clerk didn't care if his Jeep sat at the pump while he waited for her.

Allen hated calling his mom to rescue him. He was a thirty-five year old man with a family to take care of. It was his responsibility to find a job to pay the bills and he was trying. Every chance he had, he was doing freelance work on his days off from school. But it was never enough.

Allen pulled his laptop out of the backseat and was able to get an internet connection from the restaurant next door. Not caring if it was secure, he pulled up the bank account. His paycheck had posted yesterday and the account was fifty dollars overdrawn already. Veronica had paid her cell phone bill, bought gas for her tank, and gone to the grocery store. Other than that, there wasn't another payment on a bill in weeks. She had taken several cash withdrawals in just one day, ranging from fifty to a hundred and fifty dollars, and had apparently spent thirty dollars on lunch at an Italian restaurant.

Allen tossed the laptop in the passenger seat and called his mother.

"I just can't do this anymore. I swear she's trying to sabotage our marriage."

"I doubt it. Maybe she's looking for attention. People do strange things when they love someone."

Allen knew his mother wouldn't understand. She married her high school sweetheart in a small town in Iowa over forty years ago. A God-fearing Christian, she believed in the sanctity of marriage. All four of his sisters had managed to get through the hard times. Whenever he mentioned the word divorce, his mother would raise her voice, insisting it was against the word of God and he would end up in hell.

"I think we tied the knot too early. I was stupid. Three months wasn't long enough to get to know someone."

"Well you're married and have a family. You'll be fine when you finish school. Things will change for the better. Lucas and I will be there shortly."

Later he walked into in the living room to find Veronica sleeping on the couch, the television blaring. He turned off the noise and shook her awake to let her know he was home. When she opened her eyes, he knew immediately what she had been doing. She was stoned again.

"Are you going to be okay to watch Lucas tonight? I've got to go to class."

Rubbing her eyes, Veronica shook her head. "I'm fine, just tired."

"The bank is overdrawn again. I thought you should know. I had to borrow some money from Mom again to fill my tank."

"Yeah." She yawned sleepily as she stretched her arms. "I keep forgetting to put my paycheck in the bank."

"What do you mean forgetting? You set it up with automatic deposit, remember?"

Veronica stood and walked into the kitchen. Dirty dishes cluttered sticky kitchen counters, and an overflowing trashcan spilled onto the unwashed floor. That morning, Allen had taken out two full trash bags that sat in the kitchen for two days. Veronica opened the refrigerator and grabbed a soda.

"We changed payroll companies. I haven't set it back up yet. I've been busy."

Allen knew how busy she was. She went to work, came home, and slept. The rest of the time she was waking up from a nap or arguing with him. He learned a long time ago not to start a fight when she woke up. It was about the only time she was calm and they could talk.

"I've got to go or I'll be late."

Waving her hand, she walked over to Lucas. "It's time for bed sweetie."

Cursing under his breath, he knew he couldn't leave. Lucas had just woken up from a nap when he called his mother to rescue him at the gas station. He didn't know how much longer he could handle feeling like this. He knew that things weren't going to get better.

When they got together, she promised that her brother would help out around the house. Every time he asked, the man would make nasty comments under his breath and then hide in his room. Allen had tried to talk to Veronica about her brother but she always changed the subject – that, or it started a fight. He couldn't work and go to school and still have time to clean.

"Don't worry about it. I'll ditch tonight. Why don't you go to bed?"

Without a word, his wife went into the bedroom and closed the door.

Allen went to the kitchen and started washing dishes so he could make dinner for his son.

* * *

Two days later, Allen was thankful he still had over a half tank of gas. After work, he picked his son up, and at home he found the kitchen clean and his wife making dinner.

"Dinner should be ready in ten minutes."

Allen set his laptop bag on the couch next to Jim, who held a beer, watching television. "I've got class tonight."

Veronica put her hands on her hips. "No. You're eating dinner with your family tonight."

"Put some in the refrigerator. I'm running late." He headed to the bedroom to change his clothes.

Veronica followed him. Standing at the doorway she crossed her arms and glared. "You spend too much time at school. You need to spend more time here, with your family."

He pulled on a clean shirt. "I can't tonight. I've got class."

Veronica raised her voice. "You always have something more important to do then spending time with us."

"I'm doing this for us." Allen glared back at her. "Once I graduate, I can get a better paying job and I'll have more time to spend here."

She walked over to the bed and picked up his dirty shirt. "I don't care. You're staying home tonight."

"You say that now. But when we're broke, you'll accuse me of not making enough money. I have to finish this. I'm way too close to quit now."

Veronica threw the shirt at him. "It's always about you! You're never here! You don't care about us!"

Lucas peeked around the corner. He was biting his lower lip, and his big blue eyes had turned red with tears.

Allen lowered his voice. "What do you want from me?"

"To be a good husband and take care of your family."

"That's what I'm trying to do." He squeezed past her in the doorway. He grabbed his laptop and walked out the door, hoping she was sober enough to take care of Lucas for the night.

Going to college was about the only thing keeping him sane. There he could focus on something besides his own problems.

The issues at home weren't the only motivator to make it to class tonight. Two months ago he met someone that he felt he connected to. Completely. Every time he thought of Rachel, a warm, trembly feeling ran through his body. He wanted to be near her. It was refreshing to spend time with someone that didn't judge him for working a low paying job, or going to college instead of spending time with his family; nor did she blow him off when he vented about his problems.

Allen found a parking place close to the building, grabbed his laptop and books, and ran in.

The instructor was lecturing as he sat down next to Maddi in the back row of the graphic arts classroom. He turned on his Apple and began to fight with the Adobe InDesign program. This day wasn't getting any better; he had forgotten about the assignment due by the end of class. Instead of listening to the lecture, Allen rushed to get it done, but he couldn't focus. His mind kept going in every direction other than the one he needed it to.

Twice he messed up the image and had to start over. Allen knew he needed to walk away but couldn't. He completed the edits, removing the background of his image in Photoshop and transported it to the InDesign document. Everything was perfect until he saved the file. The background he had removed reappeared. Just like my life, he thought to himself. Every time things seemed to be going good, something unexpected happens.

Thirty more minutes of class were left before they could take a break.

The instructor was giving an example of combining vector graphics with text to make advertising layouts in Adobe InDesign when Allen leaned over and whispered to Maddi, "I can't make this work."

She looked over at his computer and clicked a couple of buttons. "Try that."

Amazed that she fixed it so quickly, he moved his mouse to get the image the way he wanted it. "What did you do?"

"You had the Photoshop image saved as a psd file, not a png. Remember? When you save your picture, Photshop will default to a psd and it's not compatible with InDesign. You lose your edits."

"I knew that. I guess I was trying to hurry and forgot to rename the file." Allen rubbed his hands over his bald head and took a deep breath. "Are we done yet?" He had spent the last three years going to college, forgoing summer vacation to graduate sooner. Thankfully, Maddi had a similar goal and they were able to schedule most of their classes together.

"Two months. We're done when the summer session is over." Maddi looked back at her computer. "Are we doing this group project together?"

"What group project are you talking about?"

"The one due next week. We either stay late or get together tomorrow. We can meet up here or at my place."

"Your place?" In the entire time he had known her, she never offered to let anyone come over to her house to work on a project. Every time he asked her, she changed the subject. "Why not at my house?"

Maddi gave him a look that stopped him in his tracks. "I am NOT going back to your place. Your wife gives me the creeps."

"She's not that bad." Allen found himself defending her again.

"Are you kidding? When we were sitting at the table she kept giving me dirty looks while she was reading some book on spell casting. I was afraid she was going to curse me for intruding."

"I don't believe in that stuff. It makes her happy so I don't fight with her about it."

"Nothing makes Veronica happy." Maddi leaned back in her chair and picked up her textbook. "She's always in her own little world of misery."

He handed his cell phone to Maddi. "Type in your number. I don't have it anymore."

"Did she delete it again? One of these days you need to memorize it." She picked up her phone and pushed a few buttons. After a moment his cell vibrated.

"Thanks. I'll just save it under Matt. Maybe she won't figure out that's you."

Both of their heads popped up when the instructor said the magic word. "Break."

Smiling, Allen quickly stood up out of his chair with more enthusiasm than he had all evening. "I'll be back."

Maddi gave him an all-knowing look and rolled her eyes. "And who are you going to see?"

Allen blushed as he started for the door, using the same mocking tone. "My favorite person."

CHAPTER FOUR

Rachel was sitting in her office staring at her computer screen, twirling her hair, and daydreaming when Aimee walked in.

"Have you eaten yet?"

"No. Not yet." Rachel looked at the clock. She had been working all day and night without eating. She had a dentist appointment that morning and planned to stay late. "Shouldn't you have left by now? It's almost seven."

"I figured as much." Aimee handed her a fast-food bag. "Someone has to make sure you eat. Don't worry; I'm getting ready to leave."

Inside the bag was a cheeseburger and french fries. Rachel reached in, grabbed a fry, and shoved it into her mouth. "Thanks mmphs."

Aimee sat down at her desk. "You're welcome. Me and the girls think you need to get out and meet someone."

39

Rolling her eyes, Rachel grabbed another fry. "You buy me dinner and then tell me I need to meet someone. Is this a bribe?" She held up the fast-food bag.

"No. We were just talking earlier and thought that you needed to start meeting people."

"So my social life was the topic today?"

Aimee pulled her purse out of the drawer and set it on the desk. "Yeah, it was better than talking about how many times my husband calls every day."

"I guess you have a point."

"So, what about going out this weekend and meeting someone?"

Rachel gave the same excuse she always used. "I don't like bars and I wouldn't have any idea where to start. Remember, I met John at a bar and then he broke up with me on April Fool's Day."

"Yeah, I remember. You kept joking – obviously, I might add – how you felt like a 'fool' for spending three years with him. But I also remember he was upfront with you. He said that you were not the 'one' he was looking for and you didn't listen. So instead of meeting someone new, you spent the weekends with him playing online video games, watching movies, and occasionally going to dinner with us. He didn't change his mind, like you were hoping."

Rachel shrugged and then sighed. "You're right. It didn't work; he met someone before he broke up with me. Last I heard, they were engaged."

Aimee dug through her purse and pulled out her car keys. "If you're not going to go out to meet someone, then let's get a picture and put you on a dating site."

Shoving another fry into her mouth, Rachel gave Aimee her dirtiest look, and then softened it a bit.

"Okay. Okay. No dating site. You really should do something to meet someone. Does your karate instructor still work at the school?"

"Yeah. I checked about a month ago. He's still there." Rachel started dating Brandon a few months after she started taking tae kwon do lessons. Things were going well, until his ex-wife told him that she was six-weeks pregnant. Apparently he was trying to patch things up with her at the same time he was dating Rachel.

Aimee sighed. "But if you don't get yourself out there, how are you going to meet anyone?"

Rachel blushed when an image of Allen entered her mind.

"You have met someone? Why didn't you tell me?" Pulling her chair closer to Rachel's, she leaned forward.

Rachel almost whispered. "Because I'm not allowed to date him."

She could tell that Aimee was having a hard time processing the information. "It's complicated."

As if the entire situation could be changed with four words, Aimee picked up her purse and stood up. "Just ask him out."

"I can't. It would be inappropriate."

Aimee tilted her head and sat back down. "How? Why?"

Rachel let it out. She hadn't told anyone what she was thinking or feeling other than Maddi and her black cat, Zanza. "You have to promise me that it will not go out of this room."

Aimee's hands went to her mouth, "Oh! It's someone here on campus."

Nodding her head yes, Rachel took a bite out of the cheeseburger.

"Someone who works here?"

When she didn't reply, Aimee proceeded to list every male that worked on campus. Rachel responded with he's happily married, gay, girlfriend, not my type, or simply disgusting.

After naming everyone, Aimee hesitated. "You like girls?" and in the next breath, "He's a student!" Jumping out of the chair, she clapped her hands, as if she had just discovered one of life's greatest mysteries.

Rachel didn't answer, but her face turned red. "I can date anyone that works here as long as I'm not their boss. That's not against policy."

"But students are different. That's a conflict of interest." Aimee sat down in her chair and pulled her chair closer to Rachel's.

"Yup. That is why it's complicated."

"Who is it? You're going to tell me, aren't you?"

"Nope."

With a look of determination, Aimee grabbed her purse off of her desk and walked to the door. She looked back. "I'm going to figure this out. I am going to figure out who your Romeo is." And she left the office.

Rachel sat back in her chair, and thought of Allen. She remembered how he was dressed on Saturday – she had to admit to herself that a bad boy in a collared shirt, tie, and dress slacks was incredibly attractive. But he's married, she told herself; I have no business thinking about a married man.

When he received his scholarship, it felt perfectly natural to hug him. When she put her arms around him, she felt a strange sensation deep down inside of her, wanting to hold him longer, to never let him go. And when she pulled back, he didn't let go right away, but lowered his hands near her waist a moment longer. It made her feel small, delicate. She would have prolonged the moment if it hadn't been for the sheep.

"Are you busy?" Allen stood, leaning against the doorway, his arms crossed, with a smirk on his face.

Rachel wasn't surprised to see him; somehow she knew that he would come by tonight. She always knew. "I'm never busy." She glanced down at the pile of papers that were in front of her and smiled back at him.

Allen's eyes lit up as his smirk softened. "It's nice outside. Walk with me?"

"Sure," she replied. She tossed her pen on the papers, slipped her heels back on from under her desk, and tried to control her anxiousness to follow him.

He hadn't said a word until they got outside. With both hands shoved into the front pockets of his jeans, Allen stopped near the shaded stone bench on which they always sat. His shoulder brushed up against hers. The slight touch sparked a wave of warm energy through her.

He rubbed the palms of his hands together and she could have sworn she saw him shuffle his feet when he looked at her. "I'm incredibly attracted to you."

Rachel was stunned. Her heart raced. Was she was dreaming? It didn't matter that Maddi had only told her a few days ago how he felt. She knew that even if she had weeks to prepare, hearing him say the words would still have shocked her.

Smiling, a bit embarrassed, she looked into his amber eyes. "The feeling is mutual." Crap, she thought to herself, I shouldn't have said it that way.

Relief washed over his face as he let out the breath that neither one noticed he was holding.

"You're still planning on getting divorced?" A strange familiar feeling ran through her. She hoped to hear the word she wanted him to say.

Before he could answer, Maddi walked up to them with her classmate, Sabrina, behind her.

"Hey. How's it going?" Maddi smirked at Allen.

He glared back. "Good."

Sabrina interjected, "That project is going to be tough; have you guys started?"

Maddi smacked Allen's arm. "We start work on it tonight."

Rachel wasn't paying attention to the girls. She crossed her arms and studied the tiny rocks at her feet, kicking them around. She didn't think he would tell her this soon. She thought he would wait a little longer. If only Maddi and Sabrina hadn't walked up . . .

Rachel noticed Allen kept trying to engage in the conversation, but his eyes were continuously drawn to hers.

Maddi looked at her cellphone. "We need to get back to class."

Rachel followed them back into the building. Instead of heading to class with the others, Allen stopped and shoved his hands back into his pockets. "How late are you staying tonight?"

"I've got a big report due. I might be pretty late." She leaned against the wall next to the display case filled with ceramic pots, plates, and vases. In reality the report would only take twenty minutes, not all night.

"Wait for me." He walked away, looking back, smiling.

Suddenly Rachel felt an invisible rift forming between them. A vivid image entered her mind: She stood on one side of a gorge and Allen on the other when suddenly he disappeared. Wondering why the picture entered her mind, she began second guessing herself. Maybe the idea of someone caring for her was too good to be true. Pushing the feeling down, she turned and walked back to her office.

* * *

Three hours later Rachel turned off her computer and gathered her things. Allen hadn't stopped by.

"What am I thinking? Why would he say those things and then blow me off?" She sighed and glanced at the clock one more time, then turned off the light and locked the door. "I am not going to look desperate by walking by his classroom," she mumbled under her breath.

Since that day in April when she bumped into him at the hardware store, she had tried to convince herself that Allen wasn't Mr. Right, reminding herself that he was still married. He had a three year old. He had tattoos. But the truth was she liked kids and tattoos didn't bother her at all.

She couldn't stop thinking about what Maddi said at the Exhibit. Allen was attracted to her. And when he hugged her, she couldn't remember a time when a man put his arms around her making her feel the way he did. Time stood still; everyone in the room momentarily disappeared. Her body felt all tingly inside, and her knees went weak with his touch. He made her feel like a teenager again. She felt desirable, wanted. When he was near, her brain turned to mush.

Slowly Rachel walked toward the parking garage, avoiding the tiny pebbles lying on the cool ground. She sighed. He was, after all, still married to Veronica. Rachel had sworn that she would never put another woman in the same position that she had been in. She would never be the "other woman."

His wife was arrogant, cold and downright selfish. Rachel thought she would have been beautiful if it wasn't for her attitude. She didn't know how Allen had managed to stay with her for the past four years. He deserved to be with someone better than Veronica.

Maybe it's my turn, she thought to herself. She wondered if her past relationships were some indication she was to meet someone who was married. Could Allen be Mr. Right, or just another . . .

"What are you still doing here?" The voice startled her back to reality. She didn't realize she made it to her car on the second level of the parking structure when she heard the voice call out.

Leaning over the rail, she couldn't help but smile when she saw Allen. He stood by his slate-gray Jeep parked almost directly below her, grinning.

"I was waiting for someone to walk me to my car."

"Oh. I'm sorry. We ran late. Maddi and I were working on the project. I thought you'd left."

"Well you can't say what you said and then leave it at that."

"I'll come up and we can talk." He disappeared into the stairwell.

Stepping out on the second level, he smiled and walked toward her, rubbing his hands together. "What do you want me to say?"

"I'm not sure. It's just that you can't tell a girl you're attracted to her and not say anything else." She tried to keep her confidence and not sound desperate but her stomach felt a bit queasy and her brain turned to mush.

"It didn't help that we were interrupted."

The garage suddenly became cold. Looking down at a crack in the blacktop of the parking lot, she rubbed her arms. "You know I can't date a student." She looked up and continued, "I could lose my job – you could be expelled."

"I know. It was poor timing. I couldn't help it; I should've kept my mouth shut. I tend to speak before I think and it's gotten me into trouble a few times."

Leaning against her car, Rachel clasped her hands in front of her, wishing she had pockets to shove them into. "We will have to wait until you graduate and until you're not married."

"I have a few obstacles to overcome."

She bit her lip and peered up at him. "But that doesn't mean we can't keep talking."

They watched the cars below leaving the parking lot for the night.

She crossed her arms and studied her bare feet. "For days I've been trying to figure out how I could get you to take me for that beer when you graduate. I don't even like beer." She looked up and smiled at him. "Now all I can think about is what it would be like to kiss you." Surprised at her boldness, she took a deep breath and rubbed her arms.

Allen shoved his hands into the front pockets of his jeans and, looking down, and blushed. Rachel grinned: Oh my god! He blushed! He was as nervous as she was. Yet, she felt she had crossed some invisible boundary.

"After all," she leaned back on her car afraid to meet his eyes, "you could kiss funny. Once I dated a guy that kissed like a fish. Let's just say that I never kissed him again."

Before she could conceive her next remark, she felt his hands on both sides of her face, pulling her forward. When his full lips touched hers, she completely melted into the moment. The coarse hair of his goatee tickled her chin, and his tongue dove into her mouth, tasting every bit of her, and she eagerly responded. It was the most gentle and sweet kiss Rachel could have imagined.

Time stopped; nothing existed except for the two of them. Pressing her body against his, she wrapped her arms around his neck. His hands held her small waist and she could feel the heat of his body as his hands moved up her back, pulling her even closer. Then what felt like an eternity suddenly stopped. The kiss was for only a moment but it took her breath away.

"I'm as nervous as a schoolboy," he admitted, taking a step back. He blushed again and rubbed his hands together. "I didn't kiss like a fish, did I?"

Shaking her head no, Rachel could barely get the words out. "Definitely not." No longer cold, her body was on fire.

Wondering if they had been caught, Rachel looked around. The parking garage and the lot below were both vacant. No one was in sight.

"I think you're going to be more of a challenge than I thought."

"Why? Because I'm married?"

"No, not so much that you're married. You said you're getting a divorce. It's because you're a student. I can't date students."

"I know. You could lose your job and I could be expelled."

Rachel hugged her stomach. "How are we going to keep this a secret?"

"We're just going to have to be careful. That's all we can do until I'm done."

"Eight weeks."

"I thought it was nine?"

"The first week of class is over. Eight weeks from tonight."

"Eight weeks." He looked at the time on his phone. "I need to go."

Rachel didn't want it to end. She had been waiting for this moment since they first talked in the hardware store. He pulled her close and kissed her again, pressing her body against his. She could feel his warmth penetrating her. She couldn't hold him close enough, fearful that he would somehow disappear. Kissing him with all the passion and desire she had inside of herself, she wondered if this would be the last time his lips would touch hers.

CHAPTER FIVE

Pulling into the driveway, Allen turned off the ignition and sat back, letting the familiar feeling of the worn leather seat comfort him. Something happened tonight, something he couldn't understand. The guilt he felt was not as intense as he thought it should be. The lack of shame made him feel worse.

He took his marriage vows seriously and condemned every man that committed adultery. Men were allowed to look, not touch. They could think, but not act. And he had just violated everything he ever believed in.

Scrutinizing the house, he noticed that it looked deserted. Not even a hint of light penetrated from the windows. Just the idea of walking into the small, three-bedroom house made him feel that he was crossing a line of impending doom. Veronica didn't even leave the porch light on to welcome him home like she did when they were first married.

The place needed work but the money was not there. Instead of lush, green grass growing in the front yard, brown dirt dusted the neighborhood, trash piling up next to the wooden plank fence bordering the neighbor's. They simply couldn't afford to water the lawn and now it needed to be replanted.

The exterior needed paint and the roof, patching, from a hail storm they had a few months ago. Insurance would cover repairs, if only they could afford the thousand-dollar deductible.

Inside, Allen had started the process of remodeling one of the bathrooms. He wished they had the funds to finish laying the tile. No one could take a shower for fear of getting the drywall wet. The guest bathroom needed a new toilet. The one they had was cracked and constantly backed up. Allen hoped they didn't need to hire a plumber.

His wife inherited the house before they got married. He didn't mind the hard work that it took to maintain the house, but it was in shambles when he moved in. He did what he could with what they had but nothing ever seemed like it was enough. Veronica always complained that he wasn't doing his share, yet her half-brother stayed home all day, constantly drinking, playing on his computer, and not helping with the repairs. Apparently, she didn't see anything wrong with this.

A few months before, Allen had to turn off the internet because they couldn't afford the bill. When Jim asked what happened, Allen told him the internet wasn't as important as other bills. Jim had the audacity to say the internet was important to him. Allen couldn't believe it. The guy was 42 years old, and hadn't worked in over a decade. He shrugged it off thinking if it was that important, Jim could get a job and pay for it. Several times Allen mentioned it and each time it led to a huge fight with Veronica defending her brother. She promised her parents she would take care of him.

Sighing, Allen pulled a sketch book out of his laptop bag and searched for a blank page. Drawing helped him think and he knew he needed to put his life back into perspective. He didn't want to go inside; he knew what was waiting for him: dirty dishes in the sink, an overflowing wastebasket in the kitchen, Jim's empty beer cans on the coffee table, and an uninviting, old, broken-down sofa to sleep on.

Allen halfheartedly wished he had somewhere else he could go. But he wouldn't leave his son. And though he knew that Rachel would welcome him with open arms if he really needed it, he wouldn't do that to her. He wouldn't risk her livelihood because he was uncomfortable going home. He was a better man than that and didn't want to expose her to Veronica's wrath. Besides, he didn't have a way to contact her.

He couldn't get Rachel out of his mind and, being honest with himself, he didn't want to. It was bad enough that he put his foot in his mouth when he told her that he was attracted to her. He had no right to openly express his feelings about her. He was a married man.

But tonight went beyond anything he could imagine. Being near her was overwhelming; he could feel the sexual tension between them. More than anything he wanted to become one with her in every possible way.

Allen had no intention of letting his emotions get out of control. He remembered touching her at the exhibit. Holding her was like holding magic in his hands. Every nerve in his body reacted with a gentle energy that flowed through him. When her arms went around him he had taken a deep breath, and the unique scent of her filled him with the same magical sensation. He didn't want to release her.

The thought of holding her again consumed his thoughts and he wondered if he would have the same reaction if he touched her again. He didn't think that she had the same feelings for him until tonight when she said that all she could think about was what it would be like to kiss him. And then he couldn't resist. For some reason he couldn't explain, he needed to kiss her. Maybe he wanted to build his confidence or prove to her that he could actually perform.

Kissing her was wrong on so many levels, but when his lips touched hers he knew that he had never felt something so right. Holding her in his arms, he felt at peace.

He remembered being nervous and stepping back and telling her. Her face was flushed when she smiled at him, catching her breath before answering. Her eyes sparkled with passion and desire; at that moment he thought she looked even more beautiful. Then he realized he was the one making her glow. Smiling, he felt a sense of pride that he could affect her that way, yet at the same time he felt vulnerable.

In that instant his world came undone. It was as if someone upstairs finally listened to him and answered his prayers years too late. Or maybe fate was playing a sick joke on him, showing him what was possible and then ripping it away.

Yawning, he looked at the clock. He had been sitting outside of his house for over an hour. The morning would arrive soon and he needed sleep. As he closed his sketch book he noticed he had drawn Rachel's face. The likeness was incredible. He knew he was talented, but he focused on his masterpieces; he didn't create them subconsciously. Yet here she was, perfect in every way.

Part of him wanted to start over and paint her on canvas. Paints and canvas were expensive. Veronica had thrown most of his away, thinking they were old and because she said that they cluttered the house. He then had the urge to pull out his treasured Prismacolor pencils. Expensive as they were, he knew she was worth it. With his pencils he could easily blend, creating the perfect color of her hair, and shade where he needed to. But he knew better. If Veronica found the drawing there would be hell to pay.

His heart broke as he ripped out the page from his book and tore the image into tiny little pieces, shoving them into an empty fountain drink cup and replaced the lid. He would have to remove the evidence tomorrow morning.

Inside the house, he set his laptop case on the carpet next to the old sofa and emptied his pockets, laying his wallet, keys and cell phone on the coffee table. Lying down with his forearm over his eyes, he fell asleep with images of Rachel on his mind.

The next morning, Allen looked across the room at the time on the microwave. He had forgotten to set the alarm on his cell phone and was going to be late for work. There wasn't a clock in the living room; every time he bought one it caused another fight. She didn't believe an alarm clock should be placed in the living room. Days later it always disappeared. The mornings he overslept, he relied on Veronica to wake him up before she left for work. But this morning she let him oversleep again.

He jumped up and raced to the bedroom, got dressed, brushed his teeth and then woke up Lucas.

As his son stumbled out of his bedroom in his pajamas, Allen went to the coffee table and grabbed his wallet and keys. He didn't have time to feed Lucas or change his clothes; he would have to let his mother know when he dropped him off.

"Cell phone." He subconsciously patted his pockets. "Where's my phone?" It wasn't on the coffee table where he left it. Looking around, he noticed it was on the dining room table along with his laptop bag and a half empty coffee cup. The bag was unzipped.

Sighing, Allen knew what his wife had done. She had dug through his laptop bag and scanned through his phone looking for something to hold over his head. He knew that she would rifle through his laptop if she had the opportunity. Veronica had tried so many times to get him to tell her his password, but thankfully he caught on every time. At least he had one thing that he could keep private, not that he had anything on his computer to hide.

The spying and constant belittling was getting on Allen's nerves. He had been faithful and loyal for almost four years – at least up until last night. All he ever wanted was to be happy. He knew if he stayed with Veronica, he would never be. Grabbing Lucas, the survival bag, and his laptop, Allen locked the door behind them.

CHAPTER SIX

Rachel watched the coffee pot, wondering why it couldn't brew any faster. There were times she wished that replicators existed. Then she could say "coffee" and a full cup would instantly appear. She set the empty cup on the counter and crossed her arms as she leaned against the stove.

The past five weeks had been crazy. Rachel thought of the day in April when she sat and talked to Allen; her life was in disarray, but it was nothing compared to this past month. No one could have the streak of bad luck she was having in such a short amount of time. Lightning had struck after he kissed her that night in June.

Rachel felt frustrated. She missed their short talks in the courtyard. There wasn't anyone else she felt comfortable enough to talk to about all the weird events that were happening.

"Come on," she encouraged the coffee pot, "It can't be that hard." She hoped the power would stay on just long enough for the pot to finish.

Most of the strange happenings revolved around the nights Allen had class. Since the night he kissed her, they hadn't spent more than ten minutes alone together.

That next week, someone sent out letters to all the students stating they received a scholarship. No one on campus knew anything about scholarships being awarded. Instead of doing the research themselves or asking around, they sent everyone to her. She continuously had a line of students out the door asking questions and becoming irate when they discovered they didn't receive one.

Rachel discovered that the individual who sent the letters didn't preview them before mailing. He had accidently sent out the letter awarding the scholarship, instead of the letter asking the students to apply.

As the students filtered through her office, she would see him at her doorway. When she looked up he would smile before he left. Finally, Rachel got fed up with the inquiries and visited every classroom to explain the error and hand out the actual applications.

The week after that, Rachel thought they could spend some time together. She rearranged her schedule so she could work late and let him walk her out after class. That didn't work either. The first night he came by after class and they walked out of the building. He was upset because his wife was posting some nasty stuff about him on Facebook. He knew that potential employers surfed the internet and he didn't want them to see what she was saying. Apparently they had a big fight because she had posted that she could post whatever she wanted.

Rachel was going to ask him if his account was private, but the moment they stepped out the door, the wind picked up and the rain began to pour down hard. Instead of going back into the building, they raced to their cars to avoid getting soaked.

As they drove out of the parking lot, the rain suddenly stopped. Rachel looked at the sky and noticed it was a clear night, with only one rather large rain cloud passing over.

The next night he was on campus, Allen saw her in the hallway walking back to her office. "I have to go."

"What's going on?"

Rubbing his bald head with his free hand he said, "I'm not certain, but I think my wife is cheating on me. In fact I hope that she is because that will give me a good reason to file for a divorce."

Rachel looked at him inquisitively.

"Facebook. Some guy keeps calling her love."

"Oh I see. Remember I am here if you need me."

"How late are you here tonight?"

"Until classes are over. Are you coming back tonight?" Rachel hoped he would.

Allen smiled. "I'm not sure, but you might see me sooner than you think." He winked at her.

Rachel quickly tore a sheet of paper, wrote down her telephone number and handed it to him. "Just in case."

Allen shoved the paper in his pocket, turned, and bolted down the hallway.

He didn't come back that night. The campus closed at ten, but Rachel waited in the parking lot until ten-thirty, wondering if he was okay.

The third week her mother called because her kitchen had flooded. The pipes under the sink sprang a leak and left an inch of water on the floor. The plumber said she was lucky because without the leak, he wouldn't have found out the pipes in the wall behind the sink were eroding and would have leaked into the basement, causing even more damage. Rachel left work early to help her mother clean up the mess.

Last Wednesday they were able to sneak a few minutes alone together. Instead of staying in her office, they slipped outside and walked around the campus. Finally they were able to talk face to face without distraction.

"I was wrong about the affair. Apparently, Veronica was talking to some old high school friend."

Rachel forced a smile. "Well, I guess in a way that's good news."

He sat down on the stone bench under the elm tree. "At least she's not cheating on me. I almost wish she would. I want a divorce but I don't want to be the bad guy. I don't want to hurt her."

The clouds covered the rays of the sun and made the sky appear gloomy and unwelcoming. The sensitivity he displayed made Rachel shift in her seat. "I understand."

They sat quietly, lost in their own thoughts, and watched the students fill into the courtyard. Rachel gave him a shy smile, leaned toward him, and looked in his eyes. "I wish we could be alone so you could kiss me again."

His voice grew softer. "I can't kiss you again. I have to be faithful to my wife, at least until the divorce is over. And then when we get together, you will know how loyal a man I am."

Rachel's cellphone beeped. "My boss noticed that I'm not in my office and needs to talk to me immediately."

She stood up and looked at Allen. His eyes weren't as bright as the night he kissed her. They looked sullen and glazed over. She wished she could reach over and hug him. Instead, she gave him a brief smile, squeezed his shoulder, and walked back into the campus.

The day before yesterday was the worst. Rachel needed to take the deposit to the bank. She walked to the parking structure only to discover her car was missing. For ten minutes she walked around the lot and inside the garage looking for her car. There were only two places she parked because she was good at misplacing things.

When the police came and questioned her, she noticed that her spare set of keys was missing out of her purse. No money, no credit cards, just her spare set. Why someone would take her spare instead of the ones she kept on the desk, she had no idea. Aimee was off that day and nobody had seen anyone alone in her office.

By the time she called the insurance company and found out that she could get a rental, the rental car company had closed for the evening. Luckily one of the staff members offered to drive her home, but she had to leave earlier than she had planned, missing her chance to see Allen.

Yesterday, she took the hour-and-a-half bus ride to work, hoping to get a rental car that afternoon. The guy on the phone said they would deliver it before five o'clock. Ten minutes before six, Rachel called and was told that the car they had for her wasn't ready; they asked if she would like to upgrade to a nicer car, to get one that evening. When she inquired about the cost, they said it would be an additional $24.95 a day.

Not knowing what was going on with her car, Rachel knew it could be days or weeks before it was found.

She opted to wait, letting the insurance company cover it. They promised to deliver the car to her house first thing in the morning.

About two hours ago, Rachel woke up to a call from the Denver Police Department.

"Is this Rachel Weber?"

She rubbed the sleep from her eyes. "Yes."

"This is Detective Pacas at the Denver Police Department. We found your car sitting in front of a house in the city. The homeowner didn't see anyone. We are going door-to-door interviewing other residents. Do you know anyone that lives in Denver?"

Rachel sat up in her bed. "The entire student population at the campus lives in Denver or in the surrounding cities. How's my car?"

"It looks to be totaled. The driver's side mirror is missing, the front windshield is broken, and the airbags have been deployed. Whoever stole your car hit a light pole. We found your bumper laying in the middle of the street about two-hundred feet away."

"When can I see my car?"

"We're going to hold the car as evidence. I suggest you call your insurance company. I'll be honest; it's going to be a while before they will be able to appraise it for a claim."

Rachel grabbed a pen off of her nightstand and wrote down the case number on the inside cover of a romance novel.

Finally the coffee was finished. Rachel poured herself a cup, then sipped as she walked into her living room. "Liquid heaven." She sat down at her laptop and pulled up Facebook.

The night of the crazy rainstorm, curiosity got the best of her. She wanted to see what Veronica was saying about Allen. Rachel called her friend Christian and asked him how to set up a Facebook account. He was a bit upset that it was so late for her to call, but walked her through the process anyway.

"I thought you hated social media sites." Christian had been trying to get her to join Facebook and many other social media/networking sites for the last few years. She kept telling him that she didn't want anyone to find her online. Her desire to stay hidden didn't work. She was out there, thanks to her job and other people putting stuff online. Christian became her first friend.

Rachel couldn't believe what people said online. They complained about their lives, how they hated their jobs, and their significant others. Once in a while she would see something that was positive and inspiring. She was beginning to realize how negative and enlightening social media sites were.

Instead of reading her home page, Rachel pulled up Allen's wife's page. She noticed that Allen hadn't posted anything in over a year, but his wife was different; she posted something almost every day.

The more Rachel read, the easier it was to understand Veronica.

She liked to play the victim and most of the time used Allen as her source, milking her friends and family for all the sympathy she could muster.

The night before Rachel joined Facebook, Veronica had posted, "To everyone who doesn't like what I post, you can bite me." When Rachel read this she busted out laughing. Apparently, Veronica was upset that Allen had asked her to stop posting negative comments on Facebook.

Other posts were more subtle, indicating they were broke and her husband needed a better job. When a friend of hers replied that she needed a partner who was strong and could support her physically, emotionally, and financially, Veronica "liked" the comment.

She always complained how depressed she was and how tired she was of feeling that way. Though she never indicated that she wanted a divorce, she constantly complained that all he wanted was sex, didn't support her, and she wondered why he hadn't found himself a girlfriend. If she was late for work, it was his fault. If she couldn't afford to buy lunch, it was his fault. Yet, the week before, she had posted an image of her new I-Phone.

Rachel noticed that Veronica and her friends constantly trolled Allen. They would say things like "Someone should be there for you," or "Too bad you don't have someone that can handle that." Or they would tell her how wonderful and beautiful she was and that she should live her own life instead of taking care of "others" that just don't care about her.

Rachel almost felt sorry for Veronica. No one should be in a relationship that made them that depressed. Any guilt that Rachel had falling for this woman's husband disappeared as the days went by. Only a few minutes ago, Veronica told everyone that their gas had been turned off and she didn't know how she was going to take a hot shower. She stated that "someone" didn't pay the bill. Rachel knew that her "someone" was herself. Allen told her that Veronica never let him near the bills.

Taking another sip of coffee, Rachel turned off her computer and walked to the window. It was too early for the guy to show up with the rental car but she stared at her vacant parking spot anyway.

"I fell for him," she whispered. No man had ever affected her more than Allen had. Since the night he kissed her, Rachel couldn't stop thinking about how his body felt against hers. Every morning she woke up, she realized she had just dreamt about him. Every night before she fell asleep, she thought about what it would be like to have him lying next to her.

Rachel looked at the time, almost nine in the morning; she realized her rental car should arrive soon. She quickly got dressed, set her coffee cup in the sink, and sat next to the window. Partly out of boredom and partly out of concern, Rachel picked up her cell and texted Allen.

During the last few weeks, Allen would call or text her on random occasions and afterward erase her number or the message. The conversations were quick. Generally, they would just say hello or he would call and tell her the latest and greatest problem with his wife. Not wanting to push him, she would listen, ask questions, and offer the best advice she could without sounding biased, which was becoming more and more difficult, especially now that she knew what Veronica and her friends were like.

Prior to this morning, Rachel hadn't even considered contacting him. He was still married and he was still a student. Until he filed for a divorce and he graduated, Rachel wanted to keep the relationship as mellow as possible. She knew she was failing.

She typed, "Good morning" into her cell phone and paused before hitting send. Right before her thumb touched the button, she suddenly became very nervous;

a strange tingle came over her. Rachel took a deep breath and the weird feeling disappeared. She hit send.

Maybe texting him might not have been the smartest thing to do. He could be driving to work, or maybe he forgot his phone. What if he did forget his phone and his brother-in-law saw the text? What if his wife didn't go to work today?

"No," she said out loud, "Allen is too smart to forget his phone." She took another deep breath and waited for something to happen.

Her cell phone beeped a few minutes later. Smiling, she picked it up to see what he had said.

"Good morning. Who is this?"

"Oh crap." Rachel sat stunned, her eyes transfixed on the message. "His wife has his phone. Why don't I ever listen to my instincts?"

The doorbell rang; the rental car guy was waiting outside, throwing her into a panic. Jumping up from the sofa, she quickly texted back, "Sorry, wrong number."

Rachel hoped his wife believed her and went to answer the door.

* * *

Allen sat on the old, broken down sofa clenching the X-Box controller with both hands. He moved his paladin across the screen attempting to not die, but the computer-generated dragon appeared to know his every thought and constantly won the battle, no matter how many times Allen reloaded the game.

Losing the video game was not helping his mood or giving him the distraction he was looking for. Usually he felt better taking out his frustration on dragons, but tonight he couldn't formulate a strategy to kill the oversized beast or hit the buttons on the controller fast enough. His mind wouldn't stay focused.

He arrived home at 7:30 p.m., earlier than normal, only to find the house empty.

Earlier that evening he had snuck out of class to see Rachel. For the first time in what seemed like forever, she was completely alone in her office. No one was hanging outside her door waiting to talk to her, and her co-worker had already left for the day.

When she saw him her entire demeanor changed. Her crystal blue eyes lit up as she smiled at him. All he wanted to do was gather her in his arms and kiss her until she couldn't stand and then kiss her even more.

"Hey." Her voice sounded sweet to his ears.

"Hi." He crossed his arms and leaned against the door frame, just looking at her, wanting to hold onto the peaceful moment as long as he could. "I snuck out of class. We were working on some project and I just needed to get away."

"Are you doing okay?"

"No. The gas got shut off yesterday. I guess the bill didn't get paid. Again. All she can complain about is how she can't take a shower or do laundry. Not once has she said anything about Lucas or me not being able to take a shower."

"I'm so sorry to hear that."

"And I forgot my cell phone today. I have no idea where it is. I think I might have lost it."

"No, I don't think so."

He looked at her inquisitively. "What?"

"I kind of tried to text you this morning." She looked down and rolled her hands together.

"And?"

"And, I got a text back."

"What did you say?"

"I said . . ."

The fire alarm went off, muffling her response. A woman's voice came over the intercom: "This is not a test." Rachel walked up to him, taking him by the arm, indicating they needed to leave.

The stairs were located across from her office and he lost Rachel when he exited the building. Looking back, Allen saw her directing students to the stairwell.

Outside, Allen thought over the short conversation when Maddi walked up and handed him his laptop bag.

"I thought you might want this."

"Thanks." He reached for his bag. "What's going on?"

"No idea. But we were just told that we needed to check in out here and then we can go for the night."

"Check in?"

"Yeah, the instructor just needs to know that we left the building safely so the fire department doesn't start looking for us. Everyone needs to be accounted for."

Looking back at the doorway, Allen waited for Rachel to make it safely outside. A few minutes later he saw her walking out. He wanted to talk to her, but she was helping the other administrators move everyone away from the building. He realized she would have her hands full so he decided to leave for the night.

For the last few years, Allen had been miserable. His marriage was not getting any better, the bills were racking up, and Veronica never wanted to talk about anything unless it pertained strictly to her.

Six months after they were married she told him she was pregnant. He buckled down, ditching everyone he thought was a bad influence. He quit partying and began looking for a better paying job; but it didn't matter how talented he was, no one would look at his work without a degree. He really didn't like his job, but it paid the bills. At least when Veronica didn't insist on spending it before they were paid.

Tonight he didn't even bother picking his son up from his parents' house after work; a child had no business being exposed to this situation. Of course it was his fault the family had no hot water, according to Veronica. She complained the entire night that she couldn't take a hot shower, couldn't do laundry or wash the dishes. Not that Allen believed she would do laundry or the dishes. She didn't seem to care about anyone except for herself.

At 8:30 p.m. Veronica walked into the small three-bedroom house with her brother right behind her. Jim walked straight to the refrigerator, grabbed a beer and sat down on the sofa.

"Where's Lucas?" She threw her purse and keys on the kitchen table.

"He's with my parents. They said he could spend the night."

Veronica put her hands on her hips. "You need to bring him home. I want to see my son."

"No. He's fine where he is. He does not need to be here to see this."

"But he's my son."

Allen tossed the controller on top of the coffee table. "He's my son too. And he is safe."

Throwing her hands in the air, Veronica walked away. Just like she always did.

This time Allen followed her into the bedroom. "You told me last week that we would go through the bills together. Then you said they were all paid and that I didn't have to worry about them."

"I did pay them. With all the money that we had."

Allen slapped his hand against the wall. "You're lying. I checked our account earlier today. You made all kinds of transactions at convenience stores and fast food restaurants. You paid very little on the bills. And now we're broke again."

She crossed her arms again. "If you would get a better job, we could pay all of them."

"So it's always about me."

"Yes! You need to make more money."

"I'm trying." Allen was sick and tired of hearing her say this. He was thankful to have a job at all.

"You're not trying hard enough. You expect me to fix everything. I have to take care of the bills, of you, of our son, of our house. You don't do a damn thing except drink and play video games. I have to do EVERYTHING else."

His eyebrows shot up. "No you don't and you know it. All you do is smoke your pot, hide away in your own little world, and not care about anything!"

"What I do is none of your business."

"You don't care about me. You don't care about Lucas." He lowered his voice, bringing up something that hurt him the most: "If you really cared then why was Lucas born with THC in his system? You swore to me that you stopped smoking."

As always, Veronica changed the subject. "Then maybe you should find someone who will take care of you. Why don't you go and visit one of your girlfriends! How about the one that I talked to today?" she had a presumptuous look on her face.

"What do you mean the girl that you talked to today?" He went over the conversation he had with Rachel earlier. She had told him that she tried to text him, but the fire alarm went off and they didn't finish the conversation.

"I talked to your girlfriend," Veronica mockingly sang in a childish voice, throwing his cell phone at him.

Watching it land, Allen looked down at the mechanical device as if it would burn him if he touched it.

He regretted leaving the campus; he knew he should have stayed and waited until everything settled down. He was completely unprepared and had no idea what they had talked about. He hadn't made a final decision about what he wanted to do. Instead he just stood there looking back at Veronica, dumbfounded, until she broke the silence.

"Why don't you tell me your side of the story?" Veronica folded her arms."

"It is just a girl on campus. We talk sometimes, that's it." Allen tried not to say too much, not knowing what Veronica knew.

"So you're cheating on me? Is that it? I talked to your mom today and told her the whole story. How you're cheating on me!" She raised her voice with every sentence.

"No! I am not cheating on you! I've never had sex with her! We talk, that's it. Good Lord, I've never seen her outside of school."

"I think you're lying."

Finally, Allen's brain caught up with his thoughts. "When? When would I have time? I'm either at work, in class, driving back and forth or here. Tell me when I would have the time!"

Instead of answering, Veronica pushed him out of the bedroom, throwing a pile of clothes at him as she slammed the door.

It was too late to go anywhere; Allen grabbed his clothes and his phone off of the floor and carried them to the living room. Jim stood up from the couch, gave Allen a dirty look and walked into his bedroom, closing the door.

Tossing everything on the coffee table, Allen laid down on the sofa and tried to fall asleep. He knew now what he needed to do.

CHAPTER SEVEN

Standing on the balcony, Rachel gazed at the stars scattered in the midnight sky. In the distance, she could see the radio towers blinking in unison on top of Lookout Mountain.

The cool breeze brushed against her knee-length skirt creating goose bumps on her thighs. She crossed her arms, rubbing them with her hands, wondering why she was here. Occasionally, she could hear the engine of a car driving down the street over the chirping crickets from the bushes below.

From behind, she felt his strong arms wrap around her waist, drawing her against his warm body. Rachel knew by the way he held her, it was Allen.

Without a word, he swept the hair away from her shoulder, gently kissing the nape of her neck. Trailing his lips toward her ear, he tickled her with his goatee, leaving a trail of fire in its wake. Her knees were weak with his touch. She leaned back, using him for warmth and support, wanting desperately to melt into him, become one with him. She couldn't remember a time more perfect than this moment. She didn't want to think, only to feel. For the first time she felt completely desirable.

He breathed into her ear. "I've found my weakness."

"Your weakness?"

"You."

Turning, she met his brilliant amber eyes, searching for answers. Caressing his smooth cheek, she realized what he meant. Again, her knees became weak, this time with the understanding that she affected him in such a way. She could see the love he had for her. His eyes pierced into her soul.

Consumed by passion and desire, she lifted herself by her toes, wrapped her arms around his neck, and drew his lips to hers. He was only a breath away, yet the distance was too far. Allen didn't share the pent up urgency she was feeling. Slowing her down, he met her lips with long, lingering, soft kisses.

Stepping back, he gazed at her for a moment, as he moved a lock of hair the breeze had blown in front of her face. "Come." His husky voice was filled with desire. Taking her by the hand he led her through the sliding glass door.

Guiding her to the sofa, he sat down. His eyes didn't leave her; they watched every step she took. Rachel didn't want to blink for fear of missing a move he would make. She knelt down on the floor between his knees, gently caressing his thighs.

When did he get a divorce? Where were they? Why couldn't she remember?

Somehow, she knew he sensed her confusion, but instead of answering, he smiled, pulled her forward, and placed her body on top of his. Feeling the length of their bodies pressed against each other, the only thing she wanted was to focus on this precious moment. Every other thought disappeared.

Her body ached with need. She wanted to become one with him. The urge to explore him was overwhelming. For what seemed like an eternity, she craved him. Rachel slowly ran her hands down his chest, unfastening each button slowly, and placed small, innocent kisses on the newly exposed skin. The warmth of his flesh underneath her lips sent a pleasurable tingly feeling through her body.

She felt his coarse, warm hands run slowly up and down the length of her arms; his eyes were filled with passion and they gave her the silent encouragement she sought. She wondered how far he would let her get before he stopped her.

Amazed at her own forwardness, she wanted to see where her boundaries lay. Lowering herself to his navel, she kissed his skin, struggling to undo his belt. Smiling in amusement, Allen reached down to the buckle, quietly showing her how to work the latch.

"Oh." Rachel was momentarily embarrassed but the feeling quickly vanished.

Silently, he watched her unbutton and unzip his jeans. Teasing him with her tongue, she explored the uncovered area. His manhood peaked and she wanted to taste him. The tightness of his pants created an obstacle, not allowing her to take all of him. Her momentary wish was granted when the barrier preventing her from going any further was eliminated with the slightest movement of his hips. She took all of him into her mouth.

Rachel felt his hands buried in her soft, long hair, holding it back, keeping it from falling into her face. She breathed in the intoxicating, musty scent of him. Hearing him quietly groan with pleasure gave her a tingling sensation; she could feel the wetness between her thighs.

Allen noticed the urgency of her wanting to please him. Pulling her up, he placed her on top of him. Lifting her skirt, he moved her panties to the side, placing himself inside of her. His lips sought hers, his tongue diving into her mouth, as their hips moved together in unison.

Loving him was all she had ever seemed to want. She couldn't believe he was finally in her arms, making love to her. Holding him tightly, she could feel her body react to his every movement. Muffling a cry, she climaxed. He held her trembling body as it shook with release.

A moment later, he slid out of her. Rachel wasn't sure what she had done wrong; Allen hadn't climaxed. She wanted to please him, as he had pleased her. Looking into his face, she saw a smirk on his lips. He maneuvered her small frame to the side and stood up.

For a split second she felt an emptiness inside, thinking he was going to leave. Instead, he knelt down between her legs and lifted her blouse. He began running his hands across her stomach followed by soft sensual kisses, moving toward her breasts. Breathing heavily, she felt his eagerness to expose her small breasts.

"Do you need help removing my bra?"

Allen gently put his finger on her lips. "Hush. It's my turn, let me explore you."

Lifting her bra, his hands cupped her small breasts, as he began teasing her nipples with his tongue. She heard herself gasp when she felt him passionately nibble at them with his teeth.

Wanting more of her, he lowered himself, placing his head between her legs. His hands gently massaged her inner thighs as he began kissing the most sensitive part of her. Rachel closed her eyes, focusing on his every touch. She felt his tongue diving inside of her, tasting every bit of her essence. Digging her nails into his shoulders, her heart pounding, she exploded again with passion.

Before she could take another breath, her eyes shot open when she felt him inside of her again. The calm teasing in his eyes was replaced with an intense hunger. He leaned forward, kissing her with rough determination. She could taste herself when his tongue dove deep into her mouth. Everything she had dreamed of was coming true at this moment. This was the man she had been waiting for all her life. Allen's groans became louder; she knew this was the moment. Wrapping her legs around his hips, she pulled him closer, wanting to feel all of him inside her. Breathing heavily, Rachel closed her eyes. The pinks and blues of the heavens filled them as he took her to another level of ecstasy. With one last thrust, he fell on top of her. It was the most amazing experience Rachel could have ever imagined. She wondered if this was the first and the last time she would ever be with him.

Rachel sat up with a sudden jolt. The alarm clock had gone off next to the bed. Her damp body was shaking and she could feel wetness between her thighs. The morning sunlight shone through the curtains of her bedroom window. Realization hit her; she was alone. She had dreamt of being with Allen.

* * *

Rachel awoke at eight in the morning, which was earlier than she had planned on waking. She wanted to work late, but the dream woke her up early and she couldn't fall back asleep. Instead of sitting in bed watching the clock, reliving the vivid images of Allen and her together, she decided to get up and be productive.

It was ten o'clock when Rachel walked into her office.

Aimee greeted her. "I am so glad you're here. Your phone has been ringing nonstop for over an hour. I had to turn off the ringer."

Rachel looked at the display; she had missed eleven calls since she left last night. "Who's been calling?"

Just then the red light on the phone began to blink. "This is Rachel." She struggled to set down her purse and coffee.

"Hey."

She recognized the voice on the other end. It made her melt, reminding her how it felt when Allen had touched her. Blushing, she looked over at Aimee, hoping that she could keep the conversation inconspicuous. "Hi."

"I just filed."

"For a divorce?"

"Yeah. She'll be served tomorrow."

"I am so sorry it came to that." She slowly sat down in her chair. Part of her was ecstatic but his tone kept her in check. He sounded hurt and disappointed.

"Are you doing okay?"

"Yeah. This is the hardest thing I've ever had to do. I didn't get married to get divorced."

"I know you didn't. I know you're not that kind of person." The silence on the other end gave her the urge to say something else. Looking at the caller ID on her phone, she recognized his number. "You found your phone?"

"Yeah. You were right. Veronica had it."

"Why didn't you call me on my cell instead of calling the campus a dozen times?"

"She deleted your number. I didn't have it so I called Maddi this morning and got the number to the school. By the way, exactly what did you and my soon to be ex-wife talk about the other day?"

Rachel told him about the text messages.

"That's it? That's all you said?"

"Yeah."

"She said the two of you had a conversation."

"No. I didn't talk to her. I just told her I had the wrong number."

There was silence on the line again. Rachel hated when he got quiet and wouldn't say what he was thinking. "What about Lucas?"

"He's with me; well, at my parents' house. They're going to let me stay there until I get a place. There was no way I was going to let her keep him. She doesn't have anyone to take care of him when she's at work, other than her alcoholic brother."

"I'm glad your parents are helping you." Rachel was a bit disappointed. She had a two-bedroom townhome they could stay in. Months ago she had cleaned out her spare room, just in case.

As if he heard her thoughts, he said, "I couldn't very well stay with you, yet. It would be confusing to Lucas and I don't want to get you involved. At least, not until the divorce is final."

"When's the hearing?"

"The first hearing is in three weeks."

"You graduate in two."

"I know." And again she heard a long silence. "Crap. Look, I'll call you later. This traffic sucks and I have a cop behind me."

"Okay, I'll talk to you later." She hung up the phone. Sitting back in her chair she didn't know what to think. He really was getting a divorce.

Aimee coughed. "Who was that?"

Blushing again, she twirled her hair. "Nobody."

"Don't tell me nobody. That was your Romeo, wasn't it?" Aimee pulled her chair closer to Rachel's.

"You were listening a bit closer than you should have, weren't you?"

"Let's see. He's married, has a kid, and is moving into his parent's house because he just filed for a divorce. Did I get that right?"

"I really said all that out loud?" Rachel sighed and picked up the papers on her desk when Aimee stopped her by pressing them back down. She looked at Aimee. "What?"

"You've been really good at keeping quiet but I have to tell you, people are talking."

"Talking about what?"

Aimee laughed. "You and your Romeo."

"Me and my Romeo?" She hardly saw him. How could anyone find out?

"I know who he is and so do a lot of other people."

Rachel leaned back in her chair and crossed her arms. "And who do you think my Romeo is?"

"Allen Sinclair."

Rachel felt her face go pale. She knew by Aimee's smug look that she didn't miss the shocked look that came over her face.

Aimee clapped her hands and jumped up from her chair. "I knew it! I knew it!"

"How?"

She waved her hand as she pushed her chair back to her own desk. "It's obvious. He always walks by the door and looks in to see if you're here. People see you guys talking all the time." Aimee laughed again. "Oh and you should see your face when he walks in. Your eyes light up and you get this mushy look on your face. It's almost comical, except I can tell how you feel about him so I try to pretend I don't see it."

"Oh God." Rachel felt the world falling down on her shoulders. If the wrong people knew . . . "I'm going to be fired."

"I doubt it. They only people that seem to know are students. I had a few ask me what was going on between the two of you."

"Students?"

"Yeah." Aimee waved again nonchalantly. "Don't worry. They all like you and Allen. Everyone knows that he needs to leave his wife and they think that the two of you would make a great couple."

Rachel was getting nervous again. "Seriously? Who knows?"

"Let's see." Aimee pressed down a finger for each person. "Maddi, Rose, Tonya, Sabrina, and I think Nicole knows too."

Rachel sighed with relief. She couldn't have asked for a better group of students to figure out her secret. She knew each and every one of them genuinely cared about her well-being. At least once a week one of them was in their office making sure that Rachel had eaten that day.

If she hadn't, they almost always came back with something in their hand, even if it was just their leftovers.

"Do me a favor?" Rachel smiled and tossed Aimee a whiteboard marker. "Write the number fourteen on the board up in the corner."

Aimee wrote the number and placed the cap back on the marker. "Why the number fourteen?"

"Because that's the number of days I have left. The number of days until he graduates."

* * *

Allen called her a half dozen more times that day. Rachel felt she spent more time giving advice, supporting his decision, and consoling him than working. Thankfully she didn't have anything imperative to do and for some odd reason, no one else seemed to want to talk to her. Other than Allen, it was a quiet day. She spent it doing menial tasks that didn't require much thought.

A few times she had checked Veronica's Facebook page. To her delight, Veronica changed her last name back to her maiden name and her status was now separated. She also had several posts about Allen stealing her son away from her, how he was cheating on her, and that he was a horrible human being. And of course all of her friends gave her inappropriate legal advice and told her she was better off without him.

She also called Christian to tell him the good news. However, Christian didn't give her the encouragement that Veronica's friends and family had. "Be careful and don't lose your heart to him until it's officially over. Trust no one."

Rachel's jaw dropped. "Why not? He's filed and moved out."

"A very old friend of mine just sold our company without my knowledge. Someone I have known for years just screwed me over." There was a beep in the receiver. "I have to take this call."

That night Allen showed up thirty minutes before class started. Rachel was shocked that he made it after the day he had. He sat in the chair across her desk and rubbed the palms of his hands together. Rachel noticed that he wasn't wearing his ring.

"I did some shopping today." Allen showed off his new white tennis shoes. "After I filed the papers I went to Walmart and bought a new pair of shoes."

"You went to Walmart to buy shoes?"

"I know they'll wear out in a month with what I do, but mine were really bad. These will work until I get paid again. I also bought myself a watch."

"A watch? Don't you use your cell phone?" She didn't know anyone that wore a watch anymore.

Allen looked down at the watch. "A few years ago, right after Lucas was born, I bought myself a watch. I know it's crazy but I've always wanted a nice watch. It wasn't that expensive, only about two-hundred dollars. My son was just born and I had been accepted into college. I wanted something nice for myself.

"That night when I got home and showed her, she got really upset with me. She started screaming at me, asking me what the hell I was thinking, telling me we couldn't afford it. She told me I had to return it. So the next day I did. It wasn't so bad that I had to return it. If we didn't have the money, we didn't have the money." Allen paused for a minute, rubbing his cheap ten-dollar watch.

He glanced back up at Rachel. "It wasn't so bad, except two days later she went out and financed a brand new truck. Do you remember the one I told you about a while ago?"

Rachel leaned forward. "The one that was repossessed and then she went out and got another one?"

"Yeah. We couldn't afford a watch for me, but we could afford a payment on a brand new truck. Her car was still in good shape. She said she needed a truck for the winter."

He looked back down at his treasured purchase and smiled. "So I bought one today."

Rachel couldn't help but grin. He was as giddy as a school boy with a brand new bike. She was happy that he was happy. Rachel stood when he picked up his belongings to head to class. Walking him to the door, she suddenly stopped, and looked at the clock.

"What's wrong?"

She looked around in disarray. "We've been sitting here talking for almost a half hour. No one came in, no phone calls, nothing." Crossing her arms, her face red she said, "I guess I was wondering if something was going to happen."

"Yeah, I know what you mean. By the way, what happened the other night with the fire alarm?"

"One of the students failed his exam and pulled the alarm because he was angry with his instructor."

"Not cool."

Letting his laptop bag slide to the floor, Allen reached out and pulled her into his arms. Rachel let her guard down for a moment and didn't pull herself out of his arms until she heard him growling in her ear. Giggling, she released him. "Get to class."

She watched him walk down the hallway. He stopped and looked over his shoulder. "One down. One to go."

Rachel knew he was talking about the barriers keeping them from being together. He was getting a divorce; the only thing left was graduation.

CHAPTER EIGHT

Sitting in his Jeep in the parking lot at campus, Allen watched the cars, looking for Maddi's. He had texted her earlier asking her to get to campus early. He needed someone to talk to. Someone to help him put everything in perspective.

The last week everything he had worked toward spiraled out of control. They had a final exam in two days and he couldn't focus on anything except for the two women in his life.

He had one woman that he would give almost anything to be with. When he was near her he felt that he had found the other half of himself. What he felt for her was completely unexpected. He never imagined having these feelings for someone. If this was what love felt like, he wanted more of it.

But he still had a connection to Veronica. Veronica tugged at something deep down that he couldn't let go.

He remembered the feelings he had for her when they met and got married. She was everything to him; he wanted to spend the rest of his life with her. Most of all, he felt guilty for breaking his commitment. When he said his vows, he meant every single word. Even though their relationship had gotten worse he continued to feel an obligation to the promise he made on their wedding day. To love, honor, and cherish her until death do they part.

Months ago Rachel had asked if he ever told Veronica how he felt. He remembered Rachel saying that if he was hers, she would sit up all night talking about their problems and then about their dreams and goals.

Taking her advice, he took Lucas to see Veronica over the weekend. He tried to explain why he wasn't happy. He told her they didn't communicate like he needed them to; he wanted to be involved with the entire relationship, including the finances. He explained that by not taking responsibility, they were not teaching their son the right way to live. He also explained that he wasn't happy with his job either, but at times, he felt the only thing she heard was that he wasn't happy about his job.

After hours of talking, they agreed to try again. She agreed to the few things he asked of her and in return he had to promise to refrain from thinking about or wanting to have sex with her for a while.

The only problem was that when he left to pick up his things from his parents' house, he felt trapped and drained. The conversation made him tired. Lacking the motivation to hurry back, Allen drove around for a while, thinking about what he had just recommitted to and how he was going to break the news to Rachel.

Deciding that the decision was temporary and everything would depend upon how Veronica acted the next few days, he drove home. When he got there everyone was asleep. Peeking in the bedroom, he noticed his son sleeping next to his wife. Considering there was no room for him, he curled up on the sofa and fell asleep.

* * *

When he saw Maddi pull up, he jumped out of his Jeep and met her at the sidewalk next to the building.

Rubbing his hand over his bald head, Allen pulled out a pack of cigarettes. "I've got no clue what I'm going to do."

Maddi looked at him and laughed. "So when did you start smoking again?"

He looked at the pack in his hand. "Right now. You got a lighter? I forgot to buy one."

Maddi sat her bag on the ground, dug one out and handed it to him.

He took the lighter from her hands. "Since when do you carry around a lighter?"

Maddi laughed again. "Since right now." She folded her arms across her chest.

Allen lit the cigarette, took a few drags, and coughed. He hadn't smoked a cigarette since he left the military. "Now I remember why I hated these things so much." He took another drag and began to pace.

"Okay. Enough procrastinating. You told me to get to campus early because you needed to talk to me. What's the problem? It's obviously not the quiz we have tonight."

"I don't know what I'm going to do. I feel trapped and confused. I just needed some female advice."

"So you call me? What do I know about being female?" She adjusted her baseball cap. "I should've been born a boy."

Smiling, Allen looked around, to make sure they were out of earshot of everyone hanging around outside before class started.

"I have serious female problems. And you're the only one that knows anything."

"What's so serious? I thought you filed for a divorce? You only have two more days before you and Rachel can get together."

"That's the problem." Allen began pacing again, not sure how to explain his feelings. Finally, he broke the silence. "I have a wife and I have a girlfriend and I don't want to hurt either one of them. I just don't know what to do."

Maddi gave him a confused look. "Wait. What about the divorce?"

Sighing, Allen finally stood still. "We've been talking. She can't pay the bills by herself and I just can't leave her with all that debt."

"But those are her bills. She is the one that is in debt. Not you."

"But she is my wife. We are married."

"Yeah. On paper." Maddi grabbed the pack of cigarettes out of Allen's hand and pulled one out for herself.

"So when did you start smoking?"

"Just now, like you." She lit the cigarette, but didn't cough like Allen had a few moments earlier. He gave her a curious look and she shook her head. "Don't even give me that look." She shoved his pack into the pocket of her hoodie, and sat down on the curb. "Okay. So tell me exactly what's going on."

Allen followed her lead and sat down next to her. He picked up rocks lying on the pavement and tossed them to where they belonged. "We've been talking all weekend."

"Who is we?"

"Me and Veronica." He sighed. "She really wants to get back together. She told me she would start the court ordered check-writing classes and even made an appointment to see her therapist for this morning. And she actually went."

"Do you really want to stay married to her?"

Allen rubbed his hands together. "I don't know. I have to try one more time. If I don't, I know I'll regret it. I have to do everything I can to make this work. Someone needs to be there to support her if she is going to change. And I am her husband."

"So, you're deciding to stay."

Allen shrugged and nodded.

Maddi took a drag of her cigarette. "And what if it doesn't work?"

"Then it doesn't work. I can only take so much before I have to leave. I don't want to look like the bad guy."

"And what about Rachel?"

He hesitated and looked at her.

Maddi stared at him. "You fell for her didn't you?"

Allen didn't answer Maddi. Staring at the cracks in the pavement, a vision of Rachel came to his mind. She was all he could think about. Frequently, these past few months, he would wake up realizing he had dreamt about her.

Allen picked up another rock on the pavement and tossed it. "I have these strange dreams and they're always the same. Rachel's standing on the bank of a river watching me. We're too far away to hear each other.

The entire dream, I walk up and down the bank on the other side trying to find my way across. Every time I look up, she's directly across from me. I know she's waiting for me – that she needs me – but I can't find a way across. I feel frustrated, guilty, and almost in a panic because I can't get to her. After a while, she finally turns around and walks away. I watch her until she's out of site. As she disappears, I wake up."

"Why don't you jump in the water and swim across?"

Dumfounded, Allen gave her the strangest look. "I have no idea. I guess I don't want to get wet."

"Men." Maddi started laughing. "You guys are lost without us." Allen joined in the laughter a moment before she became serious. "What are you going to do about Rachel?"

"I have no idea. I don't want to hurt her."

"So you do know she has the same feelings?"

Allen nodded in agreement before he realized what Maddi had said. He felt like he was in high school. "How do you know?"

Maddi rolled her eyes. "You're kidding right? Every time I see the two of you together it's written all over her face."

"When? We hardly see each other anymore."

"Okay the few times I've seen the two of you together. We've talked a couple of times. I can see it in her eyes when I bring you up in conversation. I finally broke down and asked her last week."

He tried to sound aloof. "And what did she say?"

"That's between me and her. If you want to know, then you'll have to ask her."

"I don't know. I have to tell her about Veronica and I don't know what to say."

"Ah. So the truth finally comes out. That's what you want to know?"

Allen sighed, "Yeah."

Pulling out her phone, Maddi checked the time and grabbed her bags. "My best advice; tell her the truth and don't keep her hanging on. That is the worst thing you can do."

He grabbed his bag. "Just the truth? Nothing else? It's going to hurt her."

"Better to hurt her with the truth than to hurt her with a lie. Besides, Rachel is the most open-minded and understanding person that I've ever met. I think she'll understand."

"I hope so. We better get to class. I'll talk to her on break if she's still here."

Two hours later Allen walked into Rachel's office, thankful that nothing weird had happened to make her leave early. She was sitting at her desk going through a stack of papers. Before he could say hello, she closed the file, looked up, and smiled at him.

"Hey." He could hear the relief in her voice; it made him wonder if he was making the right decision.

She stood up and walked to her office door, and pulled off a piece of paper stuck to the back of it. Smiling, she showed him her sign. "This is to make sure we're not disturbed for at least a few minutes."

The sign simply stated: "In a meeting, please do not disturb."

Her smile disappeared when she closed the door and looked at him with frustration. "I am so sick to death of this." She stomped her foot. "I am sick and tired of not having the ability to talk to you without watching every word I say. I feel like everything I tell you is calculated because I'm so afraid someone will hear. I feel like I don't even have the opportunity to tell you what I'm thinking. I'm only able to say half a thought or half a sentence."

Allen took a step back. "You're not mad at me are you?"

"No." Her demeanor softened. "It's just that every time we start to have a conversation someone walks up or something happens. I wish I could see you outside of here so you could get to know who I am. Allen, you need to decide what's going to make you happy."

She looked down, lifted his left hand, and looked at the ring on his finger. He had put his wedding ring on the night before when he was at the house with Lucas. The look on her face broke his heart.

"You're wearing your ring." Her voice was filled with disappointment and confusion.

"We've been talking over the weekend. Veronica doesn't want to get divorced." Taking a deep breath, he decided to test Maddi's advice. "She went to counseling today and promised to get her court-ordered classes done. I can't leave her like this. Not when she's willing to change. She's going to need all the support she can get." He looked into Rachel's eyes. "I am a loyal man. And she is my wife."

"I know, Allen. But what's going to make you happy? Do you want to stay with her? You've wanted to leave for a very long time. Her problems are going to take longer than a few counseling sessions to fix."

"I don't know. I'm going back and forth. I'm not sure what I want to do. I realized this past week that the problems we were having fall on my shoulders too. I have spent a lot more time with Lucas. I discovered how hard it is to raise a child. I see what Veronica was going through when I would ignore both of them."

"It is hard being a single parent."

"I've also realized that I have anger issues. I need counseling. You've seen my temper."

Rachel smiled. "Um. No. I've seen you upset, never angry. Just do me a favor. Wait a few weeks before you pull the divorce papers and see what happens." Sighing, she hugged herself and her eyes filled with tears. "I'm not going to let go of this until it's final. Until I'm sure this is what you want and that you are happy."

He looked at the clock, "I need to get to class." Allen had never seen her upset like this but he understood. He felt like he had led her on. He felt like he had a wife and a girlfriend and did not know who he wanted to be with more.

CHAPTER NINE

Rachel tapped on her keyboard but couldn't focus on work. Her thoughts were on the last conversation she had with Allen. He was teetering, completely unsure of what he wanted.

"Going back to his wife," Rachel mumbled. She looked up at her whiteboard across the room. The first thing Aimee had done every morning was decrease the number. Today it was a big fat zero with a smiley face drawn inside.

If he could only hold on a few more hours, she could openly express every feeling, every pent-up emotion she had. She knew if she could talk to him outside of campus, away from all the distractions, she could get him to see reason. His wife wasn't healthy for him. Rachel knew he would never achieve his goals and his dreams if he stayed with Veronica. He would always be beaten down, never be good enough, and always broke.

Over the weekend, Rachel had spent what little money she had left from her paycheck on a haircut and a new outfit. She bought a new, black knee-length skirt and a beautiful emerald green, short-sleeve, silky blouse with a rounded neck. She knew his favorite color was green. She even went to Victoria's Secret for a matching bra and panties. Finding a set that even came close to the color of the blouse was a challenge, but though she finally had to drag the sales clerk around the store, she left smiling; Allen's last night of class would be a night to remember.

Rachel even stopped at a few jewelry stores looking for the perfect man's watch. If everything worked out the way she wanted, he would have one for his birthday in a couple of months. She planned to have it engraved with his initials and the year. Not knowing exactly what he wanted, she decided to wait.

Her hair, on the other hand, didn't fare so well. Somehow the store manager at the salon had mistaken her "barely take anything off the ends" to mean "give me layers up to my shoulders." Rachel didn't notice until she got home after running all of her errands that day. All she wanted was for Allen to hug her, tell her that her hair was not that bad, kiss her forehead and pull her tightly into his arms. She wore a baseball cap the rest of the weekend; she couldn't even look in the mirror.

Knowing she couldn't let another mishap control her emotions or her life, she hung the new clothes on the back of her bedroom door, placed undergarments on the corner of her dresser, and set her black heels next to them. She wanted everything to be in place.

The page on her computer screen finally loaded Veronica's page. Her cursor was ready to minimize the page she looked over at the door to make sure no one was going to walk in and catch her on a social media site. Rachel leaned toward the computer and began to read.

"Oh my God," Rachel sighed as tears filled her eyes. "I can't believe it." Closing her eyes, she took a deep breath to control her body from shaking. Veronica had changed her status back to "married" and her last name back to "Sinclair". Opening her eyes, she wiped away tears and looked back at the computer screen. Below, Veronica had posted, "Sighs in relief . . . Lucas is back home where he belongs." Nothing about Allen, only her son. Veronica changing her last name was enough for Rachel to realize it was over. Everything she waited for was over.

She had given into her hopes and desires. She let Allen convince her that she was someone special, someone unique, someone he wanted to be with. Every time she had tried to pull away, she would vividly recall the conversation she had with Maddi or hear him say the sweet things he told her that made her melt.

The dreams she consistently had didn't help either. She still woke up every morning realizing she had just dreamt about him, always wondering if there was some meaning behind it.

She knew better. Why didn't she listen to herself? Or at least Christian?

Wiping more tears away, Rachel let her hair down to cover her flushed face as she quickly walked to the bathroom to splash cold water on it. Thankfully, the bathroom was vacant. Turning on the cold water she looked at herself in the mirror. Her blonde hair looked curly and straggly from the layers being pulled back; her face was flushed, her nose running, her eyes red.

Raggedly breathing, she cupped her hands under the cold running water. It was colder than she expected. Veronica and Allen were back together. She turned it off, grabbed a paper towel and dabbed her face dry. In her reflection, Rachel didn't see the beautiful woman that Allen told her she was. She saw a plain, thirty-three year old girl next door. With no makeup and unstyled hair, she decided that he had every reason to go back to his wife. Rachel was not a vixen, not now. Tears filled her eyes again and she wondered what else his wife could offer, in what other ways she fell short.

How could I let go of my morals and values for some guy who says sweet things? Wiping her eyes again, she looked straight into them. "You are better than this. You knew better. You knew the risks. You knew that it could never happen. What the hell were you thinking? You weren't thinking. That was the problem. Now step up and quit being sappy about a guy you only kissed once."

Standing up straight, pulling her hair back into a makeshift bun, Rachel tried to believe what she told herself. Deep down, she knew there was more to the situation. But what, she wasn't sure.

The only thing she did know was that she wanted a new ending. Allen was going to get a piece of her mind when she saw him tonight – if he had the courage to see her.

Picking up her cell phone off of the counter, she went outside into the courtyard to call Christian.

"I've completely screwed up this time. I *can not* believe I let myself fall for him . . ."

* * *

Allen couldn't believe that tonight was the night. Finally, after three long years, he was done. One more assignment to turn in, one more exam to take, and his Bachelor's Degree was completed.

He got to campus early, telling his wife that he had to study. But preparing for his final was the last thing on his mind.

During the past two days, Allen had mulled over his decision to stay. Deep down he knew that his marriage wasn't going to get any better, but he couldn't seem to find the strength to go through with the divorce.

Veronica was doing everything she said she would do. She scheduled her court-ordered classes and went to therapy. The sessions were difficult for her; afterwards she sat on the sofa for hours in a dazed state, occasionally asking him questions. He tried to be supportive but was very careful to watch every word he said, not wanting to make things worse. She wanted to know if she was controlling, if their problems were her fault, and if he still loved her.

What could he say? He told her that she was controlling at times but knew that what she did was for everyone's best interest. That the problems they were having were both of their faults and he promised to work harder. And when she asked him if he loved her, he lied.

Allen was shocked to realize he didn't love her anymore. He hadn't really considered it. Loyalty, commitment, and the dedication to family dominated his thoughts. When he realized that he didn't love her anymore, he wondered if he ever really loved her or if it was just lust. He was drawn to her in a way he couldn't explain. It wasn't an intimate connection but there was something he was tied to, and he couldn't let her go.

What he did know was that he was about to see the most beautiful woman he had ever met. The golden speckles danced in her crystal blue eyes when she saw him. Her body fit perfectly against his and the sound of her voice filled him. He simply couldn't get her out of his mind.

Letting go of Rachel was going to be the most self-destructive thing he would ever do. He knew that he had the opportunity to be with the woman of his dreams yet he had to let her go, knowing something like this would never happen to him again in his lifetime. For his son, for his family, he was willing to give up his happiness.

The day before yesterday he had tried to explain to her that he needed to stay with his wife. But the hurt in her eyes and the distress in her voice made him second guess himself. The last thing he wanted do was cause her pain. It would be better this way, he tried to convince himself, better for everyone. She deserved to know.

Walking by her office, he took a deep breath, and glanced in. She wasn't at her desk, but he heard noise coming from the room. Peeking his head around the door, he saw her standing at the filing cabinet. She held a rather large stack of papers in one hand and thumbed through files with the other.

Had he made the right decision? Her emerald green blouse brought out the highlights in her beautiful blonde hair. He vividly remembered how soft it felt against his hands and how it smelled when she had her arms around him. Being near her, he felt at peace. For a moment he didn't remember why he was standing there quietly watching her, and then the guilt washed over him. He was there to tell her that he had made his decision.

Gently, he closed the door. "Hello."

Startled, she turned rather quickly and the papers in her hand fell to the floor.

"Crap," she muttered under her breath, looking down at the mess.

Allen smiled; it was nice to know he had that effect on her. He wanted to touch her again.

She knelt down and picked up the papers. "Is there something that you want to tell me?"

"Tell you?" He had been so engrossed with inappropriate thoughts that he forgot again why he was standing there.

Pulling the stack of papers together, Rachel tried to stand up. The next thing Allen heard was her head hitting underneath the file drawer she had left open.

Rachel stumbled as her knees buckled and her face turned white.

"Are you okay?" Allen lunged forward to catch her before she fell.

"You weren't going to tell me that you and Veronica are back together?"

"Oh that? I came in to tell you." She just had to bring up Veronica, he thought to himself. He felt guilty for looking at Rachel that way, given he had just made his final decision a few hours ago. He couldn't fathom how she found out so quickly; she always seemed to know what was going on before he told her.

Pulling her into his arms, he tried to walk her to the chair but she wouldn't move. "You need to sit down."

"But you haven't told me." She touched his face. "As your friend, Allen, I want you to be happy."

"That means a lot to me," he said, thankful she wasn't going to start crying or say she hated him.

Rachel looked away. "But as the woman that is attracted to you . . ." She paused, and began to pull his face forward.

He knew what she was about to do, but he was faster. He leaned forward and met her lips, drawing her closer. He kissed her with all of the passion and desire he was feeling, knowing this would be the last time his lips would ever meet hers. And then she collapsed in his arms.

CHAPTER TEN

The half-day's ride to the Drovere Estate would have taken twice as long had he opted for the carriage. Alexander Dohetry appraised the sky; not a cloud in sight. If the weather continued to cooperate, this year's annual hunt would be a success.

Slowing his horse, he surveyed the estate on the horizon. Through the tall trees he could see the gray-stoned, three-story modest home of the well-to-do wool merchant, Arthur Drovere. After hours of riding, the beauty of terrain had become dull and boring. Alexander knew why he wasn't enjoying the scenery; his mind was on his last conversation with his mother. This morning they parted on the most unfavorable terms. The moment she stepped into her coach for her journey home, Alexander grabbed his belongings and prepared to leave. Much to his manservant's dismay, he decided to ride instead of being locked in the slow carriage.

During the week's visit, his mother could only speak of one thing: Viola Bryant. As far as she was concerned, Viola was sent from the heavens to marry one of her sons. The events of the last year now put the responsibility of the union on him.

As far back as Alexander could remember, Viola was promised to his older brother George. As children, the boys chased her around the estate, pulling her hair and teasing her. Not once did Viola tattle, though she had every reason to. Instead, she would play tricks on them, once getting George to eat a dirt pie. For years after, they would all giggle about the expression on his face when he tasted the dirt.

She was as smart and daring as any boy, constantly trying to show them up during practice sword fights using small branches. Most of the time, the boys won, but once in a while she was able to use their cocky attitude to her advantage. Afterward, they would roll on the ground laughing about how a "mere girl" could best them.

Years later, the boys saw her in a new light. Viola wasn't a mere girl with whom they played with when her parents came to visit. She was becoming an attractive, sensitive, young woman. During one visit, the boys came across her crying, holding a wounded bird in her small hands. The bird had a broken wing and couldn't fly away; Viola was devastated. Instead of teasing her for crying, the boys helped her take care of the little bird until it healed enough to fly. That was the last happy memory he had of the woman.

Her cousin James came to live with them; shortly thereafter her mother passed away. In a matter of mere months, Viola went from a sweet girl to a she-devil. At first it was small things. When her father wasn't present, she demanded attention from those around her. Viola became irate when they visited and George trained with the guard in the courtyard, as if her betrothed had a responsibility to attend to her.

At first Alexander felt sympathy for her but as they grew into adulthood, the more he got to know her the less he wanted to do with her.

Six months ago George passed away; Alexander had a hard time adjusting to his brother's death. During a family picnic, George had fallen from a cliff near their childhood home. The accident still didn't make sense to Alexander. When they were young, they had constantly been whipped for sneaking off to play near the cliffs. George knew the area better than anyone. Anytime their mother couldn't find the boy, she sent someone to the ridge in search of him. As George grew older, the cliffs became his favorite place to impress one of the serving girls. Alexander felt that his brother knew every blade of grass, every loose stone, and how George could have slipped to his death was a mystery.

Now his mother wanted Alexander to step in, uphold the agreement, and marry Viola. He had to admit the union would be a move up. Any other man of his station would jump at the opportunity. She was beautiful, wealthy, and a distant cousin to the Queen.

Her thick, long black hair, dark brown eyes, and aristocratic face made her the catch of The Season. Viola was petite and God blessed her in all of the right areas, except for one. She was, quite simply, vile.

After several days of listening to his mother praise Viola, he could tell she was frustrated with his lack of response. Alexander could say the word "no" only so many times before he quit saying anything at all. Several times during her visit, he came home to find Viola in the drawing room and twice he found her unexpectedly at supper. Those meals were long and excruciating. Had she invited herself? He would have confronted her but he couldn't be sure his mother wasn't behind it.

When that didn't work, his mother reminded him the family had already taken possession of the livestock from Viola's dowry shortly before George passed away. There were plans for the Bryant land that bordered their estate once the union took place.

Last night Alexander told her to take the issue to his oldest brother Richard, who inherited the title and most of the small fortune when their father passed away. He realized his response was not the one she wanted to hear when she accused him of having no honor, loyalty, commitment, or responsibility to his family. Those words had been pounded into his head since he was a small boy.

This morning she did something unforgivable. She challenged his loyalty to his brother, how George would want Alexander to take his place, and uphold the families' agreement. For the first time during her visit, he felt he was losing the battle.

Had anyone else said those words, Alexander would have started laughing. George felt the same way about Viola and if given the choice, he would have broken off the engagement. He confided to Alexander that he had no plans to reside with her. Once she became pregnant, he planned to do exactly what their father had done, live in separate households and have several mistresses attending him.

When Alexander disagreed that George wouldn't ask this of him, his mother finally told him the truth. She had already spoken to Viola's father and in his stead agreed to the engagement.

At that moment, his world came crashing around him. His mother's actions made sense. The engagement had been accepted on behalf of the family, and she was trying to convince him that it was his idea. Realizing he was trapped, Alexander persuaded his mother that the end of The Season would be a better opportunity to announce the engagement that he had no intention of following through with.

He hoped Viola would find someone else to set her interests upon, not him. He couldn't imagine spending the rest of his life with that woman.

Alexander's thoughts were interrupted when he heard a faint scream in the distance. Shaking his mind back to reality, he looked around for the source of the cry. Ahead of him, standing in the field next to an oak tree, stood a woman with long blonde hair, yelling while flapping her arms about.

Alexander turned his horse, gave him a swift kick, and raced toward the girl.

* * *

Rachel heard faint voices over the ringing in her ears; she tried again to open her eyes. Her body felt weak, and she tried to determine whether or not opening her eyes would invite more pain then she could tolerate at the moment.

The state between sleeping and waking was the worst; as Rachel tried to move her sore shoulders, attempting to pull her mind out of the foggy realm of sleep, a sudden sharp pain shot through her neck. She grimaced as her body tensed, riding through another spasm. Not wanting to move her upper body again, she rolled her ankles and stretched out the stiff muscles in her lower legs.

With the slightest movement of her body she could feel her mind beginning to clear as she made another attempt to open her eyes. Finally, she was able to barely crack them open – only to have the bright light shock them closed again. Since the pain of waking up was worse than the ringing in her ears, she directed her energy to the distant voices becoming clearer.

"'Tis time you awoke, scaring me by falling out of the tree like that. Papa will be upset when he finds out you were climbing trees at your age." Rachel wished she could open her eyes just enough to see who the scolding woman was.

She heard the voice of a male. "Has she awoken?"

"Of course she is awake, she moved. Come. We need to get back and cleaned up before all the guests arrive." Rachel knew the woman was talking to her when she felt someone tugging at her arm, but had no idea what she was talking about.

Curiosity took over. She forced herself to open her eyes. Lifting her arm to shield the light, she was able to crack them open enough to see what was around her. Everything was a colorful blur. After she blinked several times, her surroundings began to take shape.

Where the hell am I? Rachel asked herself. I have to be dreaming. When she looked up she saw a rather large tree filled with big green leaves, the clear crystal blue sky, and thick, luscious, green grass as far as she could see.

Her survey of the area was disrupted when the woman began pulling at her arms. Rachel's legs wouldn't cooperate; looking down she saw they were bound tightly within the folds of a blanket. Blinking again, she realized that she was wearing a long dress.

Why am I wearing a dress? She thought to herself. Disoriented, Rachel did her best to assist, thankful that most of the pain had subsided.

Using the woman for support, she knew that her body was still weak. Once she was upright, the woman released her. Rachel's legs collapsed. Before she realized that she was falling, the ground beneath her disappeared. Looking up, she gazed into the most amazing amber eyes she had ever seen.

"Allen," she whispered breathlessly. Her world went black for the second time.

CHAPTER ELEVEN

Stretching, Rachel wondered what time it was. The alarm clock hadn't gone off so it had to be early. Deciding that she didn't care, she reached out for her pillow, wanting to pull it back under her head. With her eyes closed, she couldn't find it; she wondered if it fell on the floor, but searching required more effort than she was willing to exert at the moment.

As the haze of sleep lifted, she could smell the sweet scent of burning wood, and wondered which one of her neighbors had a fire going.

She opened her eyes and spotted red embers flickering in a fireplace. Confused, she looked around and saw a blond-haired girl asleep on a rocking chair with a handmade quilt lying in her lap.

I must be dreaming, she thought, rubbing the sleep from her eyes. She opened them again, but the scene in front of her didn't change.

Rachel sat up, immediately regretting the sudden movement from the stabbing pain in the head, and the dizzy, nauseous feeling in her stomach. Taking a good look at her surroundings, she noticed she was lying on a soft bed that resembled a canopy, with only two poles at the head. The walls held simple, faded tapestries, which once were colorful designs of Celtic knots, draping over dark wooden panels. Wooden shutters covered the windows, preventing the bright sunlight from entering the room. Beneath the window a small wooden table held a white pitcher and bowl. Near the door sat a small cabinet reminding her of an old-fashion ice chest her mother owned.

Pulling the thin sheet away from her body and turning to get up, she noticed she wore a long, thin night gown. The movement must have been louder than she thought when the girl awoke and moved quickly to help her.

"You should not sit up too fast." The young girl spoke with a thick English accent. "I will go get mother. She is beside herself with worry."

"Wait." The girl turned at the sound of Rachel's voice. "Give me a moment to adjust myself."

The girl stepped back to the bed and knelt down, putting her hand on Rachel's arm. Rachel could see the worry in her eyes but she couldn't console the girl; Rachel had no idea where she was.

She looked around again. "Where am I?"

A stunned expression covered the girls face. "You do not know where you are? You are in your bedroom," she stated flatly. "Do you not remember Lord Alexander carrying you? Everyone has been in an uproar, such improper behavior. I shall get mother." With that she raced out of the room.

This is not my bedroom, Rachel thought. I must still be dreaming.

Moments later an older woman with long graying hair walked through the door with a short balding man carrying a small, brown leather bag.

The young girl ran in behind them. "She does not seem to know where she is and she cannot recall Lord Alexander."

The older woman waved her hand. "Hush now, Abigail. The physic is here."

Not knowing what else to do, Rachel let the bald man examine her while she tried to put everything together, what happened and why she needed a doctor.

"The bump on her head may be contributing to her memory loss. Otherwise she appears to be fine." The physic concluded, "Are you hungry, lass?"

Rachel shook her head no; the dizziness and nausea made her not want to speak.

"Give her some bread, broth, and eyebright infusion. Let her rest and her memory will return soon enough. I will be back in a few days' time to check on her."

In the spirit of the strange diagnosis, she quizzed herself. Her name was Rachel Weber. She was thirty-three years old and born in Kansas. She lived in Lakewood, just outside Denver; had a younger brother, a black cat named Zanza, and the last thing she remembered was kissing Allen in her office.

Wanting to disagree with the man and tell him her memory was fine, she decided to keep quiet instead. She didn't know where she was or who these strange people were.

Finally the gray-haired woman and the physic left the room, leaving Rachel alone with Abigail.

The girl gave Rachel a timid look. "Does it hurt?"

Rachel nodded. "Yeah."

The minutes passed by as the two girls sat there quietly looking at each other. A knock on the door brought the timid girl to her feet. Taking a tray from a serving girl, Abigail set it on the bed next to Rachel. Rachel picked up some flatbread and cheese, and tried to recall the last time she had eaten.

Stuffing the food in her mouth, she thought back to the last thing she remembered. She had grabbed a stack of papers and started filing them to kill time before Allen arrived on campus. All she could think about was how he had broken her heart when she heard him say hello from behind her. Turning, she dropped the stack of papers . . .

"Holy Crap!" Rachel rubbed the bump on her head.

"Rachel! If mother catches you blaspheming in this house that bump on your head will be the least of your troubles."

"Sorry," she said solemnly, wondering how Abigail knew her first name.

"Abigail, where's the bathroom?"

Abigail jumped from her seat and clapped her hands. "You remember me!" She paused, "I dare say, what is a bathroom?"

"Seriously?" The dumfounded look on Abigail's face made Rachel realize that she really didn't have any idea what she was talking about.

"Um, restroom?" Abigail shook her head no.

"Facilities?" Again she shook her head.

"Privy?" Abigail had a look of understanding, pointing to the cabinet that resembled the old-fashioned ice chest.

Opening the small door, Abigail collected a rather large, white ceramic bowl with a handle on it. Realization led to distress in Rachel's face; it was a chamber pot. But she had to use what was available, and then maybe she could think. Embarrassed, Rachel lifted her shift and carefully crouched over the oversized bowl. Trying not to miss and thereby mess the floor, she wished that she was outside with a large bush she could hide behind.

Feeling better, Rachel examined the room in detail. There were no lamps or light fixtures hanging from the ceiling. Next to the pitcher on the table sat a small comb with various colored ribbons attached to it. She noticed that there weren't any mirrors in the bedroom and the only light came from the fireplace and the edge of the shutters. Other than its color, Abigail's dress resembled a wedding gown with its long sleeves, tight bust and full skirt.

Rachel walked over to the shutters, opened them, and peered outside. A cart pulled by two horses trod off in the distance down a dirt road. There was no pavement and there were no cars. Looking closer, she didn't see any telephone poles or power lines scattered across the landscape, either.

Rachel felt her heart fall into her stomach. She turned around to look at Abigail. "Where am I?"

"I told you before, silly, in your room."

"No. What town, what city?"

"Near Bedminster."

"England?" Rachel looked back upon the scenery.

"See! You do remember."

Rachel turned quickly. "The date? What is the year?"

Putting a finger to her lip she took a moment to think. "It is the hundredth-and-twenty-fourth day, in the Year of Our Lord 1564."

"Hundred-and-twenty-fourth day?"

"That is what I said. The hundredth-and-twenty-fourth day, in the Year of Our Lord 1564."

It took a moment to register in Rachel's mind. She turned white, and almost passed out before Abigail caught her and sat her back down on the bed. It took her longer than normal to do the math in her head; she was close to 450 years in the past.

"Rachel? Why do you keep calling me by my given name? You never call me Abigail unless you are upset with me."

Rachel guessed, "Um, sorry, Abby."

Abby jumped off the bed and clapped her hands again. "See, you do remember. Now you need to rest. I will be back shortly to check in on you."

Alone with her own thoughts, Rachel couldn't comprehend how she ended up almost 450 years in the past. She laughed when she thought about the work left on her desk, and wondered who was going to finish it while she was missing. Of course, she mused, the work hadn't exactly been created yet.

The thought of her desk lead her to the last minutes she spent with Allen. She told him that she wanted him to be happy before she kissed him . . . or did he kiss her?

It didn't matter. He made his decision; he went back to his wife. Tears filled her eyes as she pulled the thin linen sheet around her, thinking about the last time she'd seen his face, wondering if she would ever see him again.

* * *

Rachel couldn't fall asleep. Every time she began to drift off, someone walked in attempting to engage her in a conversation. First it was the chambermaid, Alice, who came in to check on the fire, arrange her bedding, and offer to dress her. Though she tried to shoo the young woman away, Alice continued asking if there was anything else that she could help her with.

Several times her new mother, Eleanor, whisked in and out of the room only to make sure Rachel was awake and to update her about the preparations for the nobles attending the annual hunt.

Abby's visits were calmer and longer than those of Eleanor. Her new sister's vibrant personality made her easy to talk to. Though Rachel had asked her strange questions, Abby willingly answer them without complaint or passing judgment. She revealed the most basic information with a smile and sometimes a giggle.

Rachel discovered her name was Rachel Drovere, nineteen summers old with Abby two summers younger. Her father was Arthur Drovere, who had several small holdings in addition to his main estate. He was known for the quality of wool his estate produced. Last summer he had an accident, injuring his leg. According to Abby, it still hadn't healed properly and now he used a cane.

The day after tomorrow was the first day of the Drovere Estate's annual three-day hunt. The majority of the guests would arrive by supper tomorrow night, with a few trickling in afterward. Most of the fourteen nobles expected had attended in years past.

This year was even more exciting for Arthur's girls, for they were allowed to participate and they were both of marrying age. Abby confessed there would be several eligible bachelors attending, and she hoped to meet a potential suitor.

Yesterday, Abby had dared Rachel to climb the large oak tree south of the house, to see any guests arriving, specifically one of the men. She had no idea that Lord Alexander was in the vicinity; but Abby was thankful he was. Laughing, she told Rachel that Lord Alexander carried her the entire way back while Abby led his horse. Once inside, much to their mother's distress, he carried her into her bedroom and laid her down on the bed.

Rachel moved the quilt around. "Why would mother be distressed?"

A horrified look came over Abby's face and then she began giggling again. "It is improper for an unmarried man to enter an unmarried girls room. Thankfully none of the other guests had arrived to witness."

As Abby, Alice, and her new mother raced in and out of her room at different times and for varying intervals, Rachel tried to lie down in between, hoping to fall asleep. Whenever she thought about her present circumstances, her head would begin to throb with excruciating pain. Instead, she decided to let her thoughts drift; most of the time they returned to Allen.

All she needed was one more day to tell him how she felt, to show him how much he meant to her – and with only hours left, he ripped her dreams away, tearing her heart into little tiny pieces. She planned to give him a piece of her mind, to tell him how she felt no matter what the circumstances.

Instead she had reached up, kissing him with everything she had building inside. The release of passion had given her a strange tingling feeling and for a moment, she had felt as if she had connected to him completely. The next thing she remembered was waking up in a strange bedroom in 1564.

* * *

Rachel looked out at, but didn't see the beautiful English landscape. Her mind was distracted with the events of the last twenty four hours. Waking up this morning, she realized that she wasn't dreaming. Somehow she fell out of her time and into the past.

Attempting to adjust to her new reality, Rachel surveyed her new home from her new bedroom window. She could see a dirt road lead into the grand circular driveway of the main entrance just beneath her. In its center sat an enormous oak tree, its giant branches shading the multi-colored stone perimeter. On either side of the drive, a wing of the house jutted forward, each a three-story square with five evenly spaced rectangular windows per level, and a triangular roof.

The Drovere estate reminded her of a large, silvery gray stone house she had seen on a PBS Special. Across the drive, as far as the eye could see, were rolling hills of green grass with clusters of trees and small herds of sheep grazing in the pasture.

Hearing the sound of horses, Rachel automatically turned toward the road where she saw an elegant carriage approaching. It reminded her of something Prince William and Kate would have ridden in. The large black vehicle had seven windows; three on each side and one in the back. The driver sat high on its front, holding the reins of two magnificent draft horses trotting in unison down the driveway.

Black curtains adorned the windows to keep prying eyes from seeing its occupants. On the side, the carriage doors featured what looked like extra-large brass buttons, pressed into the shape of the letter B.

She watched as the guests and workers approached the newcomer. Whoever was arriving must be someone incredibly important, Rachel thought to herself.

Mesmerized, Rachel stared as the horses came to a halt at the front of the entrance. A young man with red hair opened the carriage door, extending his hand to the visitor. A delicate hand was placed in his, as the most exquisite woman Rachel had ever seen stepped out. "Regal" was the first word she could think of to describe the mysterious woman. She had the most luxurious long dark hair, covered by only a petite cap draped with netting. Her long, sapphire-blue gown shimmered in the sun, exposing enough cleavage that Rachel blushed for even noticing. The most impressive thing was how she carried herself. Her back was straight and when she moved it was slight and with purpose.

As Rachel caught herself leaning out the window to take a closer look, Abby burst into her room dropping a basket filled with sewing supplies onto the floor next to the bed.

"Oh my, Oh my." Abby tried to catch her breath. "Did you see her?"

Looking back outside, Rachel noticed that the woman was no longer below. "Her?"

"Yes. The Lady Viola. Mother is beside herself, rearranging everyone."

"Rearranging everyone?" Rachel was completely confused.

"Yes, silly. We have to move everyone for Lady Viola."

"Slow down. What are you talking about?"

Taking a deep breath, Abby explained that the highest ranking individual gets the best room with the next highest sleeping in the second best room and so on.

"Viola was not expected. We have to move the rooms. Mother gave up her sewing room for Lord Edmond. Father wanted to move Charity into your room, but she told him that it was not necessary because of your condition. She said she would bunk with me. It will be just like old times when she would sneak into my room and we would stay up until dawn."

Abby talked so fast with her English accent, Rachel wasn't sure if she heard her right. People in this time actually moved their guests around based upon status? In her time, if someone crashed the party, they could sleep on the floor and no one cared.

Rachel had to know. "So who has the highest status?"

"The Lady Viola, for her father is an Earl."

Somehow Abby's response didn't surprise Rachel. She thought back to how everyone amassed toward the carriage when Lady Viola arrived and how regal she appeared when she stepped out of the carriage.

Sitting down on the bed, Rachel looked into the basket Abby set on the floor. Picking up a white piece of lace, she caressed it carefully between her fingers. "This is beautiful." Rachel whispered in amazement.

"You are funny." Abby giggled. "Just yesterday morn you said that was the ugliest piece of lace you have ever made."

"I made this?"

"Of course silly, this is your sewing basket; mother said I should bring it to you."

Looking back down at the simple piece of lace, Rachel couldn't see how anyone could call it ugly.

"Mother says you are expected for supper. I had best be assisting her with the preparations." Abby closed the door.

The last thing Rachel wanted was to be around so many people when she didn't know how to act or what to do. For a moment she thought about running away, but the thought was fleeting. Even if she could find her way to the front door unnoticed, she didn't know where she would run to. She had no family in England; her ancestors were Volga Germans – or at least they would be in a few hundred years.

CHAPTER TWELVE

Shortly after Abby left, Rachel's chambermaid walked into the room to dress her for supper. The forest green gown Alice carried made her giggle with delight.

Rachel wished that she could bathe, knowing that soaking in a tub would be out of the question; she remembered people bathed a few times a year, believing that it would harm their health. Instead, she used the pitcher of water and a rough linen cloth simulating a sponge bath. Though it wasn't the most wonderful experience, it did make her feel better.

Her excitement faded when she noticed the massive amount of clothing lying on the bed. Pulling off the thin nightdress that she'd been wearing since she arrived, Rachel took a deep breath as the young girl started dressing her.

First was a thin shift, similar to the one she had removed. Then the corset; she didn't realize it would be so heavy. The tabs held thin strips of flexible steel designed to flatten her torso and give her a tiny waist. Expecting the worst, Rachel held her breath as Alice tightened the laces. When she exhaled to take another, the girl tugged, decreasing her waist by another inch.

Unable to take another deep breath, Rachel stepped over to the fireplace, holding onto the mantel, wondering if she was going to pass out. Focusing on inhaling and exhaling, she calmed down, realizing that the corset made her stand up straight, giving her an hourglass shape.

The entire ordeal took almost two hours. Rachel lost count of the number of layers Alice had buttoned and tied to her. She gave up making small talk over an hour ago; every time she asked a question, Alice gave her a peculiar look.

Nonetheless, Rachel was giddy as a schoolgirl. She felt like a little kid dressing up for Halloween. The taffeta fabric shimmered in the light while she practiced walking back and forth in the small room. Wearing close to thirty pounds of clothing, she still felt naked underneath not wearing underwear. Too embarrassed to ask, Rachel figured if she was supposed to wear underwear, Alice would have handed her some.

Her mother walked in while Alice combed her long blonde hair. "Rachel, does your head still bother you? You have been awfully quiet."

"Yes. It's just a headache. I'm sure it will pass."

She gave Rachel a strange look. "Are you quite sure? Your speech seems odd this day." Waving her hand in dismissal, Eleanor continued. "The guests are beginning to gather in the parlor. Your father expects you to arrive in a quarter hour." She left the room, closing the door.

Rachel's enthusiasm immediately turned into panic. She didn't know what she had said wrong to receive such an odd look. Besides, she hadn't stepped out of the bedroom since she arrived; she should've been paying more attention, figuring out how to act in this time period instead of thinking about where she belonged. Now she had to do it in front of at least a dozen people and the only person she had been somewhat relaxed with was Abby.

What would happen if she did something stupid? What if they discovered she was an imposter? She would rather give a speech in front of a thousand people in her own time then go to supper tonight in this one. Faking it was her only option. She resolved to speak when spoken to and try to remember the phrases Abby had said. If anyone noticed, she would use her memory loss as an excuse.

The final touches were completed. Rachel stood up and glanced down at herself. Had she not been so nervous, she would have felt like a princess in a fairy tale. The gown fit snug against her waist, a bit of cleavage showing from her small chest, and her hair was put up on top of her head with ringlets falling down. She tried to take a deep breath but the corset prevented it. Rachel gave a shallow sigh and began the long walk to the door. Opening it, she almost ran into Abby.

Protectively taking Rachel by the hand, Abby took a few steps then suddenly stopped. "Wait." She turned and raced into Rachel's room.

Looking around for the first time, Rachel saw the hallways on both sides of her room lead to small stairs at each end, merging into one grand staircase. Black iron sconces held several lit candles, spaced evenly down the hallways. Past the wooden railing, a grand chandelier featured crystals and candles lighting the foyer. Tapestries and large portraits covered the painted wood paneling.

Abby grabbed her hand again, placing a small gold ring on her finger. The tiny ring held a small, baroque pearl. Its lumpy teardrop shape held a luster unlike she'd ever seen before. Gazing at the gem, Rachel became absorbed in the translucent nacre.

"'Tis your favorite, do you not remember?"

Rachel shook her head no without looking away from the ring.

Abby tugged on her sleeve. "Come along before mother goes into another fit."

Carefully descending the stairs, Rachel narrowly avoided tripping on the hem of her gown when Abby caught her arm. "We cannot have you falling again."

Holding Abby's arm, Rachel smiled.

At the base of the stairs, the two turned left and walked slowly into the parlor.

"Here are my girls!" Arthur greeted his daughters with a bit too much enthusiasm.

This must be my father, Rachel thought. The short, heavy-set man didn't look much older than forty, other than graying hair at his temples and the cane he used to help him walk.

Over a dozen people filled the room. All of the women wore beautiful gowns. Rachel felt self-conscious, wondering if hers was appropriate. She wanted to gawk at everyone but the embarrassment of not knowing what to do made her roll her hands together quietly in front of her, keeping her gaze locked on the floor, standing very closely to Abby and her father.

Rachel's curiosity got the best of her. Peeking up, she took in her surroundings.

Dozens of flickering candles adorned the room. Two sofas faced the fireplace where four older women sat talking amongst themselves. A couple men stood at the mantel under a beautifully painted portrait of her mother. Rachel had to take a second look when she noticed the men wearing tightly fitted woolen jackets, puffy long balloon shorts that reached their knees, and tights. She giggled, then corrected herself – they're called hose – as she tried to suppress a memory of a movie she'd seen several times, in which woodsmen danced in green tights.

Continuing to take subtle glances, she noticed several other small groups standing together in quiet conversation. Rachel caught her breath; out of the corner of her eye she thought she had seen Allen. She turned to look and it was as if time had stopped. The man looked directly at her with the amber eyes she remembered. For an instance she didn't hear the noises around her or see the guests. It was as if they were on another plane of existence meant for only them.

Her sister pulled on her sleeve, bringing Rachel back to reality. "Rachel. 'Tis not polite to stare. Do you not hear me?"

Blushing, Rachel shook her head. "Who is that?"

"*That* is Lord Alexander. Do you not recall him? He carried you to your bedroom after you fell out of the tree." Looking down at the floor, Rachel shook her head no.

Taking one more subtle glance, she saw that now his back was to her, so she couldn't determine if what she had seen was an illusion. She wondered if she recognized him from her dream the day before.

Rachel had been in the parlor less than ten minutes and she was finally beginning to feel slightly more confident. Mimicking Abby was easier than she thought it would be. Other than asking Abby who Lord Alexander was, she hadn't uttered another word. Smiling and nodding her head were the only responses she had the courage to use.

A man who had been standing near Lord Alexander approached the small group greeting them. "Good den, Miss Abigail, Miss Rachel."

Recognizing the man as the one who helped Viola out of the carriage, Rachel noticed he was a couple of inches shorter than most of the men in the room. His strawberry blonde hair and freckles made him look more like a kid up to no good rather than several years older. His eyes portrayed intelligence and confidence that she rarely saw for men his age in her own time. Rachel guessed that children were expected to grow up faster during this period of time rather than coddled. After all, Romeo and Juliet were only about fourteen years old.

"Good den, Mr. Parker," Abby responded, smiling. Turning to Rachel, she asked, "You do remember Mr.

Parker?" Rachel looked down, embarrassed, shaking her head no.

Mr. Parker gave Rachel an inquisitive look before Abby regained his attention and whispered, "My sister had an accident yesterday and has lost her memory."

The look that came across his face was of genuine concern. "You are well otherwise, I assume?"

Nodding her head yes, Rachel smiled.

"Ah. 'Tis no wonder that you are shyer this evening than on the other occasions when we have spoken."

Abby leaned toward him and lowered her voice. "Mr. Parker, my sister is to sit next to you. Would you be so kind as to watch over her for me? I fear leaving her alone for she does not remember the simplest of things."

"Do not fear, Miss Abigail, I will tend to her." Mr. Parker's face turned a bit pink. "Miss Rachel, could I be so forward as to request to escort you to supper?"

Rachel nodded, taking his arm as the guests proceeded to the dining room.

Supper was a grand event at the Drovere Estate. Huge silver trays filled with various meats and with rich sauces were placed with great ceremony. Each course held a variety of different foods. Cups were filled with soup which was, Rachel learned, drunk instead of eaten with a spoon. She enjoyed most of the foods other than the vegetables; they were cooked to a pulp and she didn't like how the slimy texture felt on her tongue.

Mr. Parker was a perfect supper companion. He didn't press her by asking questions that required more than a nod. At one point, she had asked his first name. He laughed and whispered that it was inappropriate to ask, but answered her just the same, "Henry."

Rachel found herself enjoying Henry's stories, thankful she had kept his attention so she would not have to speak to anyone else. When the first course was served, Rachel had difficulty trying to eat with only a knife, a spoon, and her fingers. Without making a spectacle of Rachel's memory loss, Henry silently guided her. She felt as if she had met a friend in 1564.

Lord Alexander sat several places down on the same side of the long table, next to the woman Rachel had seen step out of the carriage. Rachel found that the seating arrangement suited her. With Mr. Parker on the other side, she was not tempted to stare at the man.

The conversation turned easily from politics to the events of the next three days, to the upcoming balls in Bristol. It appeared that everyone present would be traveling to Bristol after the hunt.

"Will the unknown artist be painting?" asked an older woman, one of the chaperones.

"Anon," a man across her with dark eyes corrected.

The older woman lifted her brow. "Anon?"

"Aye. That is the name Lord Henry Berkeley has dubbed the anonymous artist." The man responded confidently.

"Interesting," she mused, "Shall we be seeing Anon, anon?" A handful of the guests who heard the comment chuckled.

Dumbfounded, Rachel leaned over to Henry. "What did I miss?"

Henry lowered his voice. "Shortened from anonymous. Lord Berkeley felt that the unknown artist needed a shorter name to identify him, thus Anon. Miss Bush asked if we would be seeing the unknown artist soon."

"Oh." Before Rachel could process all of the information, the conversation turned to the latest news from the Queen's court. Rumor suggested Queen Elizabeth was prepared to declare Mary Stuart as her heir on the condition she marry Robert Dudley.

* * *

After everyone had their fill, the dining table was cleared of the evening meal. The women moved into the parlor while the men were caught up in a discussion about the heroics of past hunts. Alexander moved closer to Nicholas Mattingly, the Yeoman, who planned the events each year for the Drovere Estate hunt.

Alexander and Nic had known each other for years. Most of Britain's high society wouldn't have considered befriending someone of such low rank. However, Alexander looked beyond a man's status. He believed a man should be judged by his actions, not by the title he inherited.

Since Viola's arrival, Alexander had not shown much enthusiasm about the upcoming activities. The urge to pack his bags and ride back to his cottage in Bristol that evening was overwhelming. He hoped three days in the country hunting deer would give him an opportunity to come to terms with his mother's agreement. He did not see how he could marry a woman he couldn't stand being near.

The moment Viola stepped into the parlor she burdened him with idle conversation. Her older, widowed cousin James Bryant was only a few feet away. Alexander assumed he was acting as Viola's chaperone as the elderly woman he met last week was not present.

During the meal she politely kept him conversing with their host and guests seated near them. Alexander did not know how she managed to have him seated next to her, as there were others of higher rank in attendance. Not letting his emotions override his sense of duty, he managed to get through supper without incident.

However, he had difficulty keeping his eyes from occasionally glancing at the woman a few seats down.

His mind would not let him forget the events of the morning before. When he had heard the scream, he raced to see what had happened to make a grown woman shriek the way she did. Alexander recognized Arthur's daughter Abigail, but he didn't immediately recognize the girl she was scolding as she was trying to pull her to a standing position. He knew Arthur had two daughters, for he had met both of them on prior occasions.

The girls were alone with no escort. He quickly dismounted to help the lass. When they had finally gotten her to stand, she looked at him and called him Allen just before she collapsed.

The moment he swept her into his arms, he felt a strange sensation come over him. The woman he carried was exquisite. The moment she looked at him he felt as if he had known her for an eternity. Never in his life had he felt such an immediate connection.

When Alexander carried Rachel over the threshold, her father tried removing the lass from his arms. Alexander remembered glancing at the cane and then at the man. The look was not lost on her father. Realization and then embarrassment came over Arthur's face; with his injured leg, he could not have carried her.

Following her mother Eleanor into the bedroom, Alexander laid the girl on her bed. Gently moving a lock of blonde hair from her face, he had the sudden urge to kiss her before her mother interrupted his thoughts. Thanking him, she began tending to her daughter. Alexander quietly left the room.

Alexander leaned toward Nic. "Tell me more about the blonde wearing the green dress."

"Miss Rachel?" Nic cleared his throat and gave Alexander a curious look. "She is the eldest daughter of Mr. Drovere. They will be in attendance for the rest of The Season." His friend leaned forward, lowering his voice. "I have heard it said that this may be the girls only Season. If they do not find a match in a few months' time, their father may marry them off to the highest bidder."

Alexander's eyes shot up. "Highest bidder?"

"'Tis rumored Arthur has borrowed every penny to stay afloat. Old man Goodwin offered to pay off his debts if he would let him marry the younger lass."

"Goodwin? Why he is older than . . ."

Nic cut him off, "Exactly. He has yet to acquire an heir, for his wife and child died in childbirth several years ago."

"Why the younger girl?"

"Did you not notice? Miss Abigail is the more appealing of the two."

Alexander shook his head no. He thought Abigail was pretty, but her beauty did not compare to that of Rachel.

CHAPTER THIRTEEN

Rachel couldn't sleep, tossing and turning until dawn, images of Allen haunting her dreams. Wide awake, she remembered the first time he kissed her, the words he'd said. He was as nervous as a school boy. When he said those words, Rachel felt as if she had finally met someone she could spend the rest of her life with. He didn't want to just take her home, he wanted to get to know her, but they never had the opportunity.

Sighing, Rachel finally got up and walked to the window. Opening the shutters, she gazed at the sunrise, trying to suppress the pain she was feeling. Tears filled her eyes. Rachel felt as if he tore away the opportunity to fight for him. He knew she couldn't violate the policies.

Allen is married, she thought. She knew better than to let her guard down. Somehow, she knew he wouldn't leave his wife. If she only had one more day, just one more day to tell him how she felt. To show him how much he meant to her.

Since the night he told her he was attracted to her, the time they had spent together was limited. Every word she said to him was calculated and it felt as if the world was against them. A crazy rain storm, a fire alarm, her mother needing help with strange plumbing, even her car being stolen. Maybe all the weird things that happened were a sign. They weren't meant to be together.

She knew that she had to let go; deep in her heart it hurt too much to even think about it. Trying to justify her emotions, she remembered he wanted a divorce. He had been talking about it for months and even filed the papers weeks ago. Somehow, Veronica had talked him into staying. He made his choice. He chose to stay.

Rachel scolded herself, "I'm in 1564. I need to figure out how to get home, not think about him." She crossed her arms, stomped her foot, and turned from the window.

Picking up the forest green gown from the floor, she fumbled with the fabric, trying to figure out how to get dressed when Alice entered the room. "You are awake, Miss."

Nodding her head yes, Rachel held up the gown. "Can you help me with this?"

Giving her a stunned look, and then shaking her head, Alice walked over and took the gown from Rachel.

"I am sure my lady would be more comfortable donning something a little less formal." She traded the evening gown for a simpler day dress.

The pale blue dress with little white flowers was not as elaborate as the one she wore the night before. The blue brightened the color of her eyes. Instead of placing her hair on top of her head, Alice pulled it up into a tight bun at the base of her neck. It still took over an hour to dress. And to think, she said to herself, I could be dressed and out the door with coffee in less than fifteen minutes.

Rachel was to "break fast" with Abby. Even though it was not as grand, the abundance of food shocked Rachel. The food was spread out on a buffet where everyone was allowed to fill their own plates. Grabbing a few pieces of bacon, a slice of bread, and cheese, she began looking for coffee. But to her dismay, all that was available was a week beer and watered down wine. Opting for the wine, she sat down next to Abby at the table.

"Father said that I may join the party today," Abby shifted in her seat excitely. "I have never been on a hunt."

Rachel smiled; she could not help but be happy for Abby. She was beginning to like this girl whom she had to call sister. Abby was sweet and innocent with dreams of marriage and children.

"I'm glad father is allowing you to go."

"Maybe I will be able to speak with the gentlemen," Abby offered. "You are joining us? Father said if you are feeling better you may attend."

The last thing Rachel wanted was to join the party. "I don't know, Abby. My head still hurts."

Abby lowered her voice. "We could always ask the witch lady for a cure."

Rachel looked up at Abby. "A witch?"

Rachel's mind raced, trying to remember everything she knew about witches. It's too early for the Salem witch trials. Tarot cards hadn't been invented yet. Or had they? If not, then maybe runes. Runes should have been invented by the sixteenth century. Maybe she could do a reading and tell me how I got here – and how to get home.

Mother walked up to the girls and stated firmly, "You leave the old woman alone. She is not a witch. Eat your morning meal; we have things to tend to. If Rachel feels the need, I will call for the physic."

Rachel touched her head. "I'm fine. It's just a headache."

"The lady is still feeling ill?" Turning, she saw Lord Alexander walk into the room followed by Henry Parker and Nicholas Mattingly, the Yeoman. Rachel felt her face flush.

The Yeoman looked at Rachel. "If the lady is not feeling well, it is agreeable she is excused from the day's activities."

"I concur." Mr. Parker laughed. "We do not need the lady falling off her mount. Miss Abby, you will be joining us?"

Rachel noticed that Henry almost stuttered when he addressed Abby. Both Abby and Rachel blushed.

Eleanor responded for the girls, "Abby will be attending and Rachel will be staying."

Nodding in the agreement, the men walked over to fill their own plates. They began wagering on every aspect of the hunt. Who would be the first to spot a deer? Whose arrow would be the first to hit? They even gave Mr. Parker a hard time, playfully bantering that he would be the first to fall off of his horse.

Alexander was a good looking man. Rachel could see why the women fell for him. For some crazy reason, every time she looked at him, he reminded her of Allen. It has to be the eyes, she thought, looking away, not wanting to be caught staring again.

There were distinct differences between Allen and Alexander. For one, Alexander had beautiful sandy blond hair. His nose was shaped differently and he didn't have facial hair. She wondered what Allen would look like if he shaved. They both were about the same height and build, but lots of men were about six foot tall, lean and muscular, she thought, chastising herself again for thinking about Allen.

Yet, when Alexander looked at her, it made her feel warm inside, as if he knew something she didn't. Rachel wondered if there was something between them, something Abby hadn't revealed.

The mood of the men changed from light hearted to serious when Lady Viola and Mr. Bryant entered.

"Good morrow, Lord Alexander." Viola walked over to the buffet, completely ignoring the others in the room.

Alexander frowned. "Good morrow, Lady Viola. I hope you slept well."

"Not as well as I had hoped." Viola waved her hand. "The chambermaid did not secure the shutters last evening. One swayed open and this morn I awoke earlier than anticipated with the light of the sun shining in my eyes."

Eleanor interrupted with a slight bow. "My apologies Lady Viola, I will see to the shutters being repaired."

Stunned, Rachel watched Viola turn her dark piercing eyes toward her mother; when she blinked her attention turned back to Alexander. The woman didn't nod or even accept her mother's apology.

"The room is too small for my possessions and the linens were rough, scratching my skin while I slept. I fear I should have been more prepared for a long stay at a merchant's home." Viola sighed, "Alexander, would you be so kind as to pour me a goblet of wine?"

Without a word, Alexander set his plate down on the table and proceeded to pour Viola's wine into a pewter goblet.

Viola's demeanor completely changed after she took the first sip. "What are we to expect from the day's events?"

"Come girls." Eleanor summoned Abby and Rachel from the room. Looking back as she left the room, Rachel's eyes briefly met Alexander's before he turned them back to Viola. Rachel could feel the tension and wondered what was going on between the two of them.

Shortly thereafter, the hunting party left with only a few staying behind. For the first time that day, Rachel was left alone with her thoughts. A few of the older woman were in the dayroom sewing with her mother. They asked her to join them; she politely declined, wanting to explore her new home.

The house was larger than Rachel anticipated. There were sixteen bedrooms, many of which had their own parlor that was made into another bedroom for the chaperones. The servant's quarters were behind the kitchen. When she tried to enter the kitchen she was made to feel unwelcome and politely encouraged to leave. The first floor held several rooms including the dining area, parlor, day room, ballroom, and in the back, her father's library. Each one was decorated similarly to her bedroom with paintings and tapestries hanging on the walls. The only major difference was that each one decorated with a different color scheme.

Not wanting to be stuck in the house, Rachel decided to go outside for a walk, hoping the fresh air would clear her head. Her brain still felt foggy and every now and then she felt pain in her neck from the injury.

Stepping out the front door, she looked around. The scenery was more beautiful than she imagined. The sky appeared bluer and the sun brighter than she remembered in her own time. She looked up at the oak tree. It seemed larger than it did from her bedroom window. Green grass spread out as far as she could see. It felt good to take a deep breath while the sun warmed her face. If she had to be anywhere but in her time, she felt that there could not have been a more wonderful place. Rachel enjoyed the fresh air and the absence of sounds. She had always wondered what land would look like with the absence of concrete structures and telephone poles. Now she knew.

With no one stopping her, she walked slowly around the house, taking in her surroundings. Smaller buildings stood behind the house, including the stables. Rachel found an old log to sit on against the house, facing the stables.

There was no logical explanation how she had stepped into the past. All she did was kiss Allen after she hit her head, and then blacked out. Picking up a stick off the ground, she thought about what Abby had said when she woke up: she arrived on the 124th day in 1564; that was two days ago. For some reason her mind wouldn't let her add up the numbers without looking at them. She tugged at the bun, pulling her hair free from the restraints. Drawing in the dirt, she wrote down the number of days in each month and began adding. She had arrived on May 4th – unless it was a leap year – then it would have been May 3rd.

"Wait," she whispered, remembering a conversation with the librarian on campus six months earlier. He was phenomenal in spouting useless information at random times, and engaging her in the strangest discussions. He had mentioned the Gregorian calendar was adopted in England in the mid 1700's. The people of this time were still using the Julian calendar – which meant it was ten days off.

"If leap years are perfectly divisible by four . . ." Scratching the math in the dirt, she wrote the number 391. The year 1564 was a leap year; she counted the days of the months again. Rachel had arrived on April 23rd:

the day she dropped her phone at the hardware store and bumped into Allen.

Not trusting her math, she erased the numbers and began calculating again.

A shadow appeared over her work, making her jump.

"Spending your day scribbling in dirt? What is that you draw?" Lord Alexander towered above her. She immediately scribbled through her work, not wanting him to see what she was doing.

"Yes, I mean no. It's nothing. I was thinking."

Without invitation, he sat down next to her. "I trust you are feeling better?"

"Yes."

He looked around. "Your chaperone again leaves you unattended?"

Rachel tilted her head and then remembered unmarried girls of this time should have an escort of some kind. "My mother's entertaining the women in the day room. I guess she thinks I'm in my room."

"Ah." Taking the stick out of her hand, he used it to smooth the ground at their feet.

The minutes passed as the couple sat quietly enjoying the countryside. Rachel felt comfortable sitting next to the man, relieved that he wasn't asking questions or commenting on her strange speech.

Finally her impatience kicked in, and she broke the silence. "Why aren't you with the others?"

"My horse is being tended to. He picked up a stone in his hoof. I shall join the hunt later or perhaps tomorrow."

"Oh," was the only thing she could think to say.

Rachel glanced down at the dirt; Alexander had drawn the image of a horse similar to the one standing in the coral next to the stables. Giggling, she realized that this nobleman was a big kid at heart. Seeing another stick in the distance, she playfully went to get it. "Have you ever played tic tac toe?"

The bewildered look on his face made her giggle even more. "Scoot over. I'll teach you." Not wanting to mess up his masterpiece, she drew out the grid next to the horse, and explained the rules of the game. "You be the X's . . ."

"Ah, noughts and crosses. I do know of this game." He laughed and placed a cross in the middle box.

For the next hour the two sat talking and laughing while they played. When she called him Alex for the first time, he gave her a funny look, but didn't correct her. They spoke of the hunt and he told her intimate details about the guests Abby hadn't revealed.

"Lord Edmond Severs cares not for status or wealth, as his only interest in a bride is how she appears on his arm. I believe he would marry one of his steeds if given the opportunity."

Rachel giggled.

"Whereas, Lord Gerald Goodwin flaunts his exuberant wealth. By his words, one would believe he has in possession more gold than the Queen. He does not desire a marriage of rank, but of one that will bear him an heir."

Rachel placed a circle in the last space of the grid, tying the game. "What of the Yeoman?"

"The man has an eye for business and investments."

Rachel's eyes perked up. "Why is he leading the hunt if he is a businessman?"

Alex shrugged and gave her a peculiar look. "The only interest Master Mattingly has in the hunt is acquiring new investors."

Neither could remember who won the most games when they heard someone calling Rachel's name. Not wanting to be caught, Alexander quickly disappeared into the nearest building.

That night, as the guests assembled in the parlor before supper, Rachel caught Alex watching her; he would then give a knowing smile or wink at her. The way his smile lit up his eyes reminded her of Allen.

She stood next to her father, who was engaged in conversation with several of the male guests. The handsome Lord Edmond Severs would not stop talking about the latest horses he acquired from Spain. He believed his chargers would be sought out by all of the Knights throughout England. Rachel met Alex's eyes. He winked at her again, sharing a private moment.

Rachel blushed, and thought about the afternoon they shared. When the older, more distinguished looking man, Lord Gerald Goodwin, boasted he could buy all of Lord Edmond's horses without blinking, she caught Alexander rolling his eyes. Giggling, she wished she could talk to him again without causing a scandal.

Even if she was allowed to converse with him, she didn't think she had the courage. Other than this afternoon, every time she had seen Alex, Viola appeared with her cousin behind her.

There was something about the woman that Rachel couldn't figure out. Viola was beautiful, cold, and fake. Yet several of the men were drawn to her when she entered the parlor. Men haven't changed in the last four hundred years, Rachel thought; they always look at the outside instead of the inside.

After supper everyone gathered in the parlor for entertainment. Almost everyone performed. Luckily, Henry came to her rescue when her mother encouraged her to sing, indicating that she looked pale and her injury may be bothering her. She wasn't pale because she felt unwell; it was because she couldn't hold a note to save her life.

A ting of jealousy overcame her when Viola sang in the most beautiful, angelic voice while Alex accompanied her on the lute. The instrument looked like a small guitar with a broken neck. Nic must have known what she was thinking; sitting down next to her, he made a joke about how uncomfortable Alexander appeared.

Some of the men stood and recited poetry or told a story that made her hold her stomach in laughter. By the time she went to bed, she realized she had completely forgotten that she didn't belong here.

* * *

After the evening's entertainment, Alexander stepped out the front door of the estate. He looked up into the sky only to see patches of clouds covering the stars. He closed his eyes, enjoying the silence. An image of Rachel entered his mind.

Nic interrupted his thoughts. "A most joyous evening."

"Indeed."

"You have yet to reveal your afternoon's activities."

Alexander ran his hand through his hair and started walking around the estate. "Aye. As I am sure you have already discovered my activities."

Nic's eyes twinkled with amusement. "Playing in the dirt with a merchant's daughter? Aye."

"'Twas more enjoyable than Viola's idle conversation. Is it possible for that woman to speak of something other than gossip, balls, or the latest fashion?"

They turned the corner behind the structure and Alexander peered over to the spot where he had sat earlier in the afternoon, talking and playing noughts and crosses with sticks. The girl called it by another name – in fact her entire way of speaking caught him off guard a time or two. Not once did she speak of dresses or balls. The young girl made him laugh and the conversation was natural, not forced as it always was with Viola.

Alexander sighed and walked to the stables.

Nic laughed. "Once Lady Viola discovered your absence she demanded to return. However, her cousin persuaded her to stay with the party. I believe James has every intention to win the wager of the first kill."

A stable hand approached the men and bowed with a questioning look on his face. "My Lords?"

"Go back to sleep, Timmy." Nic tossed him a coin. "We have no need for your assistance this eve."

Alexander gave Nic a curious look. "One of your men?"

"Nay." Nic looked at the young boy climbing the ladder to the loft. "Not at this time, though one never knows how valuable the lad could be."

Dozens of horses stood in the stalls which lined the path to Alexander's horse. He opened the gate and pulled an apple from his pocket. His horse sniffed the treat and then took it into his mouth. Once he finished, he nudged Alexander for more.

Nic laughed again and then became serious. "Pray tell me, were your intentions of leaving the hunt to visit Miss Rachel?"

Alexander shrugged. "Nay, though we had a most enjoyable time. One does not enjoy oneself when a woman rides so close that on occasion her mount bumps up against one's own. Viola's idle conversation began praying upon my nerves. I intentionally slowed my horse and purposely fell behind. I felt you understood when you gave me a nod."

"Aye, indeed."

"I turned my horse and raced back to the estate. 'Tis when I found Miss Rachel drawing in the dirt. I simply joined her."

Alexander did not reveal that Rachel called him Alex. Never had he let anyone shorten his name, not even his mother. For some reason he could not explain, he liked the sound of it when it came across her lips.

He gave his horse a loving pat and stepped out of the stall. "We best get back. I have manservant duties to attend to." He laughed. "It appears I was in such a rush to leave Bristol, I failed to bring him along."

"Nay, did you not hear? Your manservant arrived shortly after supper."

A look of relief crossed Alexander's face and he smiled. "Then I best not keep him waiting."

CHAPTER FOURTEEN

The next morning, Rachel woke up exhausted. She couldn't remember the last time she enjoyed herself as much as she had yesterday. The time she spent with Alex in the afternoon was worth the scolding she received from her mother after she had found her outside alone, without a chaperone.

Hearing voices outside the window, Rachel stood up and peeked out. Several of the men were practicing archery on the lawn. They strutted around trying to impress each other, which appeared to be difficult with all the laughing and jesting. She couldn't help but giggle with them when someone missed their target.

Today she knew she couldn't step outside the house without someone escorting her. The thought of having someone follow her as she walked around the estate made her feel uncomfortable. Instead of having someone watch her every move, she resolved to stay inside, hoping to find something to keep her occupied.

After the party had left for the afternoon, Rachel walked in circles, visiting every room on the main level, looking for a quiet place to think. Though she was beginning to enjoy herself, the memory of her real life kept tugging at her. She needed something productive to do; so far nothing had given her any indication as to why she was here.

Sighing, she retraced her steps into the library her father used as his study. The room was decorated for a man. Wooden planks covered the walls. Dark burgundy curtains hung over the windows, with a portrait of her father hanging over the fireplace. A tall, built-in bookcase stood behind the large oak desk. Rachel ran her fingers across several of the leather bound books.

Turning, she looked at her father's desk. Touching the polished wood, she looked up to make sure no one was watching, and then she opened each drawer. Inside of one she found her father's ledger of accounts.

The leather book was filled with handwritten columns of numbers. In her own time, she would audit student ledgers and could easily find mistakes and inconsistencies. She also had a bit of experience reading Old English. The projects she did for her friend Christian gave her the opportunity to transcribe several handwritten wills between the 1600's and the 1850's. Whenever the production company needed obscure research for a documentary, Christian called her. She had a knack for finding details others had overlooked.

Holding the sixteenth-century ledger in her hands must be how a historian felt when uncovering a piece of history. Thumbing through the pages, Rachel couldn't help but feel a bit excited. She loved to play with numbers.

Looking back at the doorway, Rachel listened intently for anyone approaching. She didn't want to be caught snooping. She stepped to the door and peeked out. Hearing no sounds to indicate someone was near, she quietly closed the door and sat down at the desk, placing the book in front of her to look at the handwritten columns and rows.

Her excitement disappeared when she realized many of the numbers were written with Roman numerals. Determined, she closed her eyes and pictured the numbers she remembered. I=1, V=5, X=10, L=50, C=100. She remembered her Grandfather explaining to her as a girl, when the little number is in front of the big one, subtract, and when it's behind, add. Opening her eyes again she went back to the ledger to decipher the transactions.

She ran her index finger down the page in deep concentration and almost didn't hear her father outside the door talking to someone. She quickly closed the book, replacing it moments before her father walked into his study, James Bryant following behind.

Her father gasped. "Rachel?"

Not knowing what to say, she lied. "I was looking for a book to read but ended up daydreaming." Well, almost a lie.

Nodding, he accepted her answer and stepped around the desk. Pouring two drinks, he handed one to Mr. Bryant and sat down at his desk with a look of defeat on his face.

"I will see if mother needs me." She excused herself and closed the door behind her.

The look on her father's face didn't sit well with Rachel. Wanting to know why Mr. Bryant had stayed behind, she decided to eavesdrop, and stood next to the closed door, quietly leaning forward, gently pressing her ear against the wooded door.

"I do not comprehend," she heard her father say. "We were steadfast this time last year. Production has not decreased."

"The demand has increased; you lack the livestock to fill the orders. We have had to lease heads at an inflated rate for the past year, of which we are behind on payment. The cost of materials has increased and so has the labor."

Her father asked, "Could we not purchase more heads?"

"There are none to be had until later this spring. However, you do not have the funds available to make such a substantial purchase."

"How bad is it?"

"You will have to borrow even more to stay afloat, unless of course you are willing to sell."

"Selling is not an option. My family has worked this land for generations. I cannot believe that we are about to lose everything. Are you sure?"

"The numbers do not lie." James paused. "If you do not plan to sell, then I suggest that you take the opportunity to find wealthy suitors for your daughters. I am sure that new in-laws will take care of your affairs. I can only stay quiet about your debts for a short time longer. Eventually, everyone will become aware of your situation. I best return before I am missed."

She heard the movement of his feet; she tried to scurry away from the door.

James opened the door before she could move very far. He saw her standing there and the look on his face turned from dismay to outrage. The guilt of overhearing the conversation must have been obvious because his eyes turned black when he looked at her.

Paralyzed, their eyes locked on each other; Rachel couldn't even blink. Her heart pounded rapidly against her chest. Guilt turned to fear. His intense stare brought a chill up her spine. She had never felt so scared in her life. Panic took over. The urge to run consumed her, but her feet were rooted to the floor.

Mr. Bryant glanced back at her father and then walked to the front door.

Rachel quickly ran up the stairs into her bedroom and sat down on her bed. Covering her face with her hand, she tried to focus on her breathing. Her heart raced and her body shook uncontrollably. After taking several deep breaths, she finally calmed down. Using the skirt of her dress to dry off her damp hands, she thought about what she just witnessed.

Mr. Bryant said that her father's estate was losing money. Abby had told her the day before that the people who worked for her father were happy and productive. People couldn't have changed that much in four hundred years; they wouldn't be happy if they knew they were not profiting from their work. They would be scared of losing their livelihood.

If her father was as broke as Mr. Bryant had implied, then why was he hosting the hunt and why was the family leaving for Bristol in two weeks to attend balls? They needed to watch every penny. Buying new dresses and feeding over a dozen guests should have been the last thing they needed to do.

She needed more information to determine what was going on with the estate. Now that she knew what was happening, she would have an easier time auditing the accounts. At least this would take her mind off of her own problems until she was able to figure out how to get back to her own time.

Rachel didn't trust James Bryant. There was something about the way he spoke to her father. His tone held no empathy and he was arrogant, just like his cousin. The way he looked at her, it seemed as if pure evil was evaluating her future. He was the one person that she never wanted to be alone with in this time. She could walk the streets of Denver in the middle of the night and not have felt the fear that she was feeling now.

CHAPTER FIFTEEN

The only thing Rachel wanted was for the hunt to be over and everyone to leave. Today was the last day and tomorrow, hopefully, every single guest would be gone. She wanted to go home but still didn't know why she was here; she thought it might have something to do with the conversation she overheard yesterday afternoon.

James Bryant gave her the creeps. Before he caught her listening in on the conversation, she hadn't given him a second thought. Several times during last night's festivities she caught him watching her. When their eyes did meet, Rachel broke the gaze by looking at the floor or pretending to be distracted by someone else. Every now and then, he would lean over to Viola, whisper something into her ear, and then Viola would turn her eyes toward Rachel.

Abby burst into her bedroom. "You missed a most delightful day."

Startled, Rachel looked up at her sister, wondering why she was up so early. Last night, Rachel didn't stay for the evening's festivities. She had excused herself with a headache, though all she wanted to do was remove herself from James's presence.

Abby crawled on the bed next to her. "Mr. Parker spotted a lone deer and everyone tried shooting it. I was having difficulty with my bow and Lord Alexander was making an adjustment to it when Lord Edmond frightened the deer away. A pigeon flew by and desecrated his new hunting jacket. He was up in arms and wanted to return to the estate immediately."

Rachel laughed, imagining the scene, wondering how Lord Edmond could spend his days mucking around horse manure and then freak out when a little bird pooped on his jacket.

"Mother says that today you need to attend. You have been hiding and she believes that being with people will brighten your spirits."

Rachel shook her head. "I'm not sure if hunting would be to my liking."

"Mother says that you need to attend and so you shall." Abby stood up and walked to the door. "Alice will be in momentarily to help you dress. We shall enjoy ourselves this day." She giggled and walked out of the room.

The last thing Rachel wanted to do was go hunting. It wasn't that she disagreed with killing an animal during hunting season; it was something that she didn't have an interest in doing. Watching an animal die or be the one killing it did not hold any appeal. More importantly, she didn't want to be near James. She had planned to stay hidden in her room, hoping that she could use her headache again as an excuse. However, hiding was not going to get her back to her own time.

Other than playing games in the dirt with Alex the other day, she hadn't stepped outside of the house. If nothing else, she would be around a dozen people and there was no chance of unexpectedly bumping into James. She would know exactly where he was.

* * *

The warm sunshine on her face did indeed brighten her spirits. The more she thought about it, the more she realized that getting out of the house was a good idea. Walking with Abby to the stables, she looked over at the spot she had sat at with Alex. She smiled when she could see that his drawing hadn't disappeared.

Most of the party was already mounted on their horses, talking amongst themselves. Both Henry and Nic were waiting for them, holding the reins of two magnificent horses.

Leaning over Abby whispered, "You do remember how to ride a horse?"

"Riding, yes. In a sidesaddle? No."

Abby laughed.

Rachel watched Henry help Abby onto her horse. When Nic stood next to her, all she could do was mimic what Abby had done. She hadn't ridden a horse in years and had never sat in a sidesaddle. It was miles before she finally adjusted to maneuvering with the horse as her ex-boyfriend Justin taught her, instead of holding on for dear life.

Justin always said that she didn't ride a horse, the horse took her for a ride. She knew he was being insulting when he made her ride what he called a Barn Baby. After the short ride, the Barn Baby would walk directly back to the barn without being guided. Rachel had dated Justin for a few years before he ran off and married his co-worker, whom he had been sleeping with nearly the whole time they had been together. The last Rachel heard, he had moved to Texas and they had two beautiful kids, one of which was almost certainly not his.

Riding in the fresh air and looking at the country side, Rachel was amazed by the beauty of it all. Abby rode in between Henry and Gerald, laughing while they flirted with her. Behind her, Viola talked with Lord Alexander, her cousin several feet behind, like a looming, ever present shadow, a dark cloud over the festivities of the entire day. Rachel kept her attention on Nic who was at the front of the party, not wanting to give James a reason to look at her.

They rode for what seemed like hours before they halted on a hill filled with trees, slightly above a pretty little meadow. Rachel stretched her aching muscles, trying to rub some of the feeling back into her rear, and then she started walking around, taking in the view.

Nic startled her when he handed her a hunting bow and a quiver full of arrows before he went to help Abby. Stunned, she looked at the empty meadow for deer and back at the bow. The last thing she wanted to do was kill Bambi; besides, she didn't know how to shoot a bow.

She had seen people use bows in the movies and at the Renaissance Festival. They always made it look so easy, but watching it and doing it were two completely different things.

Rachel fumbled with the unstrung four-foot weapon when Alex stepped up next to her.

He took the bow out of her hands. "Have you forgotten this as well?"

Rachel could feel her face turning red. She wasn't sure if it was because she didn't know what she was doing or because he was the one who noticed.

"I'm afraid so." She gave him a timid smile.

Nic disbursed the members of the party into fixed positions at the edge of the hill, behind the trees and bushes. Earlier, several huntsmen and a duo of brachets separated from the group to locate a herd of deer and drive it toward the hunting party. Rachel could hear the low pitched eerie cry of the scent hounds in the distance.

While Nic organized the placement of the noble archers, Alex took Rachel's arm. "Come."

He led her in the opposite direction, to a secluded spot behind the party. She silently watched him string the bow with ease, unsure whether she herself would have the upper body strength to bend the shaft.

Rachel touched the strange rubbery string. "What's this made of?"

"Deer intestines and catling."

She gave him a curious look. "What's catling?"

"Cat guts."

She quickly let go of the string and felt a bit ill at the description.

Glancing back, Rachel noticed Nic and James assisting Viola with her bow, while Edmond, Gerald, and Henry competed for Abby's attention. Both of the chaperones giggled while chastising the men surrounding Abby.

Alex took his time explaining each part of the bow and how to attach the arrow. He handed it to her, pointing at a tree. "Now you try."

She struggled to keep the arrow straight when she pulled the string back. Her embarrassment increased when the arrow fell from her hands a fourth time. "I can't do this."

Instead of getting frustrated, Alex gently stood behind her, whispering directions in her ear and wrapping his arms around hers while holding the bow. She felt weak when his body brushed up against her. The strangest sensation of déjà vu overcame her when he swept a loose strand of hair away from her neck. Before she was able to conceive another thought, she had the sudden urge to turn around and kiss him. With him so near, touching her, she couldn't concentrate. The dream of Allen still haunted her.

Trying desperately to keep her emotions under control, she focused long enough to hold the arrow properly as Alex helped her pull back the string.

He whispered in her ear, "Now release."

When she let go, the kickback pushed Rachel into Alex's firm chest.

Laughing, Alex instinctively placed his hand on her hip to steady her. "'Tis not difficult. Let us try again."

She took a step forward, placing her hands near his on the hunting bow. Rachel took a deep breath, refocusing her attention on the task at hand, still feeling the warmth of his hand pressed against her. Knowing what to expect, she braced herself by bending her knees and planting her feet on the ground. The next shot hit the tree.

"We did it." She had the sudden urge to hug him. When she turned, she remembered that she wasn't in her own time, and hugging a man would be considered improper.

After a short time, Rachel was able to concentrate, focus on her aim, and draw back the arrow without dropping it on the ground. Pride filled her when she was able to shoot without assistance the first time, though when she released the arrow, it often went completely off target.

Hitting the target was now the challenge. Rachel put everything she had into making it happen. With Alex's guidance and hours of practice, she could finally shoot straight. Every now and then, Rachel looked over at the other members of the party. She would see Viola avert her eyes and whisper to James who was paying attention to the hunt, not Rachel.

Lord Gerald made the only kill of the three-day hunt. His arrow had the killing blow of a sorel, a three year old buck, winning the wager the men had placed a few days before. Several attendants stayed behind to prepare and transport the animal back to the estate.

Riding back, Rachel could feel the stiffness creeping into her arms. She hoped they wouldn't be sore for the next few days. Thankfully she had been able to avoid

James. He had been occupied with Viola, and trying to win the wager. They were virtually inseparable. In the past few days, Rachel could tell James would do anything Viola asked. He acted like her body guard and she held a short leash.

On the way back to the estate, she would occasionally feel as if someone was watching her. Reasoning that the guests would have no choice but to see her if she rode in front, Rachel stayed as close as she possibly could to the Yeoman, who led the party home.

Knowing Alex was occupied with Viola, Rachel wondered why she reacted the way she did earlier. The man was only trying to teach her how to use a hunting bow. He was simply being kind, thinking that she had lost her memory. There was no logical reason for her to have those feelings running through her body. Just four days ago, Allen broke her heart and went back to his wife. Granted, Alex was a good looking man, but wasn't it too early for a rebound? Still, there was something comforting about him, something familiar, something . . . Rachel pushed the man from her mind, and gathered her thoughts. She still had to find out why she was here.

* * *

Rachel was almost asleep when Abby snuck into her room and began talking to her about the day, completely ignoring Rachel's yawns. Abby was excited about the attention she received from Lord Gerald, Lord Edmond, and Mr. Parker.

"Each of them promised to sign my dance card at the Stafford Ball."

"That's nice." Rachel yawned again and closed her eyes.

Abby was oblivious to the subtle hint, as she continued talking about the virtues of each one of her three suitors. Barely listening, Rachel found herself drifting off.

". . . and you should have seen Lady Viola fuming when he was with you."

"What?" Rachel sat up, realizing that Abby was still talking. "Who?"

"The Lady Viola. When Lord Alexander was shooting the bow with you, her face turned red and it was like she had smoke coming out of her ears." Abby giggled. "She thinks that since his older brother died that she will marry Lord Alexander."

"Oh my." For a split second, everything suddenly came together, and the next moment it disappeared as she tried to grasp the thought. "Alex doesn't want to marry Viola?"

Abby laughed again. "No silly. *Lord* Alexander does not want to marry anyone. He attends social functions to mingle and keep the rumors at bay. He never calls on any of the girls he dances with. No one knows why."

"Then why does Viola want to marry him?"

"I do not know." Abby played with the hem of her dress. "Can you believe that in two weeks we will arrive in Bristol for The Season? We have much to do."

Tuning her sister out, Rachel wondered why Alex would spend so much time in Viola's presence if he didn't want to marry her. Closing her eyes, she pondered the attraction she had for the man and why he made her feel the same way Allen had.

CHAPTER SIXTEEN

Have you seen my belt?" Alexander shuffled through his belongings, tossing the items his manservant had packed.

"My Lord?" Alexander turned to find Philip holding his belt in one hand, giving him an amusing look. "I dare say, My Lord, it is incomprehensible how you ever manage when left to your own devices."

Alexander sighed and grabbed the belt from his hand. "I *am* unaware how I manage *with* you always underfoot."

Philip laughed and walked over to the mess Alexander had created.

Alexander had found Philip begging in front of a tavern he frequented in Bristol. At first he thought the man was a peasant who had come upon hard times. After weeks of seeing him, Alexander finally tossed him a coin. The man stood up, bowed, and thanked him. Alexander was stunned with his articulate speech and stance. He discovered Philip's previous employer had died in a fire which consumed the entire home. Days before, the tenants had seen Philip speak with the herb woman and felt he had the witch cast a spell on his employer. With only the clothes on his back, Philip managed to make his way to Bristol.

The gossip of his association with a witch preceded him to Bristol; Philip was unable to find employment. Alexander didn't believe in witchcraft and he enjoyed shocking his peers. He hired the manservant immediately. Philip was capable of handling the cottage with the occasional assistance of a cook and stable hand. Otherwise it was the two of them. Alexander appreciated the privacy, knowing Philip did not disclose his master's affairs – especially the agreement his mother made to marry him to Viola.

"Shall we be departing with the caravan? Or do you prefer to ride alone again unattended?"

Alexander sighed again. "Apparently, I have agreed to travel with the party." He struggled with the belt. "I have no idea how I tend to put myself in the most unagreeable situations."

"The Lady Viola?" Philip picked up a shirt, folded it, and placed it back into the trunk.

Alexander walked to the door and opened it. "I shall see you in two hours' time."

He knew he was late for the morning meal because a few of the guests lingered at the table discussing Lord Goodwin's kill. He had no interest in the conversation; he was disappointed Rachel wasn't in the dining room.

He picked up the decanter and poured himself a goblet of ale. The past week weighed heavy on his mind. Since the moment he arrived, Miss Rachel had completely taken over his thoughts. Last night he could not fall asleep. He remembered the way she would look at him; a special smile would come across her lips making him feel as if he was the only man in the room.

"I dare say, my Lord, you appear to be distraught this morn." With a smirk on his face, Nic took the chair next to Alexander.

Alexander shifted in his seat. "'Tis been a most interesting few days."

"Indeed." Nic sat back in his chair and crossed his arms. The smirk had not left his face. "I am surprised to find the Lady Viola absent at the moment."

Alexander looked around the room; Viola was nowhere in sight. He sighed. "For that I am thankful. Have you seen Miss Rachel this morn?"

"Nay."

The two men sat in silence. Alexander stared at his pewter goblet while he turned it in circles on the table.

Nic lowered his voice. "I shall not let you avoid telling me the details. Many times I have watched your face when Henry Parker converses with Miss Rachel."

"Pray tell, what wish you to hear?" – Alexander sat back down and crossed his arms – "As I am sure you have learned Henry Parker has his sights set on Miss Abigail."

He was not about to reveal how jealous he became when he watched Henry speak with Rachel. Or how relieved he was when Henry had confessed his attentions, admitting his overprotectiveness for Rachel was at the request of her sister.

Amusement filled Nic's eyes. "Mr. Parker has competition; however, I have yet to determine who will be seeking the hand of Miss Rachel."

Alexander didn't answer.

Nic stood up and straightened his jacket. "I must see to the preparations for journey."

He sighed again. "I shall join you."

Following Nic out of the dining room, he wanted to ask how Nic managed to capture Viola's attention yesterday. He decided against it. There was no need for Nic to know how grateful he was for the opportunity to spend a few moments alone with Rachel.

Teaching Rachel to use a bow was a memorable experience, one he would soon not forget. When he held her close, he could feel the blood rushing through his body. And for a moment, it felt as if it was only the two of them on top of the hill. Alexander wondered if Nic knew him better than he knew himself.

The two friends walked around checking the horses and carriages, inquiring of the fretful groomsmen the state of their transports. He knew they were adequately cared for, but he wanted to avoid Viola and arrive in Bristol without incident.

He bent down to look at the wheel of his own carriage when a shadow appeared. He looked up, expecting to see his manservant, when he saw Rachel standing there, her hands clasped in front of her, watching him.

Alexander stood up quickly. "Good morrow, Miss Rachel."

She looked around and turned back to him. "Good morning Alex."

He laughed. "Is your chaperone missing again?"

"No, not missing." She looked around again and smiled. "I don't have one."

Alexander winked and a grin crossed his lips. "Do not fear Miss Rachel, I shall remain honorable."

Her eyes lit up when she smiled and he noticed the golden speckles dancing in her crystal blue eyes.

"I, um . . . I just wanted to wish you a safe trip home."

"Thank you. I believe in a fortnight you will also be traveling to Bristol?"

Just then, Viola interrupted the conversation by taking his arm. "Good morrow, Lord Alexander."

"Good morrow, Lady Viola," he nodded. "Mr. Bryant."

James nodded back and gave Rachel a stern look.

Alexander looked back at Rachel; she had nervously taken a step back and her face flushed. A moment later she stepped forward and lifted her chin.

"Lady Viola and Mr. Bryant." Rachel looked back at Alexander. "Have a safe journey." She simply nodded and walked away.

Viola gave Rachel a piercing look. "People of her status should learn how to respect their betters."

Alexander watched her walk away and wished Viola was the one who had left.

Viola jerked on his arm, regaining his attention. "You must ride with us to Bristol. We will have such a pleasant journey. Eleanor has prepared the grandest dinner. We shall set up a picnic."

"I had planned to lead the party alongside the Yeoman." Alexander tried to regain possession of his arm, but she gripped it tighter, and began walking.

"Nonsense, your station is above such menial tasks." She stopped and looked at him. "James and I will be expecting you to join us in our carriage when we depart."

She walked away, James following silently behind her. Alexander stood stunned, wondering again how he was capable of getting himself into the most unagreeable situations.

Nic appeared next to him. "Have you not spoken to Lady Viola?"

Alexander shrugged. "Nay, she is as stubborn as her mother was and will not take no for an answer. I feel my actions are obvious."

"Do you plan to ride with Viola?"

He laughed, "Nay, my good friend. Nothing would possess me to spend the journey back to Bristol in her carriage." Alexander slapped Nic on the back and started walking into the house. "I plan to lead the party with your idle conversation to annoy me for hours, you old hag."

Nic busted out laughing.

Alexander looked up before they walked through the front door. He spotted Rachel peering out of the window. When she saw him, she smiled. He hoped she was feeling better and wondered when he would have the opportunity to see her again. She was addicting and he found himself wanting more.

CHAPTER SEVENTEEN

The size of Bristol was amazing. Nothing prepared Rachel for the abundance of people and buildings that lined the streets. Everything she had seen or read about the Elizabethan age gave her the impression that it was a time of peasants tending the land with Lords and Ladies living in grand castles; not cities with vast shipping docks, glorious chapels, beautiful parks, and small homes surrounding the city.

The family had traveled to the city two weeks after the hunting party had left. With only a few months of The Season left, Abby and their mother raced around making the necessary preparations. Between the packing and traveling Rachel was exhausted. She did her best to assist the family with preparations to leave, but felt that she got in the way. Once they arrived, they had gowns to purchase, the theater to attend, and invitations to accept.

When Abby said they were staying with their Aunt Lilly at her cottage, Rachel imagined a tiny home with a couple of bedrooms, a white picket fence, and colorful flowers adorning the front entrance. She was right on target with the flowers and fence, but not the house.

The tiny cottage was larger than her parents' two-story house in the suburbs of Denver. The six-bedroom cottage was complete with a kitchen, dining room, parlor, library, and a large stable in the back for the horses and carriage.

Lilly Thayer, a social extrovert incapable of being alone, always kept a full house, whether of family or guests from out of town, presumably out of the need to replace her children who had all married and moved away from the city, or her husband, always in London on business.

After their first appointment with the seamstress, the women spent their day walking and window shopping around the merchant quarter. Aunt Lilly and their mother didn't appear to care where the girls went, so they followed behind. They kept busy talking and catching up on the latest gossip, continuously stopping and visiting with acquaintances on the street. Lilly seemed to know everyone in town.

Rachel was beginning to find her experience in the past invigorating. The pedestrians on the street weren't in a constant hurry. Everyone seemed to be smiling and would nod in greeting, the gentlemen tipping their hats.

Granted, the few things she missed the most were taking a shower, having a flushing toilet, and her coffee pot. She wondered what Allen would think of this place and then she chastised herself. She hadn't thought of him in a couple of days. She knew she had seen the signs; he wasn't going to leave his wife. Why didn't she run? At times she felt as if she was finally moving on, and other times she missed him completely. The thought of letting him go broke her heart, even though she knew it was for the best.

Abby pointed across the street and said, "Father's solicitor works there."

Looking across the street, Rachel saw a big burly man walk out of a building. "That man over there works on father's books? I thought it was Mr. Bryant."

"No silly, Mr. Bryant is the solicitor's apprentice. When father was injured last year, Mr. Bryant took over seeing to the accounts." Abby nodded to the store a few doors down. "Over there is where we are going. She has the prettiest ribbons in Bristol."

Looking back, Rachel saw James Bryant step out of the door and lock it. As he adjusted his hat, he paused, staring directly at Rachel with his cold, dark eyes before he turned abruptly and walked away.

A cold, uneasy feeling swept through her body. Looking down, she noticed the goose bumps on her arms. Rachel knew without a doubt that something weird was going on. She shook it off and followed Abby into the store.

The girls spent the day shopping; their father had given them enough money to purchase new ribbons. Abby's excitement for the ball tomorrow night was contagious. Rachel hoped that she was ready, but knew she wasn't.

On their way back to the cottage, Abby wanted to take a walk through the park. "The Lady Butler is having her portrait painted. Let us see if we can discover the artist."

"He shouldn't be hard to find. He'd have a brush in his hand," Rachel mumbled. She had heard the stories about the anonymous artist. The thought baffled Rachel. How could anyone not want to get credit for the work they do, especially if they were as good as everyone said?

The girls walked slowly to the center of the park. Dozens of patrons stood in small, scattered groups watching everyone, trying to guess who the artist was. On a small bench sat an older woman, dressed in her finery, quietly looking around. She looked a bit out of place in her evening gown.

"There is the Lady Butler." Abby indicated the lady sitting on the small wooden bench.

Looking around, Rachel leaned toward Abby. "Where is the artist?"

"No one knows who he is, silly. He has his subject sit on the bench and in a fortnight or two, the portrait is completed."

"How does he paint a portrait without his subject sitting for him?"

A voice behind them startled the two girls. "That is the question that has brought so many here."

The two girls turned to see who had made the comment. Abby nodded her head. "Lord Alexander."

"Miss Abigail," Alexander kissed her hand. "Miss Rachel." As he kissed Rachel's fingers, his gaze never left her eyes; he held her hand a moment longer than necessary. As his lips touched her hand, she caught her breath looking into his amber eyes.

Rachel greeted him with a nod, not knowing what to say. Every time this man was in her presence she became nervous and her brain turned to mush.

Abby broke the silence. "Will you be attending the Stafford ball on the morrow?"

Breaking from Rachel's eyes, Alex looked at her sister. "I have yet to accept the invitation."

"Oh," Abby looked at the ground. "Will you?"

"I believe that I will be detained with . . ."

Rachel interrupted, "No one knows who the artist is?" She was trying to pull herself together and asked before she realized he was still talking to Abby. Embarrassed, she looked down and started ringing her hands together.

Without missing a beat Alex responded to Rachel, "I am afraid not." Offering his arms to the ladies he said, "Come let me escort you and I will tell you of what I know." The three strolled down the path toward the cottage, as their aunt and mother followed behind, quietly chatting to each other. Rachel didn't think their chaperones even noticed that Alex had joined them.

"It is odd, really," he paused, "A few years ago, a painting was delivered to Queen Elizabeth. The portrait was incredibly detailed, displaying her beauty like none she had seen before. The Queen demanded to meet this artist. Unfortunately, the man who delivered the portrait had vanished from the city, not to be seen again.

"Months later, another portrait was delivered, this time to Lord Berkeley. Lord Berkeley recognized the markings of the signature were the same as the anonymous artist, for he was present when the Queen received her gift. This time the delivery boy was not so lucky as to have disappeared. The only information the young lad could offer, however, was that he was given a gold coin to deliver the painting and the artist was from the area.

"After that, many of the elite sought out the artist, to no avail. No one has met him. Requests for paintings are posted and only a few accepted. The subject is asked to sit in the park for an hour or two at the bench the Lady Butler now occupies. Somehow the entire city finds out and visits the park to see if they can determine who the artist is.

"I have to admit that it has piqued my curiosity as well. I wonder who he is."

"How do you know the artist is a he and not a she?" Rachel heard Abby gasp when she made the comment; she had stepped over the invisible line of propriety yet again.

A surprised look came over Alexander's face. "Miss Rachel, how observant you are. We may have been looking at this the wrong way. The artist may very well be a female, but I doubt it."

"Why? Women can paint just as well as men."

"Women do not have the business sense, nor could they keep such a grand secret. Women gossip and sew."

That was not an answer that Rachel thought she would hear from this man, especially after they had talked while playing games in the dirt. Other men, yes. Even in her own time, she had met many men who thought a woman should be barefoot and pregnant.

"You *seriously* don't believe that," she demanded, crossing her arms with as much anger as she could muster without causing a scene as Abby and their chaperones stood there stunned, not sure if they should involve themselves in the conversation.

Laughing, Alex looked in her eyes. "No. My mother would beat me if I believed as such." Collecting the two girls back into the crooks of his arms, he began walking. "To be honest, 'tis more of a sense I get when I look at the work."

Rachel was relieved that he was not a chauvinist pig. "Do you own one of his portraits?"

"Aye, I own several."

"Several?" Rachel was stunned. "You must be very wealthy."

"No. I am not as wealthy as my older brother Richard. I was not born to that privilege. I own several businesses, one of which displays art. I own a few pieces that must have been his first works. They were on my doorstep with a note describing how to compensate him. I kept the ones that I favored and the others I had displayed."

"How could anyone create such work as you describe and not want to receive the credit? He must be a recluse."

Alex winked. "That, my dear, is the core of the mystery."

The party arrived at their aunt's cottage. Standing in front of the gate, Alex tipped his hat and bid the girl's good day.

"Rachel, why did you say those words to Lord Alexander? I am surprised he did not bid us farewell long before," Abby whispered, not wanting Alexander to overhear her scolding her sister.

Rachel laughed at Abby's statement; she couldn't believe Abby was embarrassed for her actions. She patted Abby on the arm. "No worries Abby; I don't plan to seek Lord Alexander as a suitor."

Sighing, Abby gave Rachel a worried look. "Ever since you hit your head you say the strangest things."

Rachel took her arm and walked into the cottage with their purchases.

Abby glanced at her. "I am relieved to hear you are not setting your sites on Lord Alexander."

"Why?" Rachel stopped and asked as she looked back, watching Alex in the distance walking back toward the park.

Abby's jaw dropped. "Because he is not of our status. Besides, he does not want to marry and if he did, he certainly would choose to marry the Lady Viola."

* * *

After the family retired for the evening, Rachel sat on her bed watching the flames in the fireplace sputter. She finally felt better. Her head wasn't as foggy as it had been since she arrived.

The last week had been busy and tiring. Rachel couldn't remember having so many different things to do in just one day. There were fittings to attend and invitations to accept. Before they left, the girls even had dance lessons; and due to her lack of memory, she was forced to relearn certain social etiquettes. Her mother was so distraught with the amount of things that Rachel had forgotten that she almost canceled the entire trip.

Rachel felt bad for Abby, who had been looking forward to this trip for months. Rachel promised her mother that she would quickly learn what she needed to, saying she felt that her memory would return. Once in a while she was able to give her mother the impression that her memory was returning. Rachel was thankful that she was picking up on everything so quickly, but it had been difficult. Without Abby, she knew her scheme would have been discovered by now.

Rachel paced in her bedroom. She had been in the sixteenth century for over two weeks, with no indication as to why. Her thoughts drifted to how different everything was compared to her small townhome in Lakewood, Colorado. She had to wake up earlier in the morning just to get ready for the day. Granted, it was wonderful that someone else cooked all of the meals and cleaned the house, but she missed taking a warm shower and washing her hair. She missed her firm mattress and fluffy pillows, not to mention the ability to leave her home without someone constantly following her, watching her every move.

Still, Aunt Lilly had to be the most lenient chaperone in existence, Rachel thought to herself. Anytime the girls wanted to go somewhere, Lilly was ready and willing, not really caring where they went or who they stopped to talk with. She seemed to always find enjoyment in the smallest things.

Rachel wondered what she was going to do. What she was supposed to do? She couldn't get back home if she sat here idly.

Sitting back down on the bed, she replayed the past days in her mind; who she met, what was said, anything that could give her some indication as to why she was here.

Realization hit her. The third day in the dining room before Viola walked in, Abby had mentioned a witch. But then Rachel overheard the conversation between her father and Mr. Bryant and completely forgot about the witch. Grabbing her robe, she snuck to Abby's bedroom and opened the door without knocking.

Abby lay on her bed, staring at the ceiling when she walked in.

Rachel whispered, "Tell me about the witch."

Sitting up, Abby gave her a strange look. "The witch? Does your head still hurt?"

"Yes," Rachel lied before she realized what she said. "Yes, it hurts a bit, but I'm trying to remember."

"You know the old lady that lives in the woods west of our estate. You do remember the tales?"

"No." Rachel sat down on the bed next to Abby. "I must have hit my head harder than I thought. I remember bits and pieces, but you might be able to help me fill in the blanks."

Thankfully, Abby liked a little gossip and trusted her completely, Rachel thought. Otherwise she might be in big trouble. How could she explain to anyone here in this time that she was from the future? They would burn her at the stake.

"Well," Abby leaned forward and lowered her voice, "they say that people sneak to her house seeking potions for their illnesses when the physic cannot find a cure."

An herbalist, Rachel thought to herself. People in my day act like natural cures are new.

"They also say she can cast spells and curses on people." Abby's eyes went wide. "And tell the future. Some even say she can turn you into a toad with one look."

"Have you ever seen her?"

Abby laughed, "You really do not remember, do you?"

Rachel shook her head.

"We use to play pranks on the old lady when we were children. Once she caught us and threatened to give us nightmares, after which I had nightmares for a week."

Rachel bid her sister goodnight and headed back to her bedroom, lost in thought. But what choice did she have? She had no idea why she was here, who these people were, or how to get back to her own time. She resolved to find this witch-lady and see if she knew anything.

The spark of hope fizzled however, as Rachel tried to figure out how to visit the witch. The family was in Bristol, a day's ride from home. Even if they were home, Rachel hadn't paid enough attention to remember the terrain. Sighing, she crawled back into bed and resolved to ask Abby more detailed questions later.

CHAPTER EIGHTEEN

Rachel's mother ran around the house making last minute preparations before the ball. The girls, apparently, were taking their time. Though being late was socially acceptable, being the last to arrive was not.

"Come along girls," she called again. "We are prepared to leave."

As Rachel and Abby descended the stairs, their mother clapped her hands and exclaimed, "They are beautiful, Arthur. Our little ones have grown up before our eyes."

Abby almost tripped over the white lace of her peach-colored gown. Luckily, Rachel noticed and caught her, and to their mother's dismay, they both started laughing.

Rachel's gown was low cut in a stunning royal blue. At first she had begged the seamstress for the gown to cover her cleavage; the dressmaker insisted this was the latest fashion; anything higher would be considered dated.

Now she was glad she lost the argument. Rachel had never felt so beautiful in her life. Her long blonde hair was placed on top of her head with small glass beads intertwined, ringlets falling down her back. If she only had some mascara, she thought to herself.

The family did arrive fashionably late. It seemed everyone who was someone attended. Tonight, everyone dressed as if the Queen herself would appear.

According to Abby, the event was grand, but not as grand as the ones they would attend in the coming months. Rachel couldn't imagine anything more elaborate than this. Fresh flowers adorned the room, the food and drink were fabulous, and everyone seemed to be having a good time.

Rachel was thankful for their mother's reminders about the social proprieties on their way to the ball and the dance lessons they had a few weeks before. She had forgotten it was considered scandalous to dance with the same man more than twice in one evening. Rachel wished that she had paid more attention to the historical romance novels she had read in her own time.

Once she had gotten over her surprise and awe of the event, she observed that it wasn't much different than a high school dance. Granted, no one had dates – they were using dance cards – and a few social etiquettes were different. The people separated into small cliques. She overheard the women gossiping, pointing out little things they did not like about their competition.

Though all the single women were scouting husbands, it seemed the men were evaluating them as if investing in a car or looking at a slab of meat. Apparently, Rachel thought to herself, men haven't changed.

Abby's vibrant personality lit up the room. She seemed to always have something nice to say about everyone they spoke to. Unlike many of the other women Rachel overheard, Abby was sincere and the men were drawn toward her, filling her dance card up quickly.

When she had a free moment, Abby complemented a woman's dress or accessories. Abby even took the time to speak with a young, homely looking girl hiding in the corner who looked even more uncomfortable than Rachel did. By the time she left, the young girl was laughing and smiling. Shortly thereafter, Rachel found to her surprise that Lord Edmond, Henry Parker, and Lord Gerald had all signed her dance card. Rachel knew Abby had asked the men to dance with her; she seemed to be looking out for everyone.

Rachel was not there for a husband. She was simply following along, trying to figure out how to get home. Yet, deep down she knew she needed to be wary of her actions. She didn't want to ruin the reputation of the woman whose body she was using. She decided to stay as unnoticeable as possible, hoping it would benefit the both of them. For a brief moment, she felt she could understand why the anonymous painter chose anonymity.

Looking around, she saw Viola for the first time that evening. Viola gave her a little smile as if she knew something Rachel didn't. Rachel smiled back and then quickly turned her attention to those standing next to her.

* * *

Normally Alexander did not attend so many functions during The Season. He felt his time would be better spent working. He had accounts to oversee, requests to consider, a trip to his mother to plan. The last thing he wanted was to spend time with Viola. While dressing for the ball, he had one thought in his mind – to see Rachel again. He donned his coat and stepped into his carriage.

When Abby mentioned the Stafford ball, Alexander made sure he accepted the invitation. The request had been sitting on his desk for several weeks. It was not unlike him to accept at the last moment.

Normally, Alexander felt pride when he was announced and all eyes turned to him. Tonight, he wished he could have gone unnoticed, like the painter in the park. Scanning the guests, he recognized a friendly face. Apparently, Nic had acquired an invitation.

Grabbing a drink, he walked over to his longtime friend. "Looking for a wealthy bride?"

Nic laughed. "No, a rich Lord to invest in my latest venture. Do you know of such a man?"

Alexander had invested in some of Nic's ideas which ended up being profitable for the both of them. The look on Nic's face told him he had something to offer. "Visit me on the morrow and we will discuss your latest venture. Tonight I plan to enjoy myself."

Nic followed Alexander's gaze. "Enjoyment with Arthur's daughter, by any chance?"

He felt his face flush. It was either obvious or the two men had spent too much time together. He reasoned the latter.

"She is remarkable."

Nic rolled his eyes. "A woman who has completely lost her memory and you call her remarkable. Maybe you like the idea that she does not remember your reputation."

Alexander smiled at the jab. He spent his time mildly flirting with women but never called on them and had broken more hearts than he wished to count.

"I shall return momentarily." Nic bowed slightly, turned, and walked toward Lord Stafford, the gentleman of the house, leaving Alexander standing alone.

Alexander barely heard Nic leave. He was watching Rachel from across the room, trying not to be obvious. As men approached her, he became jealous, thinking about all the things he wanted to say to her, do to her.

"Hello Lord Alexander," he heard from behind him. Turning, he saw Viola with her cousin.

"Good den, Lady Viola, Mr. Bryant. Are you enjoying the ball?" He tried to be polite and not let his real emotions for her show.

"Indeed, quite the time." Her voice dripped with sarcasm.

They stood there in silence watching the dancers on the floor. Neither spoke until the next dance began. Finally, Viola continued the conversation. "You plan to give your decision soon, I hope."

Alexander could not fight his emotions any longer. He needed to tell her and let this play out. "I am sure my decision will please you. There is no reason for us to be wed. I believe you are setting your sights far too low and would find a more suitable companion."

"I disagree." She looked around the room. "You are more than suitable."

Her reaction was not the one Alexander hoped for.

Mr. Bryant stepped forward. "There is the livestock to consider. Your family has taken ownership before your brother George left us. Along with the land and the rest of her dowry, you would benefit more than our family."

Sighing, Alexander ran his hand through his hair. He knew that James was right. He simply did not want to marry Viola. The dowry was unimportant to him. Nor did he find her distant relationship to the Queen appealing, as he had no interest in attending Court. He was about to break social etiquette and tell her how he felt when Nic came to the rescue.

"I beg your pardon." Nic bowed, looking at Viola and her cousin, then turned to face Alexander. "My Lord, the Lord Stafford has requested your presence in the drawing room."

Alexander bowed to Lady Viola and Mr. Bryant. "I thank you for the conversation." Following Nic to the drawing room, he whispered, "How did you know?"

Nic smiled. "I can tell when you are ready to say something inappropriate. The two are up to no good. I am not sure what gives me that impression, but something tells me there is more going on. A rich Lord from London called on her and she would not give him the time of day. She is not looking for wealth, but something else. I simply cannot figure out what she wants from you, but . . ."

Looking over his shoulder, Alexander did not like the way she looked at him or how she talked to her cousin. Nic was right; something was amiss.

An hour had passed and Alexander had engaged in several conversations, not really caring who he spoke to, avoiding Viola and her cousin as much as possible.

Finally, he decided he had waited long enough; he walked over to Rachel, who sat alone near the corner of the room, as if trying to hide. Alexander bowed. "I believe this is my dance."

He could see the color change in her eyes. A moment ago, they were a clear blue and now they sparkled like the sun hitting the ocean. He hoped that they had lit up because he was standing in front of her.

Smiling, she took his hand and stood. A shocked look came over his face before he realized what was happening; he hoped she had not witnessed it. Her warm hand fit perfectly in his. He felt the warmth of her penetrating touch tingle through his arm. His entire body responded. Never had a woman had this effect on him. He stood there, gazing into her eyes when she spoke.

"Dance?" Was the only word he heard as he remembered where he was and what he should be doing.

He led her onto the dance floor. Alexander was thankful he was able to dance with her during the Volte; it was the only dance where couples were allowed to closely embrace.

"I hope you are doing well this evening, Miss Rachel." He walked her out to the dance floor. The music started and they began to dance.

Alexander noticed Rachel watching the other dancers out of the corner of her eye; she was counting the steps, and doing her best to follow his lead. They took several steps and then he lifted her into the air. He felt the same penetrating feeling, her thighs pressing against his, and then he set her down on the last beat of the measure. They turned and repeated the steps. She was light as a feather and her body felt perfectly natural against his. The dance was too short for his liking. Afterward, he escorted her back to her mother, and signed Abby's dance card.

Alexander refilled his drink and joined Nic in conversation with Lord Butler. They were speaking of his wife sitting for the painting in the park the day before. His eyes did not leave Rachel for long, yet the conversation he was listening to caught his attention long enough for him to lose sight of her. Scanning the dance floor, he spotted her again, dancing with James Bryant.

Her body was stiff and her smile appeared to be forced. The couples were dancing to the Pavane, where they would lightly touch their partner's fingers as they paraded around the dance floor. Out of reflex his right hand went to his side for his sword before he remembered he left it at the cottage.

After James returned her to her mother, Rachel carefully slipped away toward the balcony. Alexander, having observed her escape, waited a few minutes longer, handed his drink to Nic, and followed her.

Alexander had not stayed at a ball for the duration in many years. He usually left early, and danced with a few woman just for gossip.

Alexander quietly stood at the doorway, watching her lean against the white, wooden railing at the edge of the balcony overlooking the garden below.

"'Tis not lady-like to be here alone. A lesser man than I may take advantage of a beautiful woman."

Rachel faced him. Her eyes showed relief when she looked at him, and she placed her hand over her heart, blushing. "It gets stuffy inside."

"That it does. I appear to have startled you."

She looked toward the door leading back into the ballroom. "Yes. I mean no. I mean . . ." Pausing, she looked down and straightened her dress, brushing out wrinkles that did not exist. "I am glad it's you."

Alexander tilted his head. She continued, "There are some that I wouldn't like to be alone with."

His stomach lurched. How could this mere woman who had completely lost her memory affect him this way? The urge to hold her and keep her safe overwhelmed his thoughts. He wanted to be the one to show her and teach her all the things she had forgotten. He wanted to move her away from everything that caused her fear.

"Walk with me." Motioning to the gardens below, he took her arm in his and escorted her down the stairs. "Have you visited the garden?"

"No. Though I was admiring it from afar." She looked back at the balcony where they had stood only a moment ago.

The gardens before them were a rectangle labyrinth of scented evergreens with boxes of assorted herbs and flowers forming the inside. "Close your eyes," he whispered as they approached the shrubbery. He wanted her to experience the fullness of the exotic scents.

Slowly, he led her onto a pebbled path of tiny, colored stones. The four-foot evergreens outlined the perimeter; smaller plants created the outline of a Celtic knot on the inside. As they walked, the aroma of the herbs and flowers changed in each area. The herbs were chosen for their beauty as much as for their utility.

Alexander watched the changing expressions on her moonlit face. When they neared the sage and witch hazel, she wrinkled her nose at the warm, spicy fragrances. And when they walked near the foxglove and English roses, a smile came across her lips.

The night was clear with the moon lighting their way. They walked for several minutes without saying a word. He stopped at a small wooden bench next to a large silver birch tree in the center of the garden. A tree in the middle of a knot garden was unheard of, but the lady of the manor would not let her husband remove it. She had asked the gardeners to plant around the tree. Rumor suggested that it was at the silver birch tree they had shared their first kiss.

The smell of the aromas and the beautiful woman on his arm made the evening perfect. Alexander had never felt so comfortable around a woman, yet the ache in his body was anything but comfortable. That night, he had not missed a move that she made. After he had danced with her, all he could think about was touching her again. To have her on his arm, to hold her in his hands, to press his lips against hers.

Something about her intrigued him. He sensed a unique innocence in her when she looked at her surroundings. Rachel paid more attention to the women and how they conducted themselves than at the men the other women giggled about.

Everything she did was done with purpose and with thought. She was good at hiding her intentions, but Alexander could see things in people that most could not. He could tell that she was hiding something. She had a difficult time remembering simple social etiquettes, yet she was opinionated and stubborn.

"A most beautiful evening," Alexander stated, simply to break the silence.

Smiling, Rachel opened her eyes and gazed into the dark sky above her. The moonlight shone on her face and it was mesmerizing. "Yes, it is beautiful."

Alexander was at a loss of what to say. "Have you enjoyed yourself this evening?" The sound of her voice warmed his heart.

"Yes."

Think, he told himself. He could keep everyone conversing, except with her. With her, he could think of nothing intelligent to say.

"Abby appears to be enjoying herself as well. She has turned the heads of many potential suitors." Alexander liked her sister; she was fun and full of life.

"Abby has no idea what she is in for." Rachel sighed regretfully. "Pray tell me: as I understand, you are to wed Viola."

The moment that was so perfect changed abruptly. The last thing Alexander wanted to talk about was Viola. He wanted to know more about Rachel. What she thought, what she was hiding, and how she would feel wrapped in his arms.

Running his free hand through his hair, he parried the question. "My engagement is none of your concern. Tell me about James Bryant. Is he one of your many suitors?" The moment he said those words, he regretted them. At the mention of James Bryant's name the brightness in her eyes turned dark.

She hastily stood up. "None of my concern? We may be causing a scandal by standing here in the garden unattended. You dare ruin my reputation and say it's none of my concern?" Stomping her foot, she began walking back through the labyrinth toward the ball.

Alexander knew she was right. He should not have sought her out on the balcony. Ruining her reputation could mean that he would be forced to marry her instead of Viola. The thought of spending the rest of his life with Rachel was appealing; however, he did not want her to be pressured into a union in such a way. Besides, his family would be unhappy, as the marriage to Viola would bring land and livestock which his mother had already accepted on behalf of George. Alexander was still unsure how he would break the agreement. His thoughts returned to Rachel. When he asked her about James, her entire demeanor changed. The fear in Rachel's eyes made him want to know what was scaring her. He needed to find out.

Instead of letting her run off, he caught her by the arm and spun her around. As she turned, she lost her balance, catching herself by placing her hand on his chest. Instinctively, his arm curled around her waist. As she looked up into his face, Alexander could not help himself; pulling her closer, he bent down, pressing his lips upon hers. Her soft lips tasted sweet as he felt his body react to her touch.

As he moved away, she put her arm around his neck and pulled him back to her lips. Another taste of heaven, and his body tingled once again. Instead of a simple kiss, it felt as if Rachel was taking control of the moment. Parting her lips, she began to taste him with her tongue. This was not what he had expected. Using her teeth, she began to gently bite his lower lip until he responded to her with his tongue. The kiss only took a moment but every second was engraved into his mind. It ended all too suddenly when he felt her move away.

A young woman's voice called out Rachel's name. Blushing, Rachel lowered her voice. "I'm sorry. I shouldn't have done that." Nervously, she straightened her gown and walked toward the voice.

Consumed with guilt, Alexander rubbed his hands together as he quietly stepped into the darkness and watched her walk away. What was I thinking? he thought to himself. There was no logical explanation for my actions. I knew better than to take advantage of the situation. Rachel deserves more than a rogue of a man; a man more honorable than I.

Shaking his head, he walked toward his carriage, hoping the chill of the evening air would cool down his body. He still felt the passion beneath the kiss they shared. Had any other woman kissed him in the way she had, he would think her a strumpet.

But she was not any other woman.

Shaking his head again, he climbed into his carriage and his driver took him home.

Since the day he carried her into her bedroom, when she had fallen from the tree, he could not get her out of his mind. Each time he saw her, he felt as if the days following were more gratifying. His friends noticed the change in his attitude. The pressures of his family did not weigh so heavily on his shoulders, other than the engagement to Viola.

Arriving at his cottage, he went straight to the attic where he kept his passion hidden away from the world. Pulling out a canvas, he arranged his supplies as he peeled off his clothes. It would do no one any good if he messed them up. He donned his old breeches, torn and splattered with paint. He did not even notice that he sat down at the canvas without a shirt, while he started outlining the image he could not get out of his mind.

As he painted, he could feel the texture of her long blonde hair. It was soft and he could almost smell its rose-water scent. Her clear blue eyes with hints of gold speckles captured the blue in her dress, making them look brighter than they really were. A few freckles covered her button nose and her lips were soft and full. As he painted he could feel her lips against his, her slender arms wrapped around his neck, and her body pressed against him. The images in his mind were so vivid that he could recall exactly how they felt.

Hours later, he noticed the sky turning pink outside the little window of the attic. Wondering where the time went, he stood back and examined his work. It was almost complete. It was then he noticed he was soaked in sweat, and the hardness of his manhood pressed against his breeches. Alexander shook his head, determining he needed to sleep. It was the alcohol he had consumed earlier in the evening that possessed him. Rachel was simply a pretty girl, he thought to himself. Gathering his clothing, he walked down the stairs to his bedroom, and crawled into bed.

* * *

"Where were you?" Abby grabbed Rachel's arm when she stepped out of the garden. "You simply cannot disappear by yourself. Mother is beside herself with worry."

"It was getting warm inside," Rachel fanned herself. "I just wanted a moment alone."

"And *were* you alone?" she asked with wide assuming eyes.

Rachel followed her sister back into the ballroom. "Of course. Why wouldn't I be?"

"Yours was not the only absence that was noted."

"Oh?"

"The Lady Viola has been inquiring as to the where-abouts of Lord Alexander. It appears both Nic Mattingly and Jonathan Butler have disappeared as well."

Rachel felt her heart fall into the pit of her stomach, wondering who noticed they were missing, or if anyone had seen them together.

Trying to be inconspicuous, Rachel found the most secluded seat in the room. The ball was far from over and the last thing she wanted was idle conversation.

Rachel sat quietly, paying attention to the suitors dancing with her sister. Abby appeared to have fun spinning around the dance floor. She had an innocence about her everyone was drawn to. Rachel was afraid that some of these men wouldn't be a good fit for her sister.

Abby blushed at the right times, made conversation when appropriate, and was very gracious. These were great traits if a man was looking for a woman to be doc-ile and a good hostess. Rachel knew it could be fun in the beginning, but a woman needed to be strong.

She needed a man to want to be with her, not need to be with her. Someone who could be her best friend, whose shoulder she could cry on, and who would help her stand on her own two feet. Someone who's eyes would light up when she walked into a room.

Rachel's thoughts turned to Allen. Her eyes filled with tears while she tried desperately to get her emo-tions under control. He was not here and moments earlier she had shared a passionate kiss with another man. Is this how Allen felt when he kissed me the first time? She wondered to herself while the guilt gnawed at her heart.

Looking around, Rachel knew she had more important issues than Allen or Alex. She needed to figure out how to get back to her own time. Until then, she needed to figure out what was going on with James Bryant; the man simply gave her the creeps.

When James asked her to dance, her first instinct was to slap him across the face and run away. He stunk of tobacco mixed with sandalwood; she would have done almost anything if she could have disappeared. However, she didn't have that option. The look on her mother's face was agreeable; apparently she thought they would make a good match. Rachel gave in and agreed to the dance. Cringing the entire time, she didn't know what to do when she had to lightly touch the man for the duration of the dance.

Though he apologized for being rash and giving her the wrong impression at the estate, Rachel wondered which time he was apologizing for. Was it when she met him outside her father's study, or the many other times he looked at her making her feel scared to death? He indicated that he would be interested in courting her, with her father's permission of course. Not knowing what to say, she told him she was flattered, managing not to actually agree, praying she could find some way to avoid him.

Why he wanted to court her, she had no idea – unless he was after her father's business. Her eyes shot up and looked at the man when the thought took hold. Thankfully, he was not looking at her when she looked at him; Rachel was sure he would see the fear in her eyes.

Hiding in the corner, Rachel cautiously monitored Viola and her cousin. Viola had a look of rage on her face as she clutched her glass of punch, whispering intensely. Every now and then, they both looked toward her. When they noticed she was watching, they averted their eyes. Something was weird, Rachel concluded, wondering if Viola noticed that she was on the balcony with Alex. Deep down, she knew there was more going on than the problems with her father's accounts and James wanting to take over the business.

* * *

The next day, Rachel sat with Abby in the dayroom learning how to make needlelace for a table runner their mother wanted completed by summer. In the future her mother and grandmother were excellent seamstresses. Rachel hadn't inherited the trait; she couldn't even sew a straight line using a machine, and now she was attempting to make lace by hand.

Each strand was attached to another with a square knot. Some of the knots had a small space between them; for others, a knot was placed directly on top. Using her left hand to apply pressure on the last stich, Rachel was able to keep the necessary tension so the thread wouldn't slide around, making the next stich with her right hand. It was a difficult process, and Rachel had to keep reminding herself that each of her hands had a distinctly separate task.

Rachel remembered seeing portraits of Queen Elizabeth. Some of the dresses she wore had yards of lace attached to the collars and bodice. As they worked, she realized the amount of lace on the dress must also reflect status and wealth, just as the color and the fabric she had read so much about.

"I hope Henry Parker calls on me." Abby giggled excitedly. "Also, Lord Gerald would be a good catch, or even Lord Edmond. Is he not handsome? "

Abby had high hopes for finding an eligible suitor that her father would approve of. The attention that Abby received last night was favorable. Considering their father's financial situation, her dowry would be small to say the least. Rachel had a feeling her father had been pushing both Abby and herself toward the older, more established suitors.

Rachel found herself becoming protective of the young girl. She was still having a hard time adjusting to having a younger sister. Many of the older men that their father introduced to them were Rachel's real age. If Rachel was to stay in this life, she felt she could be with a man of that age. Yet, she worried about Abby. Rachel decided that the history books were right. Marriages of this time were about gaining social status, increasing wealth, and conceiving an heir. She couldn't understand why everyone considered the Elizabethan age so romantic.

Before waking up in the sixteenth century, Rachel's knowledge of English history was limited. She did remember hearing one in three women died in child birth from complications that could have been prevented by modern medicine. If the odds were stacked against a woman producing an heir, Rachel decided Abby needed to marry for love and security, a union that would bring her happiness and joy for the rest of her life, however long that might be.

Rachel tried to work the needle without poking herself. "Lord Edmond is too arrogant. He looks at women as he does his horses. Like breeding stock."

Abby gasped and a look of shock came over her face. Rachel went on, pretending she didn't notice her sister's reaction. "If you were to marry Lord Gerald, I'm afraid that you would have many little Goodwins already running all over your estate that you don't know about."

"Of course I would know." Abby sputtered and shifted in her seat. "I would be having at least a dozen children to care for."

"I disagree. As I stood on the balcony last night, I noticed Gerald Goodwin speaking in very close proximity to a serving girl."

"Maybe he was just asking a question."

"I believe he was. After, the girl blushed, took him by the hand, and snuck toward the stables. I didn't see him until much later last evening."

The look on Abby's face was classic. She truly believed that people were honest and loving. Rachel couldn't blame her. Their parents sheltered them to the best of their ability. Growing up in a house filled with love was unusual for this time. Their parents genuinely loved each other. Rachel did not know if they had fallen in love before or after, but she knew that their situation was unique.

"As for Mr. Parker, he might be someone to consider, for the moment." He was younger than most of their suitors, attending college to become an attorney. Rachel assumed his family had money if they were able to afford to send him to college. Mr. Parker could speak with many of the men intelligently, and appeared to be respected. However, he was not the most handsome.

Every time Henry Parker looked at Abby, he flushed and became nervous, afraid that she might catch him looking. Rachel liked this quality, though her father might not. It made Rachel feel like Abby would be loved and respected.

"But what if he does not like me? What if he does not think I am pretty?"

"Any gentleman that calls obviously likes something about you Abby; otherwise he wouldn't be calling."

Rachel noticed that Abby couldn't hold her needle and thread without shaking. Setting down her work, she knelt in front of her sister.

"Abby, marriage is a commitment. You have to be absolutely positive that the man you choose will be the man you want to be with for the rest of your life. He doesn't need to be the most handsome or sought-after man of The Season. Nor does he have to be the wealthiest. You need to find someone that you can talk to, who will respect what you say. Someone whose day is not complete until he makes you smile."

"How do I achieve this? How do I find him?"

She wiped a tear away from Abby's face. "First you need to be yourself. Say what is on your mind. You can't sit there quietly when a man calls. You must speak with him, ask him questions."

Abby gasped, putting her hands to her mouth. "But that is rude!"

Rachel almost laughed at the idea of a woman finding a suitable man without having a real conversation first.

Rachel whispered most scandalously, "Who cares? This is your life Abby. How else are you going to decide if you want to be with him? Think about it. If Lord Edmond calls, ask him what he sees for your future. Are you going to want to talk about horses for the rest of your life over supper?"

Abby meekly smiled through her tears. "No."

"Okay, lesson number two."

"This is a lesson? Where did you learn this?"

"Observing other people," Rachel laughed. "Number two. You need to make sure he is listening to you and respects your opinion. Otherwise, you are doomed from the start."

"And how do I accomplish that?"

"Let's take Lord Gerald for example. If he calls on you, ask him a question. Anything, really – and then disagree with him."

"What if I agree with what he says?"

"Abby, you are testing to see what he would say. It's okay if you agree, but you want to hear his reaction. If he answers with a statement, acting as if you don't know what you are talking about, then you know he won't listen to you in the future. If he explains the topic like mother and father do, and holds a conversation, then he will respect you enough to listen."

"All right. I think I understand." Abby looked at the piece of lace in her hands.

Rachel hoped she was right. She had no room to talk; relationships in her life were not her strong point. But she knew what she was looking for and what she wanted. Guilt washed over her as she considered what she said to Abby about marriage and commitment. She must be a truly horrible person to be attracted to a married man, even if he hadn't been born yet.

Abby tugged at her thread. "If we could only see the future to see who we will marry."

The future. Rachel's head came up abruptly. She still hadn't figured out how to find the witch. She hoped that her reaction didn't reveal her thoughts. "But if you knew the future, then life wouldn't be any fun."

"Aye. I agree."

Rachel looked down at the lace in her hands, thinking that she needed to get back to her time.

CHAPTER NINETEEN

The weeks passed quickly as Rachel was swept up in the activities of The Season. She didn't have time to ponder her situation, let alone try to figure out how to get home. When their mother wasn't keeping them busy entertaining guests, they were being entertained as guests. Rachel lost count of the number of luncheons, suppers, and balls they had attended.

Every time a suitor called, their mother would go into a frenzy making sure that flowers were fresh, the decanter full of ale, and tiny little cakes served. Rachel knew the men didn't care about the little details; they were interested in acquiring a wife.

Last week when Lord Edmond called, Rachel was shocked when Abby took her advice. She really didn't think the girl had it in her to do something so completely improper. When he began speaking about his Spanish horses, Abby disagreed, stating that Arabians may prove to be a better choice.

If it hadn't been for her mother's gasp at Abby's comment, Rachel would have busted out loud with laughter. The girl had stumped him; apparently he didn't know how to respond, his face turning bright red. Somehow, their mother turned the conversation to the potential marriage of Mary Stuart and the Queen's favorite, Robert Dudley, doing her best to rectify the situation.

That night Abby snuck into Rachel's bedroom and told her she was right. He wasn't a good choice and she didn't want to spend her life talking about horses. Thankfully, Lord Edmond never called on Abby again.

The only person who called on Rachel was James Bryant. Occasionally, she found herself becoming self-conscious, wondering why the other men she had danced with didn't call. Not that it mattered. She didn't belong in this time. But, of course, she had to consider the real Rachel of 1564. She didn't want to ruin the real Rachel's chances of finding a suitor, if she, the Rachel of the future, was able to make it home. However she couldn't help but notice that the only man in Bristol interested in courting her was the one man who made her want to run away.

She had seen Alex a few times since the night they kissed. When the girls didn't have social functions to attend, Rachel frequently persuaded Aunt Lilly to show her the sites of Bristol. Occasionally, she would spot him attending church, or in the merchant quarter. She didn't know what she had done to upset him because after that night, he hadn't spoken with her. Every now and then, she caught him glancing at her and she would smile. He would then turn the other way, pretending he didn't see her. Rachel didn't know when she would find the opportunity to speak with him.

To her, it didn't make sense. Before they left the estate, Abby told her Alexander didn't want to marry Viola. Almost every time she saw him, Viola was near. For someone that didn't want to get married, they appeared to be spending a lot of time together.

Henry Parker called on Abby almost every other day. From her bedroom window, Rachel would catch him straightening his jacket, brushing his hair with his fingers, and taking a deep breath before he walked up to the door. His ritual would always bring a smile to her face.

Once, Rachel whispered to him as he was leaving that Abby liked Foxtails. The next time he arrived he held a rather large bouquet of Foxtails on his arm. Abby giggled with glee as their mother fretfully tried to keep her calm and proper.

Peeking out the window, waiting for Henry to arrive, Rachel spotted a man standing across the street.

For the last couple of weeks, she'd seen various men watching the house. She didn't know who they were or what they wanted. When she brought it up to her father, he dismissed her, stating he hadn't noticed anyone.

The first time she noticed something strange was the day James showed up unexpectedly to take her and Aunt Lilly for a carriage ride. Apparently her mother "forgot" to mention that he was arriving that day.

If it wasn't for the company, Rachel felt she might have enjoyed herself. The day was warm and the route James took was filled with beautiful architecture. For a brief moment she wondered if he really was a horrible person. The moment his hand accidently touched hers, she found herself repulsed, remembering the fear she felt when he had looked at her weeks before.

Before he left, he whispered if she was to marry him, her entire family would be taken care of. At that moment she realized James knew she overheard the conversation in her father's library.

She had been analyzing her father's ledgers for the past several weeks, when the family was sleeping. The transactions seemed to be in order, but something just didn't feel right.

With Abby's help, she suddenly became ill the next few times he called, and even let her mother call for the physic. Though the physician couldn't find anything wrong, he prescribed more of the bitter eyebright drink.

She wasn't so lucky the previous week. They were sitting in the parlor visiting with Henry, when James arrived unannounced. There was nothing she could do but endure his presence and conversation. When he quietly told her again that he was interested in marriage, she knew that there was something else. If all he wanted was her father's business, he would be speaking with her father about a union, not her. For some reason he wanted her approval, yet he didn't seem to be interested in her. The man gave her the creeps.

When he left, she knew she needed to find out exactly what James Bryant was up to. Last night she knew what she needed to do or she might get stuck with James forever. But first, she had to find a way out of the house without anyone seeing her, especially the man standing across the street.

She complained of a headache, and went to her room to lie down. Every time she heard footsteps in the hallway, she jumped into bed pretending to be sleeping. So far, her ruse was working. Peering out the window again, she saw Henry approaching with another bouquet of flowers for Abby. He straightened his jacket with one hand, ran his fingers through his hair, took a deep breath and walked to the door. Smiling, she picked up her cloak and walked to the door.

Instead of using the front door, Rachel slipped into the dayroom, knowing exactly where everyone was. Her mother would have the house in a frenzy making sure that refreshments were being served. Abby and Aunt Lilly would be sitting in the parlor entertaining Henry and her father would be in the library.

Opening the window, she climbed out just like she did as a kid, smiling at the memory. Instead of walking to the street, Rachel went toward the stables, and then cut into the neighbor's yard. Pulling her cloak over her head to hide her face, she moved quickly, focusing on her destination.

* * *

Rachel had been trying to find Alex for days. Abby thought it strange that Rachel wanted to attend church on a daily basis, and her aunt was beginning to complain about the frequent trips to the park and the merchant quarter. Rachel simply didn't want to put them out any longer.

A few days ago, Abby pointed to the cottage stating it was Lord Alexander's home, noting in particular that she thought it odd Lord Alexander had but one servant attending him. Rachel made sure she remembered how to get there.

Half an hour ago she had arrived, knocking on the door. When the manservant answered, he told her that Lord Alexander was indisposed and not receiving visitors. Rachel didn't want to go back to the cottage for fear that everyone would discover her secret.

She started walking up the street from his cottage, her thoughts drifting to her old life. Her best friend, Christian, use to call her a force of nature. Whenever she got a thought in her head, nothing stopped her from following it through. But that was in her own time, with the use of the internet and libraries. She was in the past and Alex was the only person she trusted to help her.

Hearing a carriage approach, she moved to the side of the road. Glancing at who passed, she noticed it was Alex's manservant. This was her opportunity; immediately she turned, running back to his cottage.

Rachel slipped around the back of the cottage, hoping the manservant had left the backdoor unlocked when he left. She looked around to make sure no one saw her and turned the door handle. Pushing the door open, she peeked inside to see that no one was in the kitchen. She cautiously entered the house, closing the door silently behind her.

Leaning back against the door, she let out a breath she didn't know she was holding.

The house appeared to be deserted; she couldn't hear any sounds. She walked room to room in search of Alex. If he wasn't taking visitors, maybe he was upstairs in one of the bedrooms. Aside from being immaculately decorated with beautiful fabrics covering the beds and a painting hung over the bed and mantel, every one of them was empty.

The moment she entered his bedroom she knew it belonged to him. She walked over to the bed and touched the quilt with her fingers, wondering where he was. She picked up his pillow and inhaled his masculine scent. He was engaged to be married, she reminded herself. She sighed and replaced the pillow. The attraction she had for him was uncalled for. It was silly for her to think he would want to be with her. She was from the future. Besides – she was not of his social status.

Walking back into the hallway in defeat, she spotted a small door she hadn't looked in. She opened it and followed a thin staircase into the attic.

Before her stood a well-lit room filled with canvases, painting supplies, and paintings. One side of the room held racks built into the wall separating the pieces from each other. The other side held two long tables filled with small, ceramic cups holding leaves, stone, berries; and an array of other items to be ground with the pestle and mortars nearby. Different size brushes surrounded neatly folded pieces of cloth at a table's end. Rachel recognized the flat, earthy smell of turpentine, used to clean up oil paints.

Near the circular window stood a large easel holding a half-painted portrait. She recognized the Lady Butler, the woman they saw in the park a few weeks earlier sitting on the bench in her evening gown. The detail was exquisite; the likeness, unmistakable.

Stepping over to the wall, she slid out one of the paintings, carefully balancing it with her hands, and examined it. She took her time, knowing that to truly experience a masterpiece one did not rush. She had only looked at two paintings when the sound of a carriage brought her back to the reason she was here. She glanced out the window. The manservant was returning.

"Oh my." She turned around and raced down the small stairs, quietly closing the door before descending the main staircase. She ran to the back door and cracked it open, only to see he was coming that way. Immediately she hid in the pantry, praying he wouldn't find her.

Leaving the door slightly ajar, she peered through the opening, waiting for the manservant to enter the house. Hearing the backdoor open, Rachel held her breath, her heart pounding against her chest. His footsteps, loud at first, faded.

Rachel stepped out of the tight space, quietly made it to the back door, and opened it without a sound. The moment her feet touched the ground outside, she ran.

It had been at least an hour since she broke into Alex's home. He wasn't there and she had no idea where he could be. Could his painting be the reason he was avoiding her? Now she had another reason to talk to him, if she could find him first. Rachel didn't know what to do. She walked to the park and then to the merchant quarter.

Her family wouldn't listen to her. She couldn't find Alex and she didn't want to go back to her aunt's cottage. Walking by the Solicitor's building, she saw three men walk out. James closed the door, putting his key in the lock.

Rachel pulled the hood of her cloak down so he couldn't recognize her if he looked that way. Watching the men disappear into the distance, she decided this would be her only chance. If the males in this time didn't want to help her, she would do it alone.

* * *

Pulling the pins out of her hair, Rachel looked left and then to her right, hoping that no one would notice her picking the lock of the Solicitor's office. She knocked on the door, pretending to see if they were in, just in case someone was watching.

"Stay calm and breathe." She heard the voice of her grandfather in her head as she said the words. She had spent several weeks one summer with her grandparents in Liebenthal, Kansas. To her grandmother's dismay, her grandfather taught her how to pick a lock using a bobby pin and a thin piece of metal. When she opened one, he found another in the old shed behind the house, betting her that she couldn't open it with a conspiratorial wink. With all the patience and determination a twelve-year-old could muster, she managed to open every lock he handed her.

Finally, she heard a click. Apprehension kept her from squealing in excitement for accomplishing the small task. Turning the door handle, she glanced both ways again as she stepped over the threshold and closed the door behind her.

Leaning back against the door, Rachel took several deep breaths, trying to slow down her heart beat. She wiped her damp hands against her skirt while her eyes adjusted to the dark room. No matter how many times she told herself this was important, the idea of breaking the rules gave her a queasy feeling in her stomach.

I never break the rules, Rachel thought to herself. I always count to three at a stop sign, I return wallets I find, even when filled with money – and I never have romantic relationships with students, break into Lord's houses, or sneak into Solicitor's offices.

Taking another deep breath, Rachel surveyed the room. For the most part the small space was barren. The shutters on the front window stood open, giving some light to the dark room. A simple portrait of an older, gray-haired man hung on the wall. His eyes seemed to watch her every move.

The room wasn't much bigger than her own office in the future, but instead of four filing cabinets lining one wall, a small sofa provided clients a seat. The two desks faced the front door giving whoever was working the ability to see and greet anyone who walked in. Behind them a door stood ajar. Rachel knew the office in the back didn't belong to James; he was the apprentice.

Looking at the two desks, Rachel thought that the Solicitor had two apprentices. However, one desk appeared unoccupied except for a lone candle. The other was completely cluttered with a ledger sitting open and a quill carelessly laid on the wood. The lid to the inkwell lay next to the bottle with several candles randomly placed around the papers. The disarray made Rachel think the owner of the desk had left in a hurry.

The thought made her turn back toward the front door. She convinced herself she had made it this far, so she needed to keep going. Taking another deep breath, she forced herself to take the first step toward the disorganized desk and began to pull open the drawers. One by one she opened every ledger, looked inside, and carefully replaced it, not wanting someone to discover her intrusion. She laughed at herself. She remembered how cluttered and disorganized her office in the future looked, and how she could find anything someone was looking for in a matter of minutes. "Chaos is organized," she said, and continued looking for her father's account.

Not finding what she was looking for, Rachel stepped to the barren workspace. Pulling open the bottom drawer, she was shocked to see someone was actually using the space. Kneeling down, she repeated the process of looking at each book. After previewing every one of them, she pulled the last ledger to her chest, hugging it in defeated consolation.

It's not here, she thought to herself. Where could it be? The idea of going to his home made her stomach turn. If she was caught, she knew James wouldn't forgive. He would make sure that her father found out and would make her marry him. The idea of James touching her made Rachel cringe.

Sighing, she sat back on her heels and looked around the office again. The sunlight was fading; she didn't have much time left before the room would be completely dark. She slid the ledger back inside the drawer and began closing it when she noticed the space between the spine of the book and the edge of the drawer.

Rachel analyzed both desks; they appeared to be built identically. She walked over to the first desk, opened the drawer, and looked at the distance between the journals and the edge. They weren't the same.

Rushing back to the first desk, Rachel carelessly pulled every book out, tossing them on the floor. Tugging at the thin board at the bottom, she was able to wedge it out; she found two journals with her father's name underneath. Squealing in excitement, she sat back, opening them to the last page of entries. She recognized one of the pages as a duplicate of her father's. The second book had the same transactions, but with different numbers.

Her stomach fluttered as excitement ran through her entire body. She knew it. James Bryant was cooking the books. Quickly, she replaced the false bottom, slid the other books back, and closed the drawer. She needed to get back to her aunt's cottage to show her father what she had found. Gathering the two ledgers in her arms, she realized she couldn't walk around with them out in the open. Someone might see her.

Pulling off her cloak, she wrapped them in the fabric, praying no one would give her a second glance. She stepped to the door – and stopped in her tracks when she heard someone put a key into the lock. Fear took over. She hid as quickly as possible under the cluttered desk, pulling the chair as close to her as she could.

Crap, she said to herself, I knew he was coming back and I hid under the wrong one.

Rachel knew it was too late to find another place to hide. Holding her breath, she heard footsteps coming toward her. She was certain he could hear her heart beating. She heard a desk drawer open and books being slammed on the desk.

"Bloody Hell!" a voice cursed, followed by a long moment of silence before she heard the scraping sound of a chair dragged and then thuds of ledgers put back in their place.

Slowly and carefully, Rachel released the breath she had been holding. As silently as possible, she inhaled, praying the man wouldn't hear her. She knew it was James even without peeking from her hiding place. She could smell the strong scents of sandalwood and tobacco.

The minutes felt like hours before the man stood up and she heard his feet moving across the floor. Instead of walking to the door, as she prayed he would, the sound moved closer to her. Holding her breath again, she could see his shoes from beneath the desk when she noticed the hem of her dress sticking out in view. Quickly, she gently pulled at the fabric, hoping she was fast enough and he didn't notice.

The man paced back and forth once more before rushing to the door, closing it behind him. Rachel didn't move. She didn't know if he was coming back. She was afraid he had seen the hem of her skirt, and still stood in the office, only pretending he left. But if he had left, she wanted to let him get as far away as possible. Straining her ears, she listened for any sound that would indicate she wasn't alone. She clutched the journals to her chest; her neck and arms began to ache.

She didn't know how long she had sat there after he left but the sun had set and the room was dark. Finding the courage deep down inside of herself, she climbed out from under the desk. All she could think about was getting to her aunt's cottage and showing her father what James had done to him. But she needed to get there first. Walking toward the edge of the window, she peered out into the darkness. Not seeing anyone near the office, Rachel ran to the door and gently opened it, then stepped out into the night.

CHAPTER TWENTY

Rachel knew she took a wrong turn. The walk felt longer than she remembered and her surroundings were not as familiar. She looked around trying to find her bearings with only the moon and candlelight through the windows of the buildings to guide her. Every time she encountered someone, she carefully walked to the opposite side of the road, hopeful that no one recognized her.

The night was a bit colder than it had been recently and she wished she could put on her cloak rather than hold it close to her chest. Knowing what she carried would change everything for the Drovere family, she clutched them even tighter, certain that this was her purpose in the past.

The smell of the salt water was a bit stronger than near her aunt's cottage. She could hear men yelling at each other and the sound of a carriage riding by in the distance. She decided to turn around and go back the other way before she got too close to the sounds she heard.

While retracing her steps, the thought of explaining to her family where she had gone off to consumed her mind. What was she going to say? The truth would be too far-fetched, considering what she had discovered. If she revealed that Lord Alexander was the anonymous artist, they would think her deranged – she already struggled to explain her "memory loss" – and probably throw her into a mental institution.

Thinking back, it made sense. He knew too many details about the artist and she now recognized the faint, earthy scent on him. That might have been why she felt so comfortable around him – because he smelled like turpentine. Giggling at the thought, Rachel couldn't imagine a more unromantic scent. But it reminded her of the campus, where the students still used it to clean their brushes. It reminded her of where she belonged, in the future.

Unveiling his secret to the world was not her place. She would never tell anyone what she discovered; but she knew he had too much talent to go down in history anonymously. Somehow, she had to convince him to come out of the closet and get the credit he deserved.

Deep in thought, Rachel didn't hear the two men approach from behind her until one gently grabbed her by the arm.

"Miss Rachel Drovere?"

Rachel turned toward the voice without thinking. "Yes."

"Your father has us searchin for thee. We are to conduct thee to 'em."

At the mention of her father, Rachel let down her defenses. "I'm almost home. I'll be fine." She tried to pull her arm away from the man.

"Nay, mi'lady, we are to take thee to him."

"Where is my father?" Rachel tried again to pull away.

The man tightened his grip. "Da merchant quarter."

She remembered her father went there to work on his books with James. James. She looked at the man. A red scar creased his temple, just below his greasy brown hair. The large scar made his dark, beady eyes look even more piercing. He wasn't there to take her to her father; he was there to take her to James.

She pulled her arm harder. "No thank you."

As she broke loose from him, a big, burly man grasped her waist from behind, lifting her up off the ground. Instinctively, Rachel kicked, taking a breath to scream. The first man shoved a piece of cloth into her mouth.

The ledgers were still in her arms; Rachel struggled, holding them as tightly as she could. The men tried to set her on the back of a horse. Rachel spooked it with her kicking; the nervous horse retreated backwards.

Suddenly, she saw light reflecting off a knife. The first man held it to her neck. "Nay! Stay! D'ya hear me?"

Rachel went completely still, letting the men get her on the horse, but she kept hold of the ledgers in a death grip against her chest, making the task difficult for them. They appeared not to be too bright. Instead of setting her on top of the horse, they threw her across his rump. Rachel decided to bide her time. She hoped when they felt comfortable they would let down their guard.

The men were apparently not prepared to abduct a small female and take her captive. They only had one horse, which she currently occupied. If she had the use of her hands she could have simply maneuvered herself to a sitting position and ride away, but that would have meant the journals might fall to the ground. Losing the ledgers was not a risk she was willing to take.

After a few minutes of walking alongside the horse carrying Rachel, the burly man looked at her and then quickened his pace to catch up with the first man who led the horse.

"D'ya thinks our reward be received this night?"

"Aye, when she boards the ship."

The burly one glanced back at his prize. "Where is the wench being sent?"

"The Americas. She will fetch a good price as a slave."

Holy cow, Rachel thought. That's not the way I wanted to go home.

* * *

Alexander had been scouring the city for hours with no sign of Rachel.

Earlier that evening he had returned home just before Henry Parker beat down his door. Alexander hadn't even taken off his jacket. Sometime during Henry's visit with Abby, Rachel had disappeared. Abby was petrified by the thought that something bad had happened to her sister. Henry promised to find her.

Had the situation been different, he would have thought it humorous that Henry's first inclination was to ask him for assistance. Apparently, Abby told Henry she thought Rachel had feelings for him. The idea of the small beautiful woman sharing his feelings made him feel warm inside. But he didn't have time to figure out why she made him feel that way; she was missing and they needed to find her.

Arthur was in the process of forming a search party to look for the girl. Alexander knew that Arthur's bad leg would prevent him from looking for her himself.

When Henry told him that Arthur sent his footman to inform James Bryant, he felt his stomach turn.

Alexander called to his manservant Philip and explained what Henry had said, telling him to find Nic and relay the information. In the back of his mind, Alexander knew she was in trouble. He hoped that she had simply gotten lost, but the thought of James looking for her made him suspect James was behind her disappearance. There was no telling what Alexander would do if James touched Rachel in the wrong way.

A voice called from behind him. "My Lord."

Turning his horse, Alexander recognized one of Nic's men swiftly riding toward him. Panting, the man tried to catch his breath while straightening his jacket in an attempt to look presentable in front of his better.

"Master Nic." He paused, taking another breath. "Master Nic saw James Bryant at the docks near the Jesus of Lubeck. The Jesus of Lubeck departs for the Americas in the morn. Master Nic said you needed to know."

Alexander pulled a coin from his pocket. "Thank you, the information may prove valuable."

The man waved his hand. "No, My Lord, Master Nic takes care of us. Besides, we all know what sort of man Master Bryant is."

Alexander nodded his head. "Any news of Miss Rachel?"

"No, My Lord, Master Nic has commissioned several of us in search of her. She will be found. Do not fear, My Lord." The messenger turned his horse and rode off.

Instead of going east of the city, Alexander changed his destination and raced toward the docks. Why would James be loitering near the ships? It was no secret that James' pregnant wife had drowned years ago. Since that tragic day, no one had seen James within a hundred feet of any sizable body of water.

I should be looking for Rachel, Alexander thought. Did she run away? Was she abducted? Who could kidnap her while she was in the safety of her aunt's cottage?

Alexander had asked Nic weeks ago to keep an eye on James's movements, but no one had informed him of James calling on her today. Though James had called on Rachel twice, Nic or one of his men was always near in case James decided to do something dishonorable.

Questions about Rachel raced through his mind. Henry mentioned that Rachel had feelings for him. What were her feelings toward him? Was she angry? He hadn't told her he wanted to break off the engagement with Viola; he was too busy looking at her, wanting to touch her.

The sound of a high-pitched scream interrupted his thoughts. Turning his eyes toward the sound, Alexander noticed a rather large man holding a woman from behind. A smaller man stood in front of her, blocking his view.

Alexander was not sure if the woman was Rachel, but he could tell by the movement of her skirt and how the man was trying to hold her that she wanted nothing to do with these men.

Galloping closer, Alexander jumped off his horse and ran toward the smaller man in front of the girl. She was yelling at them in a high-pitched voice, using language that would make even Nic's men blush.

The next thing he heard was her screaming his name. "Alex!"

Alexander looked up. It was Rachel. Briefly, relief washed over him – he found her. Before the smaller man turned, Rachel leaned back on the larger man, lifting both of her legs and kicking him square in the chest, knocking him down.

The larger one grabbed her by the hair and pulled out a knife. Wasting no more time, Alexander went after the man holding Rachel. He had to protect her.

"Alex!" He heard her scream. "Behind you!"

The man on the ground a moment ago had gotten back up and was ready to charge at him. Reaching for his sword, Alexander realized he had left it on his horse.

"Bloody hell!"

Using his bare hand, he punched the man in the face, drawing blood. The man stepped back, wiping the blood from his lip. Giving Alexander an evil look, he stepped forward, ready to take revenge.

Knowing what he was about to do, Alexander doubled up his fists. Letting the man swing first, he dodged the punch, then released all of his pent up emotions, beating the man until he was on the ground, not moving.

With determination, Alexander turned to the man holding Rachel. Her back was against her attacker, who held the knife at her throat. The look on Rachel's face made him pause. He noticed that she held one finger up, wanting him to stop for a moment.

"Let me go, you big oversized brute!" She pretended to struggle, but exerted very little effort. "What do you want with me?"

"My Master wants me to conduct thee to 'em." He looked at his friend lying on the ground.

Rachel's eyes didn't leave Alexander's; the man pressed the knife firmly against her throat. Motioning her hand in a circular motion, Alexander could tell she wanted him to say something.

"Who's your Master?" Alexander wanted to ram the man's head against the ground but the calm look on her face told him that she wanted him to wait.

The man pulled Rachel tighter. "Master James Bryant."

"What does James want with her?"

The man answered, but Alexander didn't hear what he said. His eyes were locked on Rachel's face. She took a deep breath, leaning back, completely relaxing in her attacker's arms. Again she motioned for Alexander to continue talking.

"Why does James want her?"

"I have spoken those words to ya!" The burly man shouted moving the knife a few inches away from her neck.

Behind Rachel's attacker, Alexander noticed Nic and one of his men walking toward them. He signaled to them to wait by lifting his hand, pretending to talk to the attacker.

Alexander tried to keep his voice as calm as he could. "Tell me again."

The man shouted angrily, "He wants to send her to the Americas. He said if he could not marry her, no one will."

As he was yelling, Alexander watched Rachel take another deep breath, calmly moving her left hand over her right. Gripping them together into one large fist, slowly she slid down the front of his body. The man fumbled, trying to pull her up. Once her head reached the level of his chest, she turned her upper body slightly, extending her hands in front of her body. Then, in one fluid, sudden motion, she pulled them back, jamming her right elbow into his groin.

The man dropped the knife as he doubled over with pain, grabbing his crotch. Rachel let herself hit the ground and roll away. Alexander wasted no time. He wrestled the man down, kicking the weapon away while Nic and his men raced forward to pin the man on the ground.

Rachel shook uncontrollably, tears filling her eyes. Stepping forward, Alexander tried to help her stand, but she pulled away from him, crawling to the bundle of fabric lying on the ground. She picked it up and held it close to her chest, hugging it for comfort.

Alexander ran his hand through his hair, not knowing what to think. He had just saved her from a couple of thugs and instead of throwing her arms around him, she was crying while hugging a clump of fabric.

Looking over at Nic, Alexander shrugged his shoulders in defeat. Nic rolled his eyes. "Attend to her, would you?"

Two men walked up carrying clubs, each holding a lantern. Nic looked at the men, snapped his fingers, and pointed to the man Alexander had beaten to a pulp. The two men rushed over to the unconscious man lying on the ground.

Kneeling down next to Rachel, Alexander rubbed the palms of his hands together nervously, afraid to touch her again. "Are you injured?"

Shaking her head no, she finally looked up at him. "Thank you." She wiped the tears from her eyes with the tips of her fingers.

"Come, let us get you home. Your family is worried."

Nodding in agreement, Rachel stood clutching the bundle to her chest. Taking a few steps toward his horse, she stumbled. Reflexively, Alexander reached out to catch her when the bundle fell to the ground with a thud.

Rachel held onto him for support, but her eyes didn't leave the ground. Alexander reached down and tried to pick up the fabric when he realized it was heavier than he thought it should be.

"No," She gasped, bending over with both hands to pick it up, tearing the fabric out of his hands.

"What do you have here?"

"You'll see." Her eyes twinkled and she made a small smile.

Alexander put his arm around her, intending to escort her to his horse.

Rachel shrugged. "I'm fine. I can make it."

He pulled his hand away from her arm, and felt something wet. Rubbing his fingers and thumb together, he noticed it felt warm and sticky. Blood.

"Nay. You're injured." He returned his arm protectively around her.

"I'm fine." She tried to pull away.

He knew she was anything but fine. She was the most stubborn, independent, beautiful woman he had ever met – and she was getting on his nerves.

"Hush," he demanded a little too sternly. "Do not say another word. Whether you agree or not, I *am* going to care for you."

He looked around and led her to the porch of a dark building. "Lantern," he called. Immediately, one of Nic's men walked over with a light.

Alexander sat Rachel down on the stoop, and used the lantern to examine the extent of her injuries. For the first time he noticed how the bodice of her dress was torn, exposing more than he wanted anyone to see. Pulling his eyes away from the cleavage of her perfectly formed, small breasts, he felt the blood rushing through his veins. Her sleeve was ripped; blood trailed down from the wound on her arm. Lifting the light, he found a nick at the base of her throat where the man had held the knife.

Alexander reached under her skirt and tore a piece of fabric from her petticoat. He used it to bind the cut on her arm.

Setting the bundle on her knees, Rachel tried stopping him. "I can do that."

"Nay," he pushed her hand away.

Wetting another piece of cloth in his mouth, he wiped the blood from her neck, imagining he could touch the same spot with his lips and his tongue, tasting her.

When he finished, he looked into her puffy, red eyes. Little golden speckles danced in the light of the lantern. Even the fear of being abducted by two thugs did not steal her spirit. Lost in her beauty, forgetting where he was, he leaned forward to kiss her when she lifted her chin, inviting his lips to hers. Before their lips touched, he heard Nic clear his throat.

"My men have the situation under control. The magistrate will arrive momentarily. You best get Miss Rachel home." Nic stood next to them with his arms crossed, an all-knowing smirk on his face.

Standing, Alexander removed his jacket and helped Rachel to her feet while she clutched the bundle to her chest. After wrapping his jacket around her, he took another long look into her eyes and gently kissed her forehead, letting his lips linger for a moment longer than appropriate.

As he touched her with his lips, the urge to pull her closer to him was unbearable. Instead of being proper, he wrapped his arms around her, pulling her tight, breathing in the scent of her until he was calm enough to escort her home.

* * *

Walking into her aunt's cottage, Rachel saw her father pacing with his cane. He almost skipped to the door when he heard them, and dropped his cane to the floor as he put his arms around her, hugging her tightly. After scanning her from head to toe, Arthur ordered her upstairs to wake her mother and replace her shambled clothing.

Alexander handed her father his cane as they adjourned to the study.

"Men," Rachel murmured under her breath, stomping her foot. She was not about to be ordered around. Blatantly disobeying her father, Rachel walked into the small library next to the parlor. She could hear Alex describe the events of the evening. She sat down at her Uncle's desk and noticed her father's ledgers lying open. Unwrapping her treasure, Rachel opened the other journals to the same page. She went to work auditing the books using the quill to mark each transaction that didn't match.

She didn't know how long she had sat there reviewing the numbers when the conversation in the other room caught her attention.

"Please take no offense, Mr. Drovere. Rumor states you owe more than you can afford. If need be, I will either purchase your estate or pay your debtors. If the latter, I will oversee the running of your business. Of course, you and your family will be welcome to reside at the estate."

Before her father could respond, there was a knock at the door. Nic and the magistrate were announced and she heard them walk into the parlor. She rubbed her eyes, and tore off a sleeve constantly tickling the inside of her elbow, and continued listening to the conversation in the other room.

"James Bryant has disappeared from the docks. I had my men search the Jesus of Lubeck, with permission of course." Rachel had a feeling that Nic had a bit of a bad reputation and his last sentence was meant to say he was following the law.

Rachel heard a voice she didn't recognize; she assumed it was the magistrate. "What were his interests in your daughter?"

Alexander responded instead. "Apparently, Miss Rachel dodged his proposal of marriage. It appears Mr. Bryant was willing to do anything to keep her."

The unknown voice spoke again: "Why Miss Rachel? No offense, Mr. Drovere, there are richer and higher-status women seeking his hand."

"I have no idea." There was fear in her father's voice.

Rachel had enough of the men trying to analyze the situation when she alone knew the truth. Laying all three open journals on top of each other so she wouldn't lose her place, she walked into the parlor.

"Well I do."

The men turned with a look of shock on their faces. With one sleeve missing on her torn dirty dress, dried blood on her arm, her hair unkempt and dark smudges on her face, Rachel stood in the doorway holding the ledgers. She would not be dismissed. "I have something to show you."

Her father noticed what she had in her hands; walking over to her, he reached out to take the ledgers from her.

"No!" She pulled them out of his reach.

"Those books are not for a woman's eyes."

Rachel laughed, walking over to the small table in front of the sofa where Nic and the magistrate were sitting. This is what she went to college for. She held a higher degree than any of the men in this room, yet they told her that numbers were for men. Of course, that was almost 450 years in the future.

When she reached the table, she moved the men's drinks, and proceeded to sit down on the floor like a small child. Rachel noticed men's eyes turn wide with astonishment and heard her father gasp. She was beginning to think anything she did would shock these men. Ignoring them, she opened the ledgers to the pages she had marked.

"Look here." She pointed to a column in her father's ledger. "You leased 10,000 sheep and paid one shilling per head. And here," she continued, "two months later, you paid one shilling and six pence per head." Moving over to the sister journal, she pointed. "This is the same transaction showing that you actually paid three pence. And here you paid four."

All the men leaned forward to see what she was looking at. Rachel was surprised when Alex placed his jacket around her shoulders, kneeling down on the floor next to her. The magistrate turned the ledgers for a closer inspection.

"There are many conflicting entries in the ledgers. Father, you're not poor. You're being scammed."

Her father looked at her with a questioning look. Rachel could tell he was having a hard time understanding her speech. Realization crossed his face; she knew then he understood her meaning.

"James Bryant!" He paced back and forth in front of the fireplace.

Rachel knew it was time she revealed why she had disappeared. Looking up at her father, her face covered with guilt, she asked, "Do you remember when I was sitting in the library when you and James came in? It was a few days after I fell out of the tree."

She waited for her father to nod, confirming he remembered. "I wasn't daydreaming; I was reading your ledgers. When you and James came in the room and shut the door, I stood outside listening. When he walked out, he caught me standing there. At that moment, the way he looked at me, I knew he couldn't be trusted."

Her father started lecturing her. "Have I not told you to . . .?"

"Mr. Drovere," Alex stopped him abruptly. "Let Miss Rachel continue."

Aware that Alex was still kneeling next to her, she almost forgot what she was going to say. He was so close to her she could feel the heat of his thighs next to hers. She wished he could just hold her hand, giving her strength to continue. The events of the day were finally taking their toll on her; she had truly been in danger.

Despite the impropriety of sitting on the floor next to him, she took a deep breath, refocusing her thoughts. "The rest of the visit, he was always around. That's one reason I stayed in my room as much as I could." She didn't want to admit the other reason, that she was from the future and had no idea what was going on.

Alex raised an eyebrow. "I thought you were unwell?"

"I was, but I could have been around more."

The magistrate leaned forward. "What happened next?"

"We went to the Stafford Ball where he apologized for making me uncomfortable. And then he asked to court me. Mother apparently thought highly of him at

276 | ALYSSA DEAN COPELAND

the time, so I agreed. He came by the house at least half a dozen times."

As she said this, she noticed the look Alex gave Nic. When Nic winked at Alex, she confronted Nic. "Those men outside the house when James was here, do they work for you?"

Nic hesitated. "Aye. They are mine. You noticed them?"

"Yes. But I don't think anyone else did. I was looking for something out of place. I thought it was one of James' men."

Nic smiled. "I must tell them they were caught by a mere slip of a girl."

Rachel smiled back at him. "Thank you."

Looking back at her father she continued her story. "I only let James visit twice; the other times I pretended I wasn't feeling well. Abby covered for me. On the two occasions he was here, he indicated your business was losing money and he was willing to take care of me. Every time he touched my hand, I cringed. There was no way I was going to marry him."

"You do not have the final say upon whom you marry," her father stated under his breath.

"Really Papa? If you wanted me to marry him and I told you no, would you really make me marry him?"

Rachel knew the answer before she asked the question. He was simply trying to process everything and was saying things that made him feel like he was in control of the situation.

Shaking his head, he looked down at the floor, tapping it with his cane.

Rachel took a deep breath. "I tried to tell you and mother what I was thinking and no one would listen. Mother said it was your place to deal with the business and you said that women shouldn't ask questions about the books. I had no one to talk to."

Alex glanced at her. "You could have sent a message to me."

"I tried to find you. Each time I saw you at a ball, you were across the room with Viola. I could never find you alone to speak with you without her or her cousin around. Besides, isn't it inappropriate for me to initiate a conversation?"

The men nodded. "I thought so. Anyway," she waved her hand, "today Henry came to the house and everyone was busy. I decided to figure it out on my own."

She looked at Alex. "I went to your house today but you weren't home."

A worried look came across Alex's face. Rachel was not about to tell him that she snuck in, at least not yet. She wanted to tell him in private.

"So I went to James's office and found the ledgers." She purposely omitted the fact that she broke in, considering the magistrate sat in front of her. "I think he figured out I was there because he came back. I hid under the desk. A while later I left and then I think I made a wrong turn and got myself lost. You know the rest of the story."

The Magistrate shifted in his seat. "Mr. Bryant wanted to send you to the Americas because you discovered that he was embezzling?"

"One of the thugs said he was going to sell me into servitude. I don't think he ever actually wanted to marry me."

Standing up, the Magistrate looked at her father. "My men will find Mr. Bryant and we will bring him to justice."

Nic stood up next to the magistrate. "My men are searching for him as we speak."

Shaking her father's hand, they left, leaving her father and Alex in the parlor.

Her father sat on the sofa, and placed his head in his hands. Rachel knew he felt defeated.

"You have to stop trusting everyone, father. Even if you think you trust them, always pay attention to what is going on. Always keep your nose in it and double check."

He lifted his head. "We are not broke? I do not have to sell?"

Rachel smiled.

Arthur looked over at Alex. "Please accept my apologies Lord Alexander, but I shall not be accepting your offer to purchase my estate. I believe we will be fine from here forward."

Getting up off his knees, Alex shook her father's hand. "This is good news, Mr. Drovere. Rachel has saved your business. Now that she is safely home, I shall retire to mine."

Alex walked to the door. Rachel grabbed her father's hand. "Father, I must speak with Lord Alexander for a moment, in private."

"That is not appropriate, Rachel. You should not . . ."

"Really father? After all that has happened today, you're worried about being appropriate? You can watch us, but I must speak to him privately."

Reluctantly, he nodded his head. Rachel jumped up from the floor and ran toward the door. "Alex!"

Stopping, he turned around. She stepped close to him. "There's more to what happened today."

"More than what you have spoken of this evening?"

"Yes." Guilt washed over her face. "When I came to see you earlier today, your manservant said you were indisposed. I thought you were home but not taking visitors. When he left for a bit, I kind of broke into your house."

Questionably, he looked at her. "Broke in?"

"Well, yes, I mean no, um. The back door was un-locked and I let myself in."

He crossed his arms. "And what did you do in my home?"

"I was looking for you. You're the only person I trusted, who I thought would listen. I had to find you but you weren't there."

"So you broke in?"

Rachel hesitated. She took a deep breath and slowly exhaled. "I needed to tell you that I saw something I should never have seen."

Realization crossed his face. Rachel felt incredibly guilty, more so now than when she made her discovery.

She touched his arm. "I am so sorry Alex. I was look-ing for you. I didn't mean to stumble across what I saw, and I can't go back in time to fix it."

Back in time, she thought to herself. Maybe she real-ly was here to fix something. But what? Was it her fa-ther's business? Finding Alex's art? Would she wake up tomorrow morning back home? If she went home, would she see Allen? No, he went back to his wife, she reminded herself. Looking at Alex, she realized she didn't want to leave him.

Alex turned and reached for the door handle. "You had no right to violate my privacy."

Grabbing his arm, she pulled him back. "You're right. I . . . what I did was wrong. But it happened. You're an amazing artist and you would be doing the world an injustice by not exposing your secret."

His face turned red. He began pacing, running his hand through his hair. "The world sees my creations; there is no need for them to know it is me."

"No need?" Her voice carried a demanding tone. Looking over at her father she noticed that he heard her outburst. Quietly she went on: "In a hundred years from now, in four hundred and fifty years from now," she corrected herself, "no one will know it was you. People will look at your work and say, I wonder who that was – and then they won't give you a second thought."

Rachel knew she was lying just a little bit. There were some scholars who tried to solve the mystery of unsigned paintings. But the artists never became house-hold names. She knew Alex could become one of the most famous artists of the Elizabethan age if he only let his secret out.

"The people of the future are none of my concern."

"But they are mine. You could become a Picasso or a Rembrandt."

"Who?"

Waving her hand she went on. "What I am trying to say is that your work is beautiful and it will last for cen-turies. You should at least consider taking credit, if not for your ego, then for future generations that will look back and say 'That's the work of Lord Alexander Dohetry of Bristol' while they admire it in a gallery."

"I will not disgrace my family's name by telling the world, as you say. This is my secret and now one more person knows, whom I will have to watch."

"Who else knows?"

"That is none of your concern. By your actions this evening, I trust my secret will never cross your lips."

"Yes. I promise I won't say a word to anyone."

Alex nodded in acceptance of her promise as he opened the door and began walking out of the house.

"Wait!" Rachel removed the jacket from her shoulders and held it out to him. "Thank you."

Alex nodded, taking the jacket from her hands. Without another word, he turned and walked away.

Rachel realized how late it was when she saw the color of the sky on the horizon. The light-blue and pink made her notice how tired she was. Rubbing her arms, trying to keep herself warm, she watched Alex mount his horse.

CHAPTER TWENTY-ONE

The sunlight through the window warmed the parlor on an early morning in June. Sitting in her mother's favorite chair, Rachel peered out onto the field. She had been struggling with needle and thread, trying to accomplish the art of making lace, and wished Abby was home to help her.

Several weeks had passed since Alex rescued her from the thugs. The day after, her father whisked her back to the estate, leaving her mother and Abby with Aunt Lilly in Bristol to finish out The Season.

For the entire carriage ride he lectured her about being a proper female. She was not to leave the house unattended. She was not to get involved with the business affairs. When they had visitors, she must quietly sit in a chair, not the floor, and she should stop using first names outside of family openly. And without a doubt, she was never again allowed to speak with an unmarried man privately.

Rachel could imagine how she would have acted if her real father had lectured her like he did when she was a rebellious teen. Arthur Drovere was lucky he had a thirty-three-year-old trapped in his daughter's body.

He was obviously embarrassed for being naive about his accounts, and that his "mere" daughter discovered the embezzlement. More importantly, he was scared. His eldest daughter had been threatened, attacked, and abducted, and he wasn't able to protect her. James Bryant hadn't been found and he was afraid the man would come for her again.

Once they arrived at the estate, she rarely saw her father. He locked himself in his library, reviewing the ledgers or speaking with one of the many visitors who randomly showed up at all hours of the day or night. She was not just being watched by one or two members of the household staff; it appeared to be everyone on the estate. On rare occasion she could sit in a room alone. Once in a while, she would look out the window, and see an unfamiliar face patrolling the estate. Knowing the man was there to protect her made her feel safe, yet she felt guilty for needing protection.

Last week, Nic arrived and was locked in her father's office for several hours. She tried to eavesdrop on the conversation, but their voices were low and she couldn't hear a word. Besides, the doorman watched her every time she stepped near the library door.

That night Nic joined them for supper. Rachel went against her father's wishes by asking Nic if James Bryant had been found. He confirmed her suspicion; James was still missing, but Nic's men had not given up the search. She wanted to ask him about Alex, but the look on her father's face when she had inquired about James told her to keep her mouth shut. She didn't want to upset her father more than necessary.

Other than supper, she sat alone in the house trying to keep herself occupied. Rachel thought she had read every book her father allowed, when she was able to catch him before he locked the library door. Instead of sitting idle, she tried assisting the cook in preparing the meals and she was shooed away. When she tried to clean, the housekeeper complained to her father that she was capable of doing the job.

Rachel missed the company of a female; really, she missed having anyone to talk to. She wasn't allowed to leave the safety of the house, and she had nothing to do except think. It was dangerous, leaving a lonely woman to her own devices. Many times she found herself pacing in her bedroom, talking to herself out loud, trying to keep her thoughts from running away and taking her sanity with them.

Her mind continuously drifted to the events that had taken place since she arrived. The night after the attack, Rachel was positive she would have woken up in her own time. She had discovered the unknown artist and saved her father's business. In essence, she changed history. Instead, she woke up to her mother opening the shutters after three hours of sleep, telling her that she was leaving for the estate.

She kept asking herself about Alex. She hadn't seen him since the night he rescued her; he hadn't come to the estate to check on her. Rachel figured she screwed up this relationship just like she had all the others.

He gave her the impression he cared about her when he bound her arm and escorted her to her aunt's. He even sat on the floor with her while she was showing everyone the discrepancies in the ledgers. She genuinely thought he had feelings for her – until she admitted that she discovered his secret.

Alex had no intention of letting his secret out. His family's name was at stake. Noblemen were not of the working class, Rachel had learned; their job was to be rich. Honor and loyalty were values she wasn't accustomed to seeing. From what Rachel had read in the tabloids, those qualities were rare. People always said one thing and did another, disgracing themselves and their families.

"Maybe not all people." Rachel sighed, thinking of Allen.

She knew of at least one person who held loyalty, commitment, and family above his own happiness. For the first time since the day she hit her head, Rachel wasn't upset with him for going back to his wife. In fact, she had more respect for him than ever before. Allen told her he wouldn't forgive himself if he didn't try one more time. He made his decision.

Rachel decided if she was ever to get back to her own time, instead of being angry with him, she was going to be there if he needed a friend.

If she couldn't get home, then she didn't know what she was going to do. The real Rachel of this time was expected to find a suitor, get married, and raise a family. If she didn't, she might end up a spinster. She didn't want to end up as an old maid if she wasn't able to make it back to her own time.

Scrutinizing the lace, she noticed she hadn't created a single stitch since she sat down. From the position of the sun it appeared to be near noon, and Rachel had no idea what to do besides think. Sighing, she tried to put at least one stitch into the lace. If she owned a magic wand, the damned lace would be done.

"A wand!" She looked at the sun again. "How could I forget about the witch again?"

Setting her work down, she went to find the door-man and let him know she had a headache, and would be retiring. When he asked if she would be at supper, she told him not to bother waking her if she didn't make it down on her own.

Racing up the stairs, Rachel arranged an extra blanket under the sheet, hoping it looked like a real person lying there with the covers over her head.

Grabbing her cloak, she peeked outside the door and quietly descended the stairs. To her relief, everyone was occupied. She opened the front door and snuck out to the stable.

Once inside, she heard a female giggling. "Timmy?" she called out, looking for the stable boy.

When she said his name the giggling stopped. Climbing down the ladder, Rachel noticed that he was covered in straw and his face was red.

"Timmy!" She scorned.

His eyes cast to the ground, he answered, "Yes, ma'am."

Thinking on her feet, she proposed, "If you help me, I will tell no one."

Meeting her eyes, he nodded in agreement.

She whispered so the female in the loft couldn't hear her. "I need to visit the witch."

The fear in Timmy's eyes made Rachel want to second guess herself. "Do you remember when I fell out of the tree?"

"Yes ma'am."

Rachel hesitated at the lie she was about to tell, then continued. "Nothing has worked. I was hoping the witch may have an herb to cure my headaches."

A bit of relief washed over his face. He must think I wanted to have him turned into a toad, she thought.

"I need a horse saddled and if you're willing, an escort." Though she wanted to go alone, she had no idea how to get there and if something happened, at least she wouldn't be by herself.

* * *

Rachel confided in Timmy that she didn't want to be seen leaving the estate. He looked her up and down before racing out of the stables. When he got back, he handed her a pair of men's pants and a shirt. When she asked where he found them, he told her they were his own. With Timmy standing guard at the door, Rachel did her best to hide while changing her clothing. Instead of a sidesaddle, Timmy provided her with a regular one.

He looked distraught; she thought he was either worried about losing his position or visiting a witch. It didn't matter to her why he was helping her, only that he was.

The journey was longer than she thought it would be, but Rachel now had some experience riding a horse, thankfully. Timmy explained the witch lived halfway to Bristol – a four-hour ride by carriage – but he felt they could do it in two. Instead of talking, they raced forward to make good time.

Nearing a grove next to the junction of the main road leading to either Bristol or the estate, Timmy slowed his horse. "Up ahead is the Forest of a Thousand Whispers."

Following his lead, Rachel looked for the forest; all she saw was a rather large patch of trees.

"That's not large enough to be a called a forest."

Timmy gave her a funny look. "All know what 'tis named."

"When I bumped my head, I lost some of my memories."

Nodding, Timmy walked his horse down the small path leading into the trees with Rachel riding behind him. Her eyes adjusted to the dark surroundings. Now she understood why Timmy called it a forest; there were so many trees packed in this tiny area, she wondered how they got enough sunlight to grow. Day turned into night; pulling her cloak around her body, she felt the temperature drop by several degrees. The wind whipped through the leaves –Rachel couldn't recall it blowing a moment ago – making it sound as if the trees moaned in pain. Frogs croaked in the distance.

As they neared the creek, Timmy slid off of his horse and pointed across the water. "Yender."

Pulling the reins back, she brought her horse to a halt next to the lad. Rachel looked the direction he pointed. "We need to walk the horses across?"

"No ma'am. I do not mind helping ya, but I go no further." Rachel gave him a questioning look. Timmy gazed at the ground and admitted, "I is . . . afeared."

Dismounting, she handed the reins of her horse to Timmy. "You will wait for me?"

"Yes ma'am. Rite here I will wait for thee."

Lifting her skirt, Rachel picked her way across the shallow water, trying not to slip on the wet stones. When the icy water touched her toes, a prickly sensation sent goose bumps over her entire body. As if to warn her, an owl hooted and flew directly across her path. She almost lost her balance.

The moment her cold wet slippers touched dry ground she heard the sounds of the forest completely disappear. She strained her ears, but couldn't hear anything other than the gentle movement of the water. Taking a deep breath, she walked down the path.

After a few minutes, Rachel could have sworn she felt someone watching her. Looking back, she could barely see Timmy through the trees, tending the horses.

"Stop it," she said, trying to counter her fear.

From a distance she could barely make out a little stone house. Taking another deep breath, she forced herself to put one foot in front of the other. In her head she went over the conversation she would have with the witch again. It didn't matter that she had thought about it the entire ride here. She tried to shake the feeling that the end result wouldn't be what she hoped for.

The cottage looked safe enough, standing in a bare area cleared of trees. It was built with differently colored stones cemented together; green moss draped the roof. A small garden of herbs and flowers was planted next to the porch. A rather large pile of wood was neatly stacked just under a window. Several feet away from the house, she noticed a hitching post with a magnificent looking Bay tied to it. She could have sworn she had seen the horse somewhere before. She looked back at the house; it wasn't at all what she had imagined a witch's house would look like.

Rachel stepped closer to the house when she heard voices inside. She didn't want to intrude if the woman had company. The last thing she wanted was to be discovered. There was no telling what her father would do to her this time.

Afraid she would be noticed if she went back the way she came, Rachel ducked behind the wood stack, praying they didn't hear her movements. Looking up, she realized she was sitting under the window. Crap, she thought to herself. I always seem to find the worst place to hide.

The fear of being spotted grew.

Peeking in the window, Rachel gasped when she saw Viola, elegantly dressed, standing in the tiny, one-room cottage, facing a short, gray-haired, middle-aged woman wearing a simple gray cloak. Quickly, she ducked down; from what she could tell, the women didn't see her.

What on earth is Viola doing here? Rachel asked herself, now understanding why she had recognized the Bay. Curiosity replaced the panic she was feeling as she settled in, straining to hear the conversation.

"This is not a spell that can be treated lightly," Rachel heard the older woman caution. "He must be the one you are willing to be with forever."

"I know that. You think me daft? I will marry him no matter what the cost. He belongs to me."

"Of this you are sure?" She laughed. It was an eerie cackle.

"Of course I am sure," Viola snapped back. "It has been foretold; when he marries he will acquire rewards worth more than King Midas' gold."

"Who told you of this?" Rachel was sure she heard surprise in the older woman's voice.

"My mother. She promised I would be his bride."

"If the prophecy was meant for you, then a spell you would not need."

"What do you know of the prophecy?" Viola asked accusingly.

Instead of answering, the witch asked another question. "You are choosing to alter your path, for mere riches?"

"To acquire wealth that will last generations? Wealth which could alter the course of all of England? Yes, this is what I choose. You will cast the spell." Viola's voice went from defensive to an authoritative whisper. "For I know the secret you keep."

"I have no secrets," the witch snapped back.

"Aye. The secret is not yours to carry, but for you to hide. I know of your sister and of her son."

"You know of her son?" The older woman's voice was shaking. There was a long pause; Viola must have silently confirmed her question.

"I am paying you a tidy sum. Do not make this personal."

"T'will be difficult, for you know, he has feelings for another."

"What do you know of his feelings?" Viola shot back.

There was another long pause; the witch did not answer. Rachel's heart sank. She knew the women were talking about Alex, but who was this woman he had feelings for? Why did he lead her on, knowing he loved someone else? Was this why she could never find Alex at home?

After a few minutes Viola broke the silence. "You will place a curse upon her. Make it so she will never find love."

Rachel heard movement and the clanking of items from inside the house. Peeking inside the window again, she saw the older woman leaning over a table with Viola watching over her shoulder. Sinking back down to her spot, Rachel wondered what they were doing.

"Take this. Careful now, if you look carefully you will see the tip of this ring has the ability to draw blood."

"Ouch," Rachel heard Viola gasp.

"You were warned."

"What am I to do with this?" Viola asked.

"Inside the ring holds a powder of thyme, rosemary, cinnamon, and more I dare not reveal. Press here and it will open. He must drink it on the eve of the full moon. You must administer it."

"I believe that shall be simple," Viola stated with confidence.

"After, you must arrive here, before the witching hour."

"You are jesting, old woman. You expect me to administer the potion and return here under the dark of night?"

"It is you who seeks the spell, it is you who wishes it cast. If this is your true desire, then you will do as instructed." The witch spoke with an authoritative tone. "You must also bring tokens, personal to both."

"Tokens?"

"Items that belong to each; a piece of jewelry, an item of clothing, a lock of hair. Blood would be the best." Rachel heard the sound of movement again. "Wear this on the eve you administer the potion."

"What is it? The scent is lovely."

"His heart belongs to another; the spell must be strong. You hold the fragrance which will capture his attention. The potion will make him desire you, will wear off by dawn, and the spell will trap his altered feelings for you for all time."

"What of her?" Viola asked.

"The curse will be cast after. Bear in mind the curse may come back threefold," the witch warned.

"I am paying you a fair amount of coin to do this; I am not paying you to lecture me. You are casting the curse; if it comes back, it will come back on you."

Rachel heard the front door slam. Peeking out from the wood pile she watched Viola walk down the path.

Somehow she made it to the creek without being spotted. Timmy said he encountered no one while waiting for her. Racing home, she hoped they would arrive with no one noticing they had left. All she could think about was what Viola was up to and who the mysterious woman was that Alex had fallen in love with. She wondered if saving this poor girl from such a fate was the reason she was here.

* * *

Looking at the sky as his horse raced down the road, Alexander hoped he would make it to his mother's estate before dusk. Weeks had passed since he last laid eyes on Rachel Drovere; the thought that she was still in danger consumed his mind.

Since the night she confessed she discovered his secret, he began questioning his reasons for hiding his talent. Did it really matter if someone of his status worked as a tradesman? Painting wasn't a chore, he thought to himself. With each commission, he closed his eyes, vividly imagining the completed masterpiece before him. The anticipation of placing the first stroke drove him; he knew the moment it touched the canvas he would become intoxicated by his newest creation.

Never did he let his passion override his duties. The income he received for the half a dozen portraits a year neared that of only one of his investments. It was a sizeable amount that was also hidden away.

Could Rachel be right? Was his work as magnificent as she stated? She seemed to think that he would be known for his art in hundreds of years, giving the impression that artists would be treated with respect sometime in the future. He remembered the look in her eyes when she said it was important to her and with that, he began second-guessing his decision.

Days later, he went back to apologize to Rachel; for what, he could not remember. All he knew was that he needed to see her again. The hurt in her eyes when he walked out of the door haunted his dreams. To his dismay, he found she had left Bristol with her father.

He then immediately sought out Nic, only to find that James Bryant had not been found. Somehow, Nic knew of Rachel's departure and had sent men to watch over the estate.

Instead of heading off to the Drovere Estate, Alexander sent a message to his mother informing her that he would be visiting within a fortnight, and sent another to his elder brother Richard asking him to join them. Though he wanted to ride straight to his mother's estate, he had people to meet and plans to put into place.

The decision was now made; nothing was going to convince him to marry Viola Bryant. He had thought long and hard about the ramifications. Though his family did not know his secret identity, he had enough saved that he could reimburse his family for the loss they would incur from the livestock they had received prior to George's death.

Dread was the only word to describe Alexander's feelings as he rode up to his mother's estate. The moment he crossed over the moat, he had forgotten the speech he had prepared. What he wanted to say suddenly did not sound convincing. Taking a deep breath, he handed the reins of his horse to the stable boy and slowly walked into his childhood home.

His mother waited in the parlor, sitting in her favorite chair near the fire. Instantly, his defenses escalated as she was positioned in her place of authority. When he was a small child, she would sit in her armchair when she disciplined the boys.

Immediately after she greeted him, she inquired when he would announce his intention to marry Viola.

Running his hand through his hair, Alexander explained that he had no intention of entering into the contract with her. Before he could give his reasoning his mother stood up fuming and lectured him about honor, loyalty, commitment, and responsibility. Again she brought up his brother, how George would want him to take his place and uphold the family's agreement.

For the better part of the evening, his mother tried to convince him not to break the engagement. Meeting with his mother didn't go as he planned; she would not listen. The only thing they agreed upon was retiring to bed.

The next morning she was still up in arms and would not speak with him. Toward noon the carriage holding Richard arrived.

Sitting in the parlor, Richard calmly listened to their mother as she reiterated the same speech she had given Alexander two months prior. When she brought up George, Richard rolled his eyes and told her the truth of her deceased son's feelings.

"Viola is a gold digger, just like her mother. No one in this family should be forced into a loveless marriage, mother. After all, have you not beaten those values into our head? How could we be loyal if we hate the women we marry?"

"He could learn to love her," his mother replied sullenly.

"Did you love father?" Richard asked.

Their mother did not answer his question. She had been forced into marrying their father. After her three sons were born, she took the two younger boys and moved into the estate that was part of her dowry in order to keep herself sane, as he would constantly parade his mistresses in front of her.

As head of the family, Richard had the final say; however, he respected his mother enough to discuss the issue instead of dictating his answer. Finally she agreed – the engagement would be broken. The three of them sat in the parlor discussing how Alexander could best give his answer to Joseph Bryant, Viola's father. When they determined how much they would offer for the livestock, Alexander stated he would make the payment from his holding.

His mother exploded again. "Pray tell me how you can afford such a debt?" She threw her arms about. "You have only the estate your father left you. It does not profit enough to cover the livestock as you spend your time gallivanting in Bristol."

"The estate steads well enough as I have a trusted man tending to the holdings." Taking a deep breath, Alexander rubbed his palms together. It was time to break down and tell his family his secret. "I am Anon."

Again, Alexander felt the pain of his mother's outburst. "We will be ruined! You cannot be employed as a mere artisan. 'Tis not appropriate for someone of your status."

Richard began laughing. It was a contagious laughter.

"Nothing more could surprise me. Today you are full of surprises, little brother. My new wife has been requesting a portrait commissioned by Anon. This will save the family coin. After all, he could complete it over the holiday this winter. It will bring Lucy happiness."

CHAPTER TWENTY-TWO

Pacing in her room at Aunt Lilly's cottage, Rachel kept going over the scene at the witch's house four days earlier. She couldn't believe Viola wanted to marry Alex for money instead of love. It boggled her mind to think that a woman in any period would pursue a man for money over love.

Thinking back, she realized that Alex hated Viola. She didn't understand how she missed it. Every time Viola was near, Alex would turn stiff and cold. She never saw him gaze into Viola's eyes, touch her longer than necessary, and Rachel was positive that she had never seen Alex approach her. Viola always sought him out.

Whatever Viola was planning to do, Rachel knew she had to be stopped. If her love spell didn't work, what other desperate measures would the woman take? The only ones Rachel could think of would dishonor his family, something that would upset Alex even more.

But what if the spell actually worked? Would he really be happy with her? Could someone under a spell be happy? Rachel didn't necessarily believe in magic, but could she afford to remain skeptical while she was living almost five hundred years in the past?

The witch said Alex's heart belonged to another. The thought of him in love with another woman gave Rachel a cold, empty feeling in the pit of her stomach, the same feeling she had when she found out Allen had gone back to his wife.

His actions made perfect sense to her now. She concluded that the reason she had not heard from him was due to the mysterious woman his heart belonged to. Lord Alexander must have hated her for breaking into his home and learning his secret.

When she followed Timmy back to the estate, her mind raced to figure out a way to contact Alex. She didn't know if she could sneak out and ride all the way to Bristol alone; or maybe write a letter – but how would she get it to him? Other than Timmy, there wasn't anyone on the estate she trusted. Chances were, no one would even consider letting her use a quill again. She decided she would simply have to find the courage to make the journey. She planned her next escape.

Luckily they arrived back at the estate unnoticed. As she decided what she needed for the long journey, her father raced into her room without knocking, waving a piece of paper. Lord Henry Berkeley had invited the Drovere family to his summer ball. The excitement in his voice was unmistakable. Apparently, the invitation was completely unexpected and she was told to pack, for they were leaving in three days' time. He didn't even notice she was still wearing men's clothing.

She had no idea who Lord Berkeley was or what it meant for her family to attend. All she knew was her prayers had been answered: she was going back to Bristol.

* * *

They arrived late in the night; Rachel hadn't even seen Abby. Deciding she had spent long enough cooped up in her room, she went to visit her sister. The moment she walked in the door, Abby started talking so fast Rachel couldn't understand half of what she said.

Sitting down on the bed, Rachel watched the seamstress trying desperately not to poke Abby with a straight pin. She was having difficulty because Abby kept moving around as she was talking.

"You have missed so much while you were gone," Abby stated excitedly. "Henry Parker has visited almost every day for weeks. He says that he is here checking on us, and mother keeps inviting him for supper."

Rachel smiled, grateful Henry was watching out for them, but more importantly that he was finally getting over his shyness and actively courting Abby.

"You missed several wonderful balls. Lady Butler's ball was a bit boring; she only wanted to talk about her portrait. She displayed it for everyone to see; Anon made her look even more beautiful."

At the mention of Alex's alias, Rachel felt her face go red. Apparently, the conversation they had before she left didn't change his mind. He was still determined to keep his secret from the world.

Walking over to the window, she spotted Nic talking to one of his men near the cottage. He looked up at her and waved before walking across the street. Rachel laughed. She really liked Nic. He reminded her of someone she couldn't place. Mentally she went through every male she knew in her own time, but couldn't place him.

"We have had several visitors. Everyone wants to know what happened. Even Viola stopped by a few times."

The sound of Viola's name brought Rachel back to reality. "Viola? Viola was here?"

"She asked mother for the cook's sugar cake recipe and we discussed the Berkeley ball. She even wanted to see my new gown. Viola was truly concerned about what happened and wanted to know if she could be of any assistance."

"I wonder what she's up to." Rachel spoke out loud rather than to herself.

"No silly, she arrived with Charity. She was not as snooty as she usually is; in fact we had a pleasant visit."

"Miss, Miss, please stand still," the young seamstress quietly requested when Abby started walking across the room. The seamstress followed on her knees, trying not to lose her place.

"What do you think?" Abby held up a burgundy gown. "I picked out the color; I hope you do not mind." The satin of the skirt opened up in the front, shimmering on top of a soft cream underskirt. Instead of the high puffy sleeves, pieces of long fabric draped down off the shoulders to just below the waist. Rachel knew she would be advertising more than she wished to, with the low-cut, square bodice. The gown Abby held couldn't have been lovelier had a famous fashion designer created it.

Between her father's reaction and Abby's excitement about the Berkeley Ball, curiosity got the best of her. "Who is Lord Berkeley?"

The look on Abby's face was comical; she was completely stunned. "You do not remember Lord Henry Berkeley?"

"I remember the name, but nothing else. I hit my head, remember?"

"Oh." Abby recovered and replaced Rachel's dress on the chair. "Why, Lord Henry Berkeley was the Godson of King Henry, and holds favor with Queen Elizabeth. There has not been a ball at the Berkeley Castle in years. Mother is still in dismay, for we cannot figure out how we received an invitation."

"Why? It's just a ball."

"No. It is not a typical ball, 'tis the ball of The Season. Everyone will be talking about it for years. Only Noblemen should have received an invitation. Papa is only a Merchant. Charity's family did not receive one. Henry Parker was invited; however his family was not and he is only a Gentleman."

"Miss. Please hold still," the seamstress requested again.

"Of course he's a gentleman," Rachel said without thinking, before she realized what Abby had said. Gentleman was a title in this time; it wasn't used to describe the good behavior of a man.

"Which means Father has a lower status than Henry?" Rachel confirmed her thought out loud.

She had been spending so much time dealing with her own problems, she hadn't really cared about social statuses. All she knew was she wasn't in the same league as Alex.

"What's Lord Alexander's title?"

"Lord Alexander did not inherit his title, for he is the younger son. Queen Elizabeth bestowed the title of Baron for his service. 'Tis rumored he received an invitation as well."

Rachel sat back down on Abby's bed, questions consuming her mind. Not only was Alex a Baron, he was clearly out of Viola's league, as her father was an Earl. The woman must believe in the ramblings of the prophecy, Rachel thought. She had always wondered if fortune telling was real; she had yet to hear of one picking the winning lottery numbers.

"Do you think Alex – I mean Lord Alexander – will attend?"

"Of course, silly. Everyone who is invited will attend unless they are pushing up daisies."

The young seamstress raised her voice: "Will you please be still?"

Both of the girls jumped, and Rachel tried to suppress her laughter at the poor girl's harried and frazzled state from having to chase Abby around the room. When she finished, it was Rachel's turn.

Wanting to get the alterations over with as fast as possible, Rachel stood perfectly still so the seamstress would hurry. She found herself lost in thought while Abby continued talking, until she mentioned Anon.

"What about Anon?" Rachel prayed that Abby didn't notice her sudden interest.

"Were you not listening?" Abby sighed before repeating herself. "'Tis rumored Lord Berkeley has discovered his true identity."

"Oh my." How did Lord Berkeley find out Alex was Anon? Rachel wondered if Alex would think it was her who revealed his secret. He had said there were only a few that knew. Dread filled her body when she realized that the next time she would see him, they would be attending the ball.

* * *

Rachel frantically rummaged through the bedroom at her Aunt Lilly's cottage. She unpacked the trunk her chambermaid carefully packed earlier that morning. She pulled out and shook each individual article of clothing, and then tossed it on the bed.

"Rachel! I dare say."

Abby stood at the door, distressed.

"The pearl ring. Have you seen it?" Rachel picked up her new corset and gave it a quick shake. "I can't find it anywhere."

Abby walked over to the bed and picked up the new slippers. "Nay, did you not take it with you to the estate?"

"I don't think so." Rachel sighed and dropped her arms in defeat. "I could have sworn I left it on the table. I know I'm good at misplacing things, but this is ridiculous." She knew the ring was not hers to lose.

Abby looked around the room and giggled. "Alice shall be furious when she sees your room in such disarray." She set the slippers aside. "Come, I shall help you look."

The girls searched through every article of clothing and every corner of the room for nearly an hour before they were summoned to the parlor by their mother.

When they entered the parlor they saw Henry standing next to the fireplace holding a small, beautifully crafted, wooden box. He nodded, "Good day, Miss Rachel." When he looked at Abby, his face turned red. "Miss Abby."

Abby smiled. "Good day, Mr. Parker." She eyed the box. "What is that you carry?"

Henry grinned and his face turned even redder when he presented it to Abby. Rachel stood next to her, peering over her shoulder. Abby carefully opened the box. She gasped and began to swoon; Rachel caught her, standing her upright.

Abby held up a necklace of at least a dozen emeralds set in gold, surrounded by tiny diamonds, and whispered, "What a beautiful carcanet!"

Eleanor walked into the parlor carrying a tray filled with goblets and a decanter of ale and almost tripped when she saw it. The pewter clattered gently against each other as she steadied herself. By their mother's re-action, Rachel knew the family didn't own anything as elegant or as expensive.

Henry nervously straightened his jacket. "I have convinced my mother to loan it to you for the ball."

Abby couldn't take her eyes off of the carcanet. "'Tis beautiful."

Eleanor regained her composure and offered Henry a cup of ale. He accepted it and sat down on the sofa. "I shall be here with the carriage at dawn. From there, we will travel to the docks and board the ship."

Rachel's eyes shot up. "Ship?"

"Aye, Mr. Mattingly has secured transport to the Berkeley Castle."

She tilted her head in confusion. "I thought the castle was near Bristol."

Henry laughed. "Nay, 'tis a five hour carriage ride north of Bristol."

"Isn't father's estate the same distance?"

Henry nodded and took a sip of his ale. "'Tis near the same distance; however, to reach your father's estate, you turn east at the Forest of a Thousand Whispers. To reach Berkeley, we would travel directly north."

"Then why are we taking a ship?"

"Mr. Mattingly felt with such a small party, it would be safer. We are lucky, for this vessel does not carry passengers up the bay under normal circumstances."

Rachel shook her head. "Under normal circumstances? And what do you mean by safer?"

Abby laughed while Henry tilted his head, confused. Rachel figured it was her strange speech that gave Henry such a look.

It took a moment before he answered slowly, "The ship is a cargo vessel and will depart for France shortly. By taking us to Berkeley, their shipment will be delayed by two days. Mr. Mattingly felt traveling by water would be safer. He fears to take any unnecessary risks, thereby placing you in danger. After all," he paused and looked at her mother, "Mr. Bryant has yet to be found."

The next morning the Drovere family and Henry Parker arrived at the cargo ship where Nic Mattingly waited to help them prepare for the voyage. The trip took only a few hours. Rachel stood at the railing and watched as they passed the land by. Abby conversed with Henry. Rachel could only think about Alexander and how he was going to react when he saw her. She worried about how angry he might be, thinking that she was the one who revealed his secret.

A few hours later, Henry drove the carriage through gates leading to the Berkeley Castle. Peeking out of the carriage window, Rachel couldn't believe the size of the warm, pink, stone walls. She noticed men on top of the parapet holding long bows, watching the guests arrive.

Arrows peeked out, ready to defend the keep, if necessary.

Everyone was nervous. As they neared the castle, their mother again recited etiquette, wanting to make a good impression on Lord Henry Berkeley and his guests. Rachel gathered from Abby that they had yet to find anyone of a lower status attending.

Rachel could not stop worrying about Alex's reaction to the news that the identity of Anon had been discovered, assuming he heard the gossip. She had gone over the conversation a hundred times in her head, hoping he would believe that she was not the one who exposed his secret.

When they entered the grand arched doors, a porter immediately escorted the family to their rooms where they were to stay the night.

Abby tugged on Rachel's sleeve. "Is this not magnificent?"

The high ceilings, stained glass windows, and stone floors were more elaborate than anything she had seen since arriving in the past. Colorful, finely woven tapestries covered the walls, displaying different scenes of the English countryside. Men on horseback chased deer across the landscape, two men fished on a riverbank, and – her favorite – knights on horseback, ready for battle, leaned over to receive favors from women.

Rachel discovered she was to share her room with her chambermaid, Alice. Several portraits hung on beautifully painted wooden paneling. Tapestries hung on the walls. Over the windows and canopy bed were extravagant drapes. A half-dozen oversized pillows, each delicately embroidered, adorned a handmade quilt covering the bed. From what Abby had mentioned two months before, she knew these were the lesser accommodations offered. Rachel didn't even want to guess how elaborate Viola Bryant's room was.

Dressing for the ball took longer than on prior occasions. The seamstress had added to her gown lace, ruffles, and buttons with tiny pearls set in gold. Alice adorned her hair with tiny, colored glass beads and burgundy ribbons.

She wondered what Allen's reaction would be if he saw her, and realized that she hadn't thought of him in days; the man she really wanted to impress was Alex.

At the last minute, a chambermaid entered her room carrying a golden, linked belt with rubies set between the squares, and a matching necklace. Rachel hadn't seen these accessories before and wondered where they came from.

She was ready when Abby knocked on the door, glowing with excitement. Their parents were waiting in the hallway; Abby clutched Rachel's arm and led her from the room. She didn't have to wait long to find out where the belt and necklace came from. Abby confided that a messenger had delivered a package with several beautiful pieces inside. The note indicated the items were a loan, not a gift, and another messenger would be sent to their estate to retrieve them. The mysterious package held a silver cuff bracelet adorned with a large sapphire and a matching necklace for her mother. They complemented her pale-yellow satin gown perfectly. They were not nearly as extravagant as Rachel's, but whoever sent them wanted her mother to reflect well on their hosts.

They slowly descended the large staircase toward the ballroom. A long line of noblemen and women patiently waited to be announced and received by the hosts. Rachel closed her eyes and took a deep breath, hoping Alexander would believe her.

CHAPTER TWENTY-THREE

Alexander arrived early – a little too early; very few guests milled around the ballroom. Henry Berkeley had not joined the reception line; his wife Katherine and her brother, the recently widowed Thomas Howard, the Fourth Duke of Norfolk, greeted the guests.

Tonight would be a night to remember. A grand ball at the Berkeley Castle was a rare occasion because the family normally resided in Yate and Callowden when they were not in attendance at the Queen's Court. The people of Gloucestershire would speak of this for years to come.

Alex stood in the grand ballroom waiting for Rachel and her family to arrive. He looked around the room and recognized many of the nobles; he had painted several of their portraits, including the Duke's.

"Have you spoken with Viola?" A familiar voice asked from behind.

"Nic." Alexander turned around and accepted the drink Nic offered. "Nay, not yet. I tried to call the other day; however she was unavailable."

Nic nodded and turned his attention toward the entrance. "And her father, how did he take the news?"

Alexander laughed. "My good man, you seem to know more than you are privy to."

Nic smiled. "'Tis my job to know everything."

"The meeting went well. Lord Bryant agreed to what we offered without hesitation. I believe the man was only doing what Viola requested. He feels her station would be better suited by marrying someone with a higher title."

"Yet, you plan to marry beneath your station," Nic noted, taking a drink from his glass, his eyes scanning the ballroom.

Alexander nodded, knowing he could not keep a secret from Nic. Weeks after the painting was delivered to Lord Berkeley, Nic had confronted him. How he solved the mystery, Nic still had yet to reveal. He assured Alexander his secret was safe; the city needed something to keep its collective mind occupied.

Bowing to Alexander he raised his voice a little louder for others to hear. "I trust you are enjoying yourself, My Lord. I must attend to my duties."

Alexander wanted to laugh when he dismissed Nic with a nod. He knew the only reason Nic was allowed to attend was to provide security of a sort. Word had spread that James Bryant was still at large.

Alexander felt his heart hit the floor when Viola entered the ballroom. She spotted him before he could find a place to hide or someone to converse with, and walked directly toward him.

"I received the most interesting letter from my father. He stated your family has had a change of heart. You plan to unkiss the bargain."

Before she stepped next to him, he could smell the sweet scent of her. An intoxicating fragrance of cinnamon, jasmine, and sandalwood caught him off guard. Not wanting to have this conversation standing in the middle of the ballroom he offered her a drink. He led her to a quiet spot near one of the tall stained glass windows, and went to retrieve an ale.

He still could feel the effects of the fragrance when he returned. Trying to shake the daze off, he offered her a glass; she reached for it with both hands, laying one over his. The moment she touched his hand, he jumped.

"Forgive me. My ring must have nicked you." She took both drinks from his hands and set them on the table next to them. Pulling out a small piece of fabric from her sleeve, Viola dabbed the blood from his finger.

Alexander did not know how to respond. He knew he needed to tell her the engagement was off, but he could not seem to find the words.

Summoning all of his strength he finally said, "You are much too beautiful to marry a man not of your station. There are richer and more powerful men that seek your hand."

Handing him back his drink, she smiled seductively. "I do not want another man as my husband."

He started to speak but Viola placed her index finger upon his lips. "Let us not speak of this here. On the morrow, if you still feel the same, I will release you of our agreement without hesitation."

Alexander could only nod as he watched her walk away. Taking a drink of the ale, he gazed around the room wondering who had arrived while he was distracted.

* * *

The Drovere family entered the grand ballroom through one of the many arched doorways. Rachel barely heard her name announced as her eyes roamed the room for Alex. She spotted him looking directly at her, smiling. Relief washed over her; she knew he wasn't upset with her about Lord Berkeley's discovery. She smiled back and followed her sister and mother, who approached the other women.

Rachel was prepared for the looks and comments forthcoming from the other guests. She knew her father would have an easier time adapting; he had met many of these men before. The women however, would be more difficult. They would stick their noses in the air, pretending to be polite, if they tried at all, and then say things behind their backs. After all, this was a popularity contest.

She watched her mother greet a woman who cut her short and walked away. Rachel felt sorry for her mother; she was completely out of her league.

Abby, on the other hand, had one of those sparkling personalities that could win anyone over in spite of themselves. Almost instantly, men gathered near her, introducing themselves to their mother, and politely asked to sign Abby's dance card. Rachel noticed Abby was unaware of the curt, snide looks from the other girls, nor did she see the insanely jealous Henry Parker across the room.

After a short time, a petite, red-haired woman wearing an emerald green gown approached them.

"Miss Eleanor Drovere?" She asked with the sweetest sounding voice.

"Yes." Her voice held a nervous curiosity.

The woman turned, signaling to a group of women across the floor, who walked toward them.

"I am the Lady Lucy Dohetry. My husband is Lord Richard Dohetry. I believe you know my husband's brother, Lord Alexander Dohetry?"

While Lady Lucy introduced the other women, Rachel wanted nothing more than to race over and hug Alex. She could feel her eyes swell up with tears, but did her best to keep them at bay, and watched her mother begin to relax and enjoy herself.

Rachel quietly listened, not wanting to scare them away with her strange speech. The women spoke of Lord Berkeley, the ball, and the grand castle. Even though she had been in the past for almost two months, people still gave her strange looks when she wasn't paying attention to her words.

When the topic of discussion changed to Lord Berkeley's discovery of Anon, Rachel focused on every word. It was rumored at midnight the identity of Anon would no longer be in question.

Rachel couldn't help but smile. Alex was finally going to let the world know who he was. She imagined the art history books filled with his name, wondering if he might end up with a collection that would travel the world.

"Have you visited the gardens?" One of the women asked. "The full moon is magnificent this eve. What a wonderful way to celebrate."

Rachel gasped and her eyes shot up. Tonight was the night. She had to warn Alex immediately. Not waiting for an escort to take her to him, Rachel slipped away from the conversation and made her way to Alex. As she neared him she saw a look of surprise come across his face.

"We cannot speak now," he whispered. "You need to stay with your mother."

"It's urgent that I speak with you," she whispered back. "In private."

Taking her by the arm he urged her back to the women. "No, not now."

Rachel stopped in her tracks; he was walking her back to her mother. She took a deep breath. Waiting for an appropriate time would be too late.

"Viola has plans to poison you this evening. She thinks the potion will make you fall in love with her."

Alex laughed. "It would take more than a potion for me to fall in love with *that* woman."

"There's more." Rachel rolled her hands. "She's having a spell cast on you at the witching hour. We have to do something to stop it."

"Rachel, Rachel." Alex spoke to her as if she had lost her mind. Taking her arm, he began walking. "Spells are a myth. I do not believe in them. There is no such thing as magic."

"Please don't drink anything anyone gives you," Rachel begged. She didn't know what else to do.

"I promise. I shall finish this one and not have another."

"Thank you." Rachel lowered her eyes; she felt that he was simply appeasing her, but it would have to do.

For the next half hour she watched the guests enter the room, wondering what was keeping Viola. Her mother, Lady Lucy, and the other women were discussing how Mary, Queen of Scots was wavering regarding the Queen's recommendation of marriage.

Finally Rachel turned to Lady Lucy. "Have you seen Viola? I've heard so much about the gown she's wearing tonight. I'm curious if it is as beautiful as I've heard."

"Viola?" She put her finger to her lip, and her eyes lit up. "Why yes, the Lady Viola was here. She left before you arrived. She mentioned she was suffering from a headache and wanted to go to her room to lie down for a spell."

Rachel shook at the news. Viola hadn't gone to her room. She tried to stay calm and scanned the room for Alex. He was refusing a drink, but he had the strangest look in his eyes when they met hers. They didn't light up; instead they were glazed over.

Rachel did her best to calmly walk up to her mother. She told her she had a headache and would be retiring to her room. Her mother quietly put up a fuss.

Instead of listening, Rachel turned and walked toward the stairs. Peering over her shoulder, she saw her father with an inquisitive look, listening to her mother. She could tell he was going to follow her as he handed his glass to her mother and took a step forward with his cane.

Rachel was at a crossroads. If she stayed, there was a possibility Viola would succeed. Somehow she knew what the real Rachel Drovere would do, and it was not what she had planned.

She was from the future, when women thought for themselves and didn't care what society thought about them — or at least she didn't care. Lifting her dress, she took the stairs two at a time, imagining the scene she was causing. She didn't care; she had to stop the spell from being cast. Alex couldn't fall in love with that woman. If he did, he'd be lost. Viola was manipulative and controlling. Alex was a strong man, but if the spell actually worked, he wouldn't be the same man she had fallen for.

She ran out the door, stopping long enough to ask the footman where the stables were. He pointed and as he began to speak, Rachel kicked off her shoes, lifted her dress and ran toward the stables. Inside she found the nearest horse still saddled. Not knowing or caring who the stallion belonged to, she shoved her bare foot into the stirrup and struggled to get on.

"Damn gown," she said to herself, moving the fabric around to get her other leg situated. The stirrups were too long; Rachel squeezed her legs and prayed, racing from the castle grounds.

CHAPTER TWENTY-FOUR

"Men!" she said out loud, galloping down the road toward her parent's estate. She had been riding for what seemed like hours, looking for the eerie grove that paralleled the road, with only the moon to light her way.

Rachel knew the distance to the witch's house coming from the opposite direction. She looked up into a starry sky. The full moon had moved noticeably to the west, so she knew that she was going the right way. If only a street sign was posted with an arrow that said, "Witches House," she thought to herself.

The road was deserted; she hadn't passed anyone for miles and the last human being she saw led a horse and cart, and had stopped dead in his tracks, mouth gaping. She couldn't imagine what he thought and really didn't care.

The only thing that mattered was finding Viola. That woman had been a pain in the ass since the day Rachel arrived in the past. She knew Viola was as smart as she was beautiful, but instead of using her brains, she used her status and beauty to get everything she wanted. Viola was, in essence, a spoiled brat.

The woman had ample opportunity to marry into even more wealth and status. From what Abby said, there were men all over England trying to court her. Marrying a man revealed as an artisan would set her at the bottom of the social scale. Rachel hoped she could change Viola's mind about having the witch cast her spell. Having a civil conversation with an obsessed, deranged, female probably wouldn't work. But she had to try.

Try as she might, she couldn't stop thinking about Alex. He was as infectious as Allen had been. Rachel knew tonight she was making the same mistake which ruined all of her previous relationships. She was trying to protect him by taking charge of the situation and fixing the problem.

She remembered the night the thugs attacked her. The pride Alex exhibited after he rescued her was unmistakable. She felt small and safe in his arms before he had taken her back to her father. It didn't matter that she was perfectly capable of walking to the steps of the building or how she could bind her own arm when he noticed she was injured.

She didn't always have to be a strong and independent woman. The concern in Alex's eyes made her feel cherished. Rachel had to admit, when he told her to be quiet and let him take care of her, she felt something she had never felt before. She felt loved.

Maybe when she got home, she would let the next guy she dated "be the man" and change the light bulb or kill a spider. She realized she needed to learn how to receive a man's attentions instead of constantly giving. Men liked being with a strong independent woman, Rachel figured; it must be more of a challenge trying to figure out how to take care of them. Yet, she never let them do the small things to make them feel wanted and needed.

Tonight was different. She warned him about Viola, and he blew her off. She had to fix this on her own.

Rachel could finally see the trees on the horizon. Urging her horse forward, she was thankful she hadn't gotten lost yet. Her destination was getting closer.

Trying to stay focused, Rachel scanned the trees looking for something familiar, anything to remind her where the path was located. A flicker of light shone in the distance.

At first she couldn't make out what she had seen. Squinting, she focused on the area where she saw the glimmer. The only noise she heard was the fall of her horse's hooves on the dirt road. He must have felt her apprehension because he slowed down.

As horse and rider neared, Rachel spotted a carriage sitting in the middle of the road. Her first instinct was to race over to make sure the driver wasn't hurt. She knew she recognized the emblem on the side of the door, when it hit her – the carriage belonged to Viola.

The little path peeked out from the trees to the left of the vehicle. Knowing Viola would have a driver waiting with the carriage, Rachel turned her horse as quickly and quietly as possible, entering the perimeter of trees.

She hadn't ridden a great distance when the bright moonlight disappeared and the temperature dropped by several degrees. The chill touched her bare arms and she realized that the breeze she felt earlier was gone. The air stood still. Other than her horse, every sound she thought she would hear in the woods was missing. There were no birds chirping, owls hooting, or leaves bristling. It was the most eerie feeling she had ever experienced.

Rachel followed the trail at a distance, not wanting to stumble upon Viola. Every now and then the moonlight would touch the ground, lighting her way, as she moved through the trees. She spotted the creek and decided to ride the horse across instead of going on foot.

Once she crossed the water, she had the same feeling as before of an odd presence watching her. Deciding her mind was playing tricks, she moved forward. She detected the smell of burning wood before the small stone house appeared in the distance. The unmistakable scent gave her a small degree of comfort.

She slid off the back of her horse, and tied him to the nearest tree, not knowing what to expect. Cautiously moving around the outskirts of the small, dark cottage, she could see the glow of fire emerge from the back. As silently as possible, using the night and the shadows of the trees to keep her hidden, Rachel approached the back of the house. Slowly, she crept toward the light, crouching down behind a rather large shrub.

Rachel peered around the branches and gasped. She couldn't believe what she was seeing. In the middle of a large circle, drawn with a white, rocky substance, stood the same middle-aged woman wearing a simple gray robe. It took a moment for Rachel to realize the circle was formed with salt. In the short time she had been in the past, she knew salt wasn't exactly cheap and couldn't comprehend how a poor witch could afford the amount of salt on the ground.

The woman was slowly turning counter clockwise, holding a rather long stick stiffly away from her body. Her eyes showed complete focus on her task while her lips moved, mumbling an incantation only she could hear.

"That's a real wand." Rachel breathed the words, mesmerized.

She almost jumped high enough to make her presence known when a loud scream shocked her back to reality.

"Meazle! You ask me to bring you these objects. Then you ignore me."

Rachel quickly turned to see Viola standing by the fire wearing a beautiful evening gown. The rage on her face turned Rachel cold.

Viola was shaking a small cloth bag clutched in her hand at the woman.

The witch didn't even flinch, but continued slowly turning.

Pacing back and forth near the fire, Viola yelled, "Od's Bodikin! Have you not finished?"

Rachel saw a small wooden table at one end of the circle cluttered with various items. Trying not to peer over the bush, she carefully stretched to see the contents. The light of the fire reflected off a silver knife next to a wooden cup and a rather fat candle. She recognized the mortar and pestle that was used to grind herbs into dust, and a staff leaning against the table. Rachel was shocked when she saw the broom.

Witches really use brooms? She thought to herself. The only things missing were a pointy hat and a large black caldron sitting inside the fire.

If it wasn't for the severity of the implications, she could have sat and watched for hours. Trying to gather her courage, she took a deep breath, planning to confront the two women when she heard a shuffling noise and Viola cursing again. Viola tripped over a small wooden basket filled with herbs and other items that Rachel couldn't see.

Viola kicked it aside and looked up at the woman again. "'Tis about bloody time."

The witch walked out of the circle toward one of the four unlit candles on the ground.

"Patience. You must have patience." The old woman took the small bag from Viola's grasp. "Sit yourself down. I will tell you when I am ready."

The old woman leaned over, picked up the debris that Viola carelessly had kicked out of her way, and placed everything back into the broken basket. The witch sat down on the ground near the fire, and held up three small dolls. She handed the bag back to Viola. "Show me what is his."

Viola emptied the contents of the bag onto her skirt and held out an object. "This is his button. I removed it from his cloak this night." She picked up a small piece of fabric. "I was able to cut his finger with the ring; this holds his blood." She handed it to the witch.

The old woman took the objects and stuffed them into the head of one of the dolls. It was dressed similarly to what Alex wore earlier in the evening. The coarse brown yarn on its head resembled his hair.

Holding one up with long yellow strands, the witch asked, "For this one?"

"I believe this is a strand of her hair."

"Believe?" The witch stated forcibly. "Believe? You must be sure."

"It came from her bedding." Viola paused and looked at the hair. "Yes, I'm sure. I was unable to get her blood. I went to visit her sister and was able to acquire this." She held out a piece of jewelry.

Rachel's hand went to her mouth. It was the pearl ring she thought she had misplaced.

Again the old woman stuffed the tokens into the doll's head. Without warning, she pulled a knife from her robe, and grabbed Viola's long brunette hair, cutting off a thin lock.

"Pray tell! What are you doing?" Viola beat the woman's hands away, trying to avoid the knife.

In response the witch grabbed her hand and slit her forefinger while Viola tried pulling away. Picking up the doll off the ground, the old woman let the blood drip onto it.

Viola tried to pull her hand away, yelling obscenities, when the witch calmly stated, "If this is what you desire, you must pay the price. The poppets must hold the power of the people they represent; otherwise 'tis all for naught."

Rachel watched the witch gently place one of the poppets into the basket. She picked up a long cord, tied the other two together, and then stood, walking back toward the circle.

Stopping, the woman turned back to Viola. "Was the potion administered correctly?"

"Yes, I slipped it into his drink at the ball. I used the ring you gave me and had no issue opening it."

Nodding, the witch walked back toward the circle.

The mention of the potion brought the image of Alex's face to mind. She wasn't here for a lesson on casting spells; she was here to stop one.

Without another thought, Rachel sprung from the bushes and yelled at the top of her lungs, "Stop!"

Stunned, both women turned and looked at Rachel. The old woman was about to speak when Viola screamed and ran through the circle toward Rachel.

"Oh crap." Rachel was so worried about finding them, she completely forgot about figuring out what to do when she got there.

Luckily, Viola was far enough away that Rachel was able to overcome her temporary shock. Viola flew straight toward Rachel with her hands formed into claws and a look of determination on her face. Rachel stood her ground until Viola was too close to stop, and then stepped to the left. Viola tripped forward, falling down into the bush Rachel had been hiding behind.

"Thank goodness for tae kwon do."

Taking a deep breath as she had been taught, she took her stance, ready to defend herself. Viola stood up, screaming at Rachel, running toward her again. This time, as Viola's arm came up to slap her, Rachel blocked it as she clenched her fist and punched Viola in the face.

Stunned, Viola took a step back. Rachel lifted her skirt and kicked Viola square in the chest, knocking her to the ground. The impact of her head hitting the ground knocked her out, at least for a moment.

With the dress caught between her legs, Rachel struggled to keep her balance. Defensively, she turned back to the old woman, preparing for an attack.

The old woman stood still, tilted her head, and gave her an all-knowing, toothless grin. "You do not belong here."

"No!" Pent up with frustration, Rachel screamed, "You don't belong here! And you need to stop what you're doing!"

Calmly the witch evaluated Rachel, holding her hands in front of her. "You are not of this time. You do not belong here."

The witch's demeanor soothed her. Taking a deep breath, Rachel somehow knew this woman wouldn't be a physical threat. "You're right. I don't."

The old woman bent down and picked up her belongings off of the ground and then from the table, and placed them into her basket. Holding the poppet with the yellow strands, she removed the ring from its head.

Handing the ring to Rachel, she gave an inquisitive look. "This does not belong to you; it belongs to the one before you. 'Tis time for you to return."

Rachel took the ring from the witch, nodding.

"Why am I here? How do I get home?"

Instead of answering, she began walking away.

"What about the spell? What about the potion?"

The old woman turned. "The potion will wear off." She looked at Viola lying on the ground. "She will no longer bring harm. She destroyed what she sought when she violated the circle."

There was something the witch wasn't telling her. Questions raced through her mind. The witch walked around the side of the cottage.

Rachel ran after her. "How do I get home?"

Only a few feet behind her, Rachel turned the corner; the witch was nowhere in sight.

CHAPTER TWENTY-FIVE

Alexander rode his horse down the path to the witch's cottage. He could barely see the structure in the distance when he reached the tiny creek. Instead of crossing, he stopped and looked at it for a moment. It was as if an invisible barrier gave him pause. Shaking it off, he kicked the horse, urging it forward. He saw his own horse tied to a tree and knew that Rachel made it to the herb woman's house safely. He was close to finding her and when he found her, he knew Viola would be near.

For the last few hours he had been trying to catch up to her, stopping everyone on the road to see if they had seen a lone woman riding south. Most just nodded and pointed in the direction that she went. A lonely old man leading his cart told him he didn't see a woman riding south, but a crazed spirit who appeared out of nowhere flying toward him. Showing the trinket hanging around his neck, he told Alexander that his talisman scared it away.

Alexander knew the crazed spirit had to be Rachel.

At the ball a few hours earlier, he watched Rachel lift her skirt and race up the stairs. The entire ball watched her; her exit was anything but peaceful. To him the incident felt like a dream, one he did not understand. His thoughts were on Viola, wondering where she was. It was Nic who elbowed him and brought his mind back to the events taking place.

Nic practically grabbed him by the collar when he raced toward the stairs following Rachel and Arthur. Once outside, the cool breeze cleared Alexander's thoughts. He tried to put the situation together in his mind.

"That is my horse," Alexander said to the men as they raced to the stables only to see Rachel charging down the road.

Arthur shouted at the stable hands, "Ready the carriage!"

Alexander looked at Arthur. "No time. I will go after her."

Arthur grasped his cane tightly. "That may be improper."

"Improper?" Alexander shook his head. "She has stolen a horse, wearing my mother's borrowed jewels, and not riding sidesaddle. You are worried about being proper?"

Nic whistled and three of his men ran toward them. "We will find her, Arthur." Turning, he explained to his men what happened, and followed Alexander to the stables.

Alexander found a horse, not caring who it belonged to, and jumped on its back. He shook his head. He knew he had to find Rachel. He recalled the conversation they had earlier. She was afraid Viola was going to cast some sort of spell. The only person within miles of Bristol known for her craft was the herb woman living in the Forest of a Thousand Whispers. Instead of telling Nic, Alexander raced south.

Hearing voices, Alexander quietly moved toward the sound, not wanting to make his presence known until he had evaluated the situation. As he neared he saw Rachel standing over Viola lying on the ground.

"At least she is not dead," he heard Rachel say to herself.

Sighing, Rachel bent down to help Viola sit up.

"He is mine," Viola hissed. "Mine! He belongs to me!"

"What do you mean, he belongs to you?"

"My mother promised him to me."

Rachel stood over Viola with her hands on her hips. "You were betrothed to George."

"My father did not listen to my mother. He picked the son more befitting my station. Richard had already been spoken for."

"If it wasn't for the accident you would have married George."

Viola smiled the most evil smile, staring into Rachel's eyes. "I was never going to marry him. He flew off of the ridge after I placed herbs in his drink."

Rachel's eyes grew wide. "You killed George?"

"It does not matter. The herbs made him loony; they made him think he could fly. I only wanted to show everyone he was not right in the mind, to give a reason to unkiss the bargain." Viola smiled again. "Alexander will be mine." She struggled to stand up.

"No you don't." Rachel pushed her back down. "Tell me about the prophecy."

Shocked, Viola scooted backwards. "What do you know of the prophecy?"

Rachel stepped forward. "More than you think I know. Now tell me the exact words."

Alexander stepped forward breaking a branch under foot. The sound made Rachel turn toward him. When he looked at her, he almost wanted to pull Rachel away from Viola but something stopped him. He felt something indescribable when he looked at her. It was beyond attraction, beyond desire. As he puzzled over his emotions, Viola spoke.

"Let it be known, once your son is wed he will discover rewards beyond the imaginings of King Midas himself. Those are the words spoken to his mother prior to his birth."

Rachel started laughing; she was laughing so hard, her eyes filled with tears.

"You know Viola, for someone as intelligent as you are, you really are stupid. Rewards could mean more than money; it could mean fame, it could mean his child would acquire wealth, it could mean . . ." she paused and looked at Alexander, "it could mean love."

Seeing the expression on Rachel's face, Alexander could almost feel the love she had for him. She explained his emotions perfectly. He was completely in love with Rachel.

"You screwed everything up," Viola hissed. "If only my brother had not failed, Alexander would have been mine by now." She struggled again to get up.

Rachel set her foot on her chest, preventing her from moving, glaring down at her. "Failed? How did he fail?"

"He did not listen to me. Had he done as he was told, you would not be here."

"What are you talking about?"

"I told him to dispose of you. Instead he tried to court you, but you threw off his advances. Then he tried to abduct you and failed. My destiny is ruined because of *you!*" Viola screamed, hitting the dirt with the palms of her hands.

Rachel eyes grew wide. "James is your brother?"

"James is my father's illegitimate son, not my cousin. As my cousin he would inherit my father's estate and leave me with nothing. As his illegitimate son, I could petition the Queen stating that I am the rightful heir to my father's holdings. James promised to give me what I wanted in exchange for my silence. Now you have ruined everything!"

Everything made sense. Alexander looked over at Rachel, her face showing the same shock as his.

He stepped forward from the shadows. "Were you behind his embezzlement as well?"

"Alexander!" Viola screamed, struggling again. "Help me! This woman is attacking me!"

"She has done no less than you deserve. You have poisoned my brother, spread rumors we were betrothed, tried to cast a love spell, and then tried to hurt Rachel. Pray tell me, were you behind the embezzlement?"

Defeated, looking down at the ground, she answered, "Aye."

"James had been stealing money for almost a year." Rachel said. "How did you know Alexander . . ."

Before she completed her thought Viola responded, "It was by luck you discovered our secret. James informed me you had been eavesdropping on his conversation with your father. James did not trust you. I heard about the little adventure when Alexander carried you into your bedroom."

Viola glanced at Alexander. "You would have never broken social graces had you not had feelings for her."

Alexander blushed. Viola was right. He had feelings for Rachel the moment he touched her.

Turning back to Rachel, Viola continued. "It was then I demanded James take care of you. He was not strong enough for the request, until he discovered you had stolen his journals."

"But how? How did he know it was me?"

"He saw you enter the establishment. Then he saw the hem of your skirt under the desk. He came to me immediately and I put the plan in place. All he had to do was get you on the ship."

"Where is James?" Alexander demanded.

"I do not know. If you find him, bring him to me, for I would love to put my hands around his scrawny neck."

Running his hands through his hair, Alexander turned to Rachel, "We best be getting back to town. Everyone will be looking for us." Walking away he added, "I will gather the horses."

* * *

Leaning over Viola, Rachel whispered, "Know this: if you ever touch Alexander again, in this life or the next, I will travel through time to right whatever you wrong, just as I have done this time."

"What do you mean 'this time'?" Viola asked with evil in her eyes, daring her to explain.

She whispered even lower to make sure Alexander didn't hear, "I meant what I said. You knew who I was prior to the hunt?"

"Yes."

"Am I the same person you remember? Would the Rachel Drovere you knew prior to the hunt have been able to evade James attack? Did she have the education to discover the discrepancies in the journals? Would she have had the audacity to chase you here in the middle of the night and stop what you were doing?"

Realization came over Viola's face. Pent up with frustration, Rachel stomped her foot, and gave Viola a discerning look. "I cannot believe how stupid you are. How could you possibly believe you could force someone to fall in with love you? And you don't love him; you were doing it for wealth. What kind of life did you expect to have being with someone whose feelings for you were fake?"

Rachel didn't know what else to say. Exasperated, she let her arms drop to her sides. Seeing Alex walking up with the horses, she bent down to help Viola stand. Once Viola was mounted, Rachel jumped up behind her, giving Alex a look that said she didn't want him within ten feet of the deranged woman.

On the way out of the grove, Alex informed Viola's footman that his employer would be riding back to Bristol. Without another word, they turned their horses and rode.

An hour later, her father's carriage caught up with them. Unlike the footman, her father demanded the women sit in the carriage and asked Rachel a hundred questions at the same time that he chastised her for leaving the ball, running off alone, and finding herself again in an inappropriate situation with Lord Alexander without a chaperone.

Only half-listening to her father, Rachel stayed awake, watching Viola like a hawk until she fell asleep. While her father was talking, Rachel sat back in her seat, wondering what changes in history she had made tonight, if Alexander would have married Viola had she not intervened. It seemed she started changing events the moment she arrived, when she fell out of the tree. It felt like a lifetime ago.

Her life in the twenty-first century almost felt like a dream, making her wonder which lifetime was reality. Sadness consumed her when she reminded herself this was not her time. She belonged in the future with running water, electricity, internet . . . but not with Allen. Sighing, she was afraid to fall asleep for fear of going home and having to face her own future alone.

On the horizon the sky was turning colors, as if cleansing the wickedness of the night with the start of a new day, giving Rachel a renewed energy.

They arrived at Aunt Lilly's cottage in Bristol where everyone she had gotten to know and love was waiting for them. Abby and Aunt Lilly were serving refreshments in the wee hours of the morning to Nic and Henry. Her mother was frantically pacing in front of the fireplace, clutching the skirt of her gown. When she saw them walk in the door, she ungraciously hurried over and wrapped her arms around Rachel and hugged her tightly. Nic and Viola's father stood up and retrieved Viola from Alexander.

Rachel and Alex sat in the parlor and revealed the events that took place after she had run away from Lord Berkeley's ball. For an hour they answered questions and described the scene. Joseph Bryant took Viola and left the cottage.

Everyone gave their opinion in small groups about James and Viola. Nic assured Arthur and Eleanor that his men were still searching for James Bryant. Abby told Henry about Viola's visit; she couldn't believe the audacity of Viola, how she pretended to be cordial.

Rachel sat down next to Alexander and handed him another cup of watered-down wine, trying to flush the rest of the potion out of his system.

"If I keep drinking I will drown and have to use the privy."

Rachel rolled her eyes, laughing. "That's the point."

Lifting the goblet, Alexander drank the entire cup; she refilled it and handed it back to him.

The tapping of the cane brought both Rachel's and Alexander's heads up. "'Tis time you make a decision." Arthur spoke to Alexander in a low voice.

"What decision?" Rachel asked out of turn.

"This is now the third time the two of you have been caught in an inappropriate situation. I have overlooked the first two due to circumstances. However, I fear Rachel's reputation will be tarnished when word of this gets out."

"No Papa. There's no need for Alex to make a decision this morn." Rachel didn't want to become betrothed to him while he still had feelings for Viola, even if they were induced and not real.

"Woman, will you ever stop stepping into things that do not concern you?"

Rachel stood up, looked at both men, crossed her arms and stomped her foot. "Concern me? The two of you are deciding my future and you say it doesn't concern me?"

Setting his goblet down, Alex stood up and placed his hands on her shoulders. Looking into her eyes, he spoke to her father.

"I had hoped to speak with you, Arthur. If it is agreeable with Rachel, I would like to make her my wife."

Before Rachel could answer, the room erupted. Everyone spoke at once. Henry caught her mother before she fainted. Abby and Aunt Lilly spouted encouraging words.

Alex stood in silence and smiled at her with a hopeful grin, waiting for her answer. All she could do was nod.

CHAPTER TWENTY-SIX

The morning sun sprawled across Rachel's face through the cracks in the shutters. Rachel sat up in bed and looked around as she stretched her arms, yawning. Each morning, for the last four days, she was surprised to find she woke up in the past.

Abby burst through the bedroom door followed by Alice. "Rachel. You must get out of bed. We have so much to do this morn. Father is preparing the carriage and mother is in the kitchen fretting about the dinner preparations. Everyone will be in attendance this day."

"I know." Rachel climbed out of bed and walked to the small vanity.

Alice reached for the forest green gown Rachel had worn to supper the second day she arrived in the past.

Abby jumped on the bed. "Mr. Mattingly visited father this morn."

351

Rachel pulled the thin shift over her head and used the wet linen cloth Alice handed her. "Why was Nic here so early?"

Abby clapped her hands and leaned forward. "I was sent from the parlor but I listened through the door." She giggled. "It appears they found every shilling stolen from father under a floorboard in the bedroom of Mr. Bryant's. They also found a ledger with each transaction matching the discrepancies you found. The money will be returned shortly."

"That's odd. Why would James keep a record of what he stole, and why would he save every penny?"

"That is not all." Abby lowered her voice. "Viola's father has whisked her away to France. He plans for Viola to be placed in a convent."

Rachel stopped in mid-cleaning. "Why on earth?" She stood there stunned and wondered why her father would want to send her to a convent.

If he planned to use love as her motivator rather than admitting it was for a prophecy, he could keep witch-craft out of the equation. Going to a convent was as close to modern therapy anyone in this time could get.

"At least she won't be beheaded or burned at the stake." Rachel sighed and let Alice dress her.

Abby walked over to the small table and opened the tiny drawer. "Rachel, where is your ring?"

"I don't remember." She waved her hand. "It's okay. I'll find it later. After all, I will get a new one today."

Their mother burst into the room. "Rachel. Have you not started dressing? The church will be filled in a few hours' time. We must not be delayed." She left as suddenly as she entered.

Abby sighed and closed the drawer. "I best be assisting mother. She is in such a tither." She walked to the door and closed it behind her.

Rachel looked over at the vanity while Alice helped her dress. The last time Rachel had seen the ring, the witch had handed it to her. She assumed she might have dropped it during the confrontation with Viola. She had planned to return to the cottage and look for it, but hadn't had the opportunity. Her thoughts drifted to Alex. He didn't have to worry about getting married to a woman he hated. Rachel still couldn't believe that she was the woman the witch had spoken about the first time she was at the cottage. She was the one he was in love with. The thought of him in love with her made Rachel feel tingly and giddy.

Word spread that Lord Alexander was Anon. Lord Berkeley had made the announcement shortly after they had left the ball. At first the town thought he was jesting – until yesterday when Alex arrived at the park with his canvas and supplies and began painting a portrait of Abby as a wedding gift. Henry had proposed to her at the ball.

Rachel had been in the past for over two months and began wondering if she would ever go home. According to what she had worked out given the calendar differences, today was her brother's birthday in her own time. It was the day Allen would admit his attraction to her.

After two hours Alice was finished. Rachel walked downstairs into the parlor where everyone was waiting to take the carriage to church.

"Dearly beloved friends, we are gathered together here in the sight of God . . ."

Nervous, Rachel looked at Alex. He stood next to her at the altar, his smile lighting up his amber eyes. She couldn't determine if the butterflies in her stomach were because she was nervous about her wedding day or if it was guilt, because she wasn't the real Rachel of this time.

Rachel looked around the church. It appeared to be filled with the entire city standing there watching them take their vows. Her mother and father were in front, her mother quietly crying. For a moment she felt she was living a fairy tale, but the thought that this really wasn't where she belonged could not be suppressed.

If she had been sent back in time to fix events, she figured everything had been completed. The Drovere Estate was back on track. Her father would be able to pay his debts and Viola wouldn't cause any more problems if she was locked in a convent. But James hadn't been found, and that worried her.

Rachel tried to enjoy her wedding, but it was all a blur. She didn't remember saying the words binding them together as man and wife. Before she knew it the ceremony was over and she was now the Lady Alexander Dohetry.

The celebration moved from the church to her Aunt's home for food and dancing. Everyone was having a wonderful time when Nic pulled Alex aside to congratulate the couple.

"I have news," he whispered. "I believe we have located James."

"You have caught the man?" Alex asked.

"No. I have word he has sailed to the Americas. I shall be leaving on the next tide to bring him home."

Rachel sighed in relief and placed her hand over her heart. "Thank you."

Nic winked at Rachel, his eyes sparkling with laughter. "Keep an eye on your husband; he easily gets himself in trouble." He leaned closer and lowered his voice. "I think you are exactly what he needs."

For a moment Rachel had déjà vu; Abby came up and told her it was time for them to go.

Rachel hugged her sister. "Thank you for everything."

* * *

Rachel stood at the front door, looking at Alex, wondering what he was thinking. Picking her up, he carried her over the threshold of his cottage.

After he set her down inside the house, she looked around at the familiar surroundings.

"You seem as if you don't want this," he said, looking down into her eyes.

"No. I mean yes, I do want this. I've dreamt of this day." But her dreams were of a future wedding with a man she would love for eternity.

"Close your eyes."

"What?"

"Will you defy me at every turn?" He smiled, stepped behind her, placed his hands over her eyes, and then whispered into her ear, "Walk forward."

Rachel giggled, doing as instructed. Feeling his body pressed against hers, she briefly recalled the dream she had of Allen the morning he filed for divorce. She wanted to turn and kiss Alex. Reminding herself that Allen was in the future and she was now a married woman, she lifted her arms, caressing the air, feeling for something solid, trying not to step on the hem of her skirt.

"Keep moving."

Still laughing, she let him guide her, afraid she would run into something. "I might fall."

"If you fall, I might catch you."

Rachel stopped walking, letting him run into her. "Might catch me?" She assumed they had entered the parlor based upon the direction he had taken her.

"Aye." He moved her legs forward with the force of his body.

"Stop here." He lifted his hands from her eyes and turned her around. "Now you may look."

A fire blazed before her; she looked around wondering what he wanted her to see.

Gently, Alex turned her head back toward the mantle and tilted her chin up.

Rachel stopped giggling when she saw the most amazing thing she had ever seen. Her eyes filled with tears – she gazed into an image of herself.

"Alex. It's beautiful."

The portrait before her captured every curve of her face, every freckle on her nose; she even noticed the tiny little golden specks in her crystal blue eyes.

"No my love, 'tis only a painting; you hold the true beauty. 'Tis my wedding gift to you."

Never in her life had she received such a gift from anyone. The portrait wasn't a mere painting; its detail was exquisite, and he had expressed the feelings he had for her with every stroke of his brush. For the first time she understood how it felt to be completely loved by another. She was overcome with a magical sensation tingling through every fiber of her body.

She caressed his face, not wanting to speak, fearful that the moment would pass by.

"This is a joyous moment, not one for tears." He reached up, wiping them from her cheek.

Rachel stepped back, blushing at the floor and then asked herself why she felt the need to look away. Gazing back into his amber eyes, she decided she would give herself wholeheartedly to this man. She pushed away the guilt she had in falling for another man; after all, she reasoned to herself, Allen hadn't been born yet.

Looking back down at the floor again, building her courage, she noticed he had shuffled his feet nervously and began rubbing his palms together.

"Oh my god," she whispered. Her head shot up, and she looked back into his eyes. Everything clicked. Alexander was Allen and Allen was Alexander. They were the same spirit. The same soul.

How could I miss it? she thought to herself. Standing in front of her was the most amazing man she had ever laid eyes upon.

Desire took over; no longer was she guarded or afraid to let herself feel. This was the man she loved enough to travel through time for.

Reaching up, she placed her hands behind his neck, pulling him to her lips. In that same instant, just like in the future, he knew what she was about to do and met her lips, kissing her before she could draw him to her.

His lips touched hers; the sensation was magical. He made her body tingle in a way she had only experienced once before. She kissed him with all of the love and passion she had inside of herself, feeling the energy around her begin to twirl, bringing them closer together. Closing her eyes, she melted into his body. She could feel the warmth of his arms around her as he picked her up, kissed her, and walked up the stairs. She felt nothing except for his presence and the love they had for each other as he laid her down on the bed.

CHAPTER TWENTY-SEVEN

Rachel felt the soft mattress below her as he drew away. She whispered, "No, don't leave."

"I'm not going anywhere," he whispered in her ear.

Rachel heard a beep. The sound was familiar, but she had no idea what could make that kind of sound in the sixteenth century. She heard the beep again and then faint voices. The voices grew louder; she couldn't make out the words. She wondered who was in Alex's bedroom.

She tried to open her eyes but the bright light shocked them closed. She tried again, blinking. The blurry room began to take shape. The first thing she could make out was Alex standing in front of her.

Rachel smiled. "Hi."

"Hi." He returned her smile.

Just then a woman got Rachel's attention by moving in front of the man she loved. "Do you know your name? How old are you? Who's the president of the United States?"

Rachel's eyes grew wide. She looked around; this was not Alex's bedroom. It was her office in the future. Her head throbbed. She tried to reach up to touch it, but her arms wouldn't move. They were held down by straps attached to a gurney. The woman was a paramedic.

Rachel looked up; it was Allen, not Alex, standing in front of her. "How long was I out?"

Allen rubbed his bald head. "About ten minutes or so."

Months had gone by in the past and it had only taken a few minutes.

The paramedics wheeled her out of her office and past an audience of bystanders in the hallway.

Rachel heard Allen behind her. "Where are you taking her? Can I go with you?"

The man pushing the gurney backed up and maneuvered it into the elevator. "University. Are you a relative?"

"No, just a friend."

"Then no. Only immediate family."

Rachel watched the doors close in the elevator mirror.

At the hospital, Rachel discovered she had hit her head hard enough to get a concussion. Her brother frantically walked into her room. The doctor told him not to leave her alone for the rest of the night, that she might have some memory loss, and to take her to the emergency room immediately if she began speaking in sentences which included random words and didn't make sense.

* * *

"When was the last time you talked to Allen?" Aimee opened her desk drawer and pulled out her purse, preparing to leave work.

Rachel sighed. "The day they took me to the hospital, so about two months."

"When are you going to call him?"

"I'm not," Rachel snapped.

"But you want to," Aimee said, taunting her.

"Yes, but no. I'm not calling him. If he wants to be with me he'll call." She sighed again. "Part of me thinks it was a dream, but sometimes the memories are so vivid."

Aimee pulled out her keys. "The dream?"

"Yeah."

"Sometimes I don't think it was a dream. Every time you mention something in the past, I search about it online. And you are always right." Aimee walked to the office door and waited for Rachel. "So, what does her Facebook page say today?"

Rachel gave her a dirty look and grabbed her purse off of her desk. "The divorce was final yesterday. According to Veronica, it was easy, no problems. They agreed about everything."

Aimee shook her head.

"What?" Rachel closed the door behind them. "As far as I'm concerned, if you post your life on a social media website and keep it public, then everyone has the right to view your page. It's kind of like being public record. Besides, it's my only window into his life."

"You have a point. I'm glad I keep mine private. Are you still going to your meeting tonight?"

Rachel pushed the down button for the elevator. "Yes, Christian said it's mandatory. Some bigwig investor wants to go over my notes and look at the new proposal. They think it might make a good mini-series." Rachel felt the story needed a new ending because Allen had simply disappeared.

The elevator doors opened and they stepped inside. "Your dream, right?"

"Yeah." They watched the floors count down on display in silence.

"Well, I don't know about you, but I think it's kind of cool. I've got class tonight. I'll see you later." Aimee gave Rachel a hug. A bell rang and the doors opened.

Rachel watched her walk away.

In the past couple of weeks, Rachel started to make connections between those she met in the sixteenth century and the people she knew and loved from her own time.

Rachel had stopped the love spell Viola wanted to cast on Alexander. Because it never happened, Veronica and Allen were no longer bound to each other. Veronica wasn't angry or obsessed with Allen anymore. She stopped posting negative, depressive, and attention-seeking posts. Instead they carried a positive undertone. Almost overnight, her brother quit drinking and decided to move to Florida. Veronica was excited to start her new life by going back to college, and had talked about a possible promotion. She also mentioned meeting a wonderful man who thought the world of her, and how she looked forward to dating him.

Christian's finances no longer appeared to be in jeopardy. A few weeks ago, he received a substantial check in the mail from the company his friend sold along with a letter expressing his sincerest apology. Christian's independent film company was getting noticed. A well-known Hollywood director expressed interest in several of Christian's projects.

Aimee, just like Abby, found a new confidence. It made her marriage stronger; her husband liked having a woman that knew what she wanted. He kept his phone calls to one a day and if she didn't answer immediately, he didn't call back. Last week she was accepted into college with a full-ride scholarship.

In her spare time, Rachel built Arthur's and Eleanor's family tree. Abby and Henry had six children, each one living to adulthood with families of their own. Alexander and Rachel had eight kids. Alex outlived his brother Richard and received the title of Earl which he passed on to his eldest son, Allen. Rachel wondered if the name came from when she first awoke in the past.

She couldn't find anything about Viola, but her brother James returned to England. All she found was a photograph of his gravestone at an old church cemetery in Bristol.

Nic Mattingly built a shipping line, a business still run today by his descendents. Though the name had changed over the years, his most recent grandson was the majority shareholder and oversaw the board of directors.

Other than feeling more depressed, Rachel didn't notice anything different about her own life. During lunch she visited the Art History section of the campus library, rummaging through the text books, reading everything she could find on Alexander Dohetry. He became one of most famous artists during the Elizabethan era. The books were filled with historians theorizing why he had revealed himself. He had been known to say, "Art is to be shared with the world and for future generations to enjoy." The images in the text books were portraits of people she remembered meeting or who were dear to her heart.

The Dohetry Exhibit left the Denver Art Museum the day she arrived home. She would have flown out of state to see it, but the exhibit had returned to England.

While she was in the sixteenth century, she changed their lives for the better. She wondered what she could have done in the past to change her own future.

Rachel arrived at the hotel, just west of Denver, with a beautiful view of the mountains on the west side and the city to the east. She texted Christian to let him know she made it. The text back told her to meet him in room 823. She gathered her laptop and book bag, and rode the elevator to the eighth floor.

She knocked on the door and Christian opened it immediately.

"Hi. Why did you want to meet in the room and not downstairs or in a conference room?"

"It's a bit more private. The guys went gambling in Blackhawk this afternoon and they're on their way back." He looked at his watch. "They should be here in a few minutes."

Rachel looked around: a king size bed took up most of the space in a small room decorated in earth tones. She walked to the table and sat down in one of the two chairs near the window, and pulled out her laptop and notes, wanting to give the impression she was prepared.

Christian stood next to her. "Did you read the e-mail I sent you today?"

She turned on her computer. "No. I didn't have a chance to check my personal email. Work was crazy."

"Do you have a wireless modem?"

"Built in. What century are you from?" While her computer booted up, Rachel pulled the stack of files onto her lap, separating the current project documents from the notes on her past life.

"Check your email first."

Once it booted up, she went to her e-mail account and logged in, scanned her mail, and opened Christian's message.

Rachel looked at Christian with her brows creased. "Just one link?" The man was not known for his short emails; they usually contained a page-long description with several links and attachments.

He looked over her shoulder. "Click it."

She gave him a funny look and turned back to the screen, watching the page load. Rachel skimmed a news article about a recently discovered World War II treasure:

"Maddison Nichols and her father Michael Nichols recently confirmed the portraits found in an old German

salt mine on August 23rd to be the original works of
Alexander Dohetry, Palma Giovane, and Raphael."

Amazed, she clicked on the slide show when she heard a knock on the door. Christian promptly went to answer it. Rachel was engrossed, completely focused on the document, and didn't look up.

Then her eyes were transfixed on an image she'd seen only once before – the night she left the sixteenth century. Tears ran down her face; she reached up and gently touched the picture, her fingers trembling. It was an image of herself. Closing her eyes, she took a deep breath and wiped the tears away.

"How did you find . . ." She looked over to Christian and cut herself short.

Allen stood leaning against the wall with his arms folded across his chest. He looked at her and his amber eyes sparkled, as if he had not seen her for an eternity.

All of her anger and frustration disappeared. She felt the energy around him, and her body tingled. The moment came to an abrupt halt when her files fell and hit the floor. The dreamy feeling she had only a moment before left her. She looked down at the disarray of papers scattered at her feet.

She was afraid to speak, hoping the moment would come back somehow. Rachel knelt down and began to pick up the papers. Allen bent down and gathered a pile;

his hand touched hers, and she looked up into his eyes. Without a word, he leaned over and kissed her. She felt his soft lips pressed against hers, his tongue tasting her, his warm hands caressing her cheeks, and she responded with an urgency she hadn't felt in months.

When the sweet kiss ended, reality took over. Rachel looked into his face and smacked him on the arm. "What the hell are you doing here? Where have you been? I was in the hospital. I could've died from a brain injury and you wouldn't have known about it." She continued hitting him on his arm.

Allen grabbed her hands and laughed. "When you're done yelling at me, I'll tell you."

"But you left me." Tears again built up in her eyes.

"First of all, I didn't leave you. The paramedics wouldn't let me go with you. I ran to class, finished my final, gave the instructor an excuse and drove straight to the hospital."

"Then why didn't you come to see me?"

He held her small hands in his. "They wouldn't let me. I sat there for hours waiting to hear something. Finally someone came out and told me that you were okay and your brother picked you up."

Frustrated, she tried to pull her hands away. He wouldn't let go. "And you didn't call me! You didn't e-mail, text, write, or send me nasty messages!"

"I couldn't. That night, everything in my life changed." He led her to the bed and sat her down on the soft mattress. "Everything happened so fast." Allen rubbed his bald head and paced. "While I was sitting in the waiting room, Veronica called. She wanted the divorce. I needed to find a place to live." He paused and rubbed his hands together. "The next day, I received a call from a producer who wanted to see my work. He's the one who wanted to buy the rights to the book cover at the exhibit. I had to leave state twice to meet the partners. I had so much to do."

Rachel crossed her arms. "And you didn't call." She looked around the room when she realized he said the word producer. "Where is Christian?"

"He is the producer."

"What?"

"Christian asked me to meet him in Golden. While I was there, I looked at his artwork and noticed a black and white photo. It was of this beautiful woman wearing a little bikini with her arms covering her chest and hair blowing away from her face. Do you know the one I'm talking about?"

Rachel's face went red. "He should *not* have shown you that picture."

"He didn't, it was hanging in his home office. That's when I realized he was the same man you introduced me to at the Exhibit. After I got the job I asked him to help me out."

"Help you?" Rachel was now confused. She had forgotten introducing them.

"Help me with you." Allen sighed. "Christian and I set this up tonight. To get you here. He's gone. Everyone is meeting at his house except for you and me."

Rachel stood up and grabbed her things. "I need to be there."

Her mind was racing, nothing was making sense. She had to go to the meeting, Christian said it was important. Rachel still didn't understand why Allen was at the hotel.

"You really are stubborn aren't you? You're just like Christian said, you get an idea in your head and you can't let it go."

Allen walked over to Rachel, turned her around, and removed the things from her hands. "You and me. Here now. I wanted to be alone with you."

"Alone? Why here? Why now?"

"You do remember when I told you that I am a loyal man?" Rachel nodded. "I didn't want you to be involved with a married man."

"So you were being loyal to your wife, to your marriage?" Those words left a bitter taste in her mouth.

Allen held her and looked straight into her eyes. "Loyal to you."

Rachel finally understood. He didn't want his wife. He had been getting his life together, following his dreams. Allen wanted to be with her as a single man. Loyalty and commitment were important to him. Rachel wiped the tears from her eyes.

Allen smiled and kissed her forehead. "I have loved you from the moment I first saw you. I don't think you remember seeing me. When I looked into your eyes, I was hopelessly lost. I didn't let myself feel what I felt and I tried to deny it, but I couldn't. Christian told me about your experience in the past. I can't help but think what he said was true. The moment you hit your head everything changed. The barriers, the boundaries, they no longer exist. I've never believed in magic until now."

Rachel looked deep into his eyes and saw Alex in Allen. She remembered seeing it once before but thought it was a dream. They were the same soul, the same spirit.

She reached up and wrapped her arms around his neck. She held him tightly, afraid he would disappear again. When he didn't, she grabbed him by the front of his pants and pulled him forward as she lifted her eyebrow. "So does this mean . . .?"

"Umm. No." He kept her from pulling him any closer.

Reaching his hand into his pocket, he knelt down. Picking up her left hand, he pressed his lips to her ring finger. "It might be longer than you think. It's not going to happen until you marry me." Allen held out a black, freshwater pearl ring, set in a gold band with curved tendrils. His hands were shaking. When he tilted the ring toward the light, the hue of the pearl turned a deep green.

Dumbfounded, Rachel couldn't breathe, let alone speak.

"Christian mentioned you lost a pearl ring. I know it's not the same but . . ." He pulled the ring back and looked down. "If you don't like it, I can get you a diamond or something different."

Rachel lifted her hand to her mouth. Tears ran down her face. The ring was far from the same, but she knew this pearl would hold a deeper meaning. "It's perfect."

Allen let out a deep breath. He slipped the ring onto her finger, stood up, and placed her head between his hands. He kissed her brow and trailed kisses down her face to her lips. He whispered, "I have always loved you. I will always love you. For an eternity, I promise we'll always be together."

This was the ending she had always wanted. As the tears ran down her face, he kissed them away.

Lord Henry Berkeley, 7th Baron of Berkeley, God-son of Henry VIII, married Katherine Howard, daughter of the poet Henry Howard, Earl of Surrey, in September 1554. The couple frequently resided at Yate when not in attendance at court. Katherine's brother, Thomas Howard, 4th Duke of Norfolk, was beheaded on a charge of high treason in 1572. The Berkeley castle still resides north of Bristol and is currently held by the Berkeley family. It is unknown if they held a ball at the Berkeley castle in 1564.

Smuggling slaves from West Africa to the colonies of the Americas was a profitable business and John Hawkins became the first English slaver. Queen Elizabeth heard of John Hawkins success and financed his next expedition giving, him the 700-ton ship, Jesus of Lubeck in 1564. Along with three other ships, he set sail in October 1564 to Borburata, Venezuela, Rio de la Hacha, and then to the French colony in Florida.

ABOUT THE AUTHOR

Photo by Woody Morelock

Alyssa Dean Copeland was born in Kansas and raised in Colorado, where she received her M.B.A. from the University of Phoenix. Copeland's passion for education led her to a career in higher education as an administrator and Associate Professor. In her free time, Copeland enjoys researching genealogy and playing Sudoku. Currently, she is working on the next book in the Pearl Heirloom Collection.

Follow her Facebook.

Made in the USA
San Bernardino, CA
21 November 2016